# VEIL OF DEATH

# VEIL OF DEATH

## Stella Whitelaw

This first world edition published in Great Britain 2004 by
SEVERN HOUSE PUBLISHERS LTD of
9–15 High Street, Sutton, Surrey SM1 1DF.
This first world edition published in the USA 2004 by
SEVERN HOUSE PUBLISHERS INC of
595 Madison Avenue, New York, N.Y. 10022.

British Library Cataloguing in Publication Data

Whitelaw, Stella, 1941-
    Veil of death
    1.   Murder - Investigation - England - Cornwall - Fiction
    2.   Detective and mystery stories
    I.   Title
    823.9'14 [F]

    ISBN 0-7278-6107-7

Typeset by Palimpsest Book Production Ltd.,
Polmont, Stirlingshire, Scotland.
Printed and bound in Great Britain by
MPG Books Ltd., Bodmin, Cornwall.

To David and Suzie,
Alexandra and Madeline,
my new Australian family.

# Prologue

A dele did not want to wake up.
If only it could be an ordinary day, not a day she had
to force herself to get through. She willed the weather to be
kind and gentle, the one detail she had been unable to plan.

She could smell the sea through the open window. The sea
was freedom. When this day was over, she would find her
freedom.

Pangs of hunger cramped Adele's starved stomach. She had
been on a strict rotation diet to be willow-slim for today and
the thought of the feast ahead made her dizzy with longing.
It would be too embarrassing if she fainted in church. Fiona
would be upset.

Adele was cushioned from the rawness of life in a comfortable pocket of Cornish affluence, wrapped in layers of good
taste. Still, she had put everything, spiritually and physically,
into the organization of Fiona's wedding.

All week the Cornish weather had been unreliable and
Adele had despaired of the lawn drying off in time for the
marquee to be erected. But now the huge tent swamped the
grass like a slumbering white elephant, a canvas Gulliver
shackled by an array of guy ropes and stakes. When Adele
woke up, a crystal clear sky heralded a dancing sun.

She had been imprisoned for long enough, she thought
wryly, but soon she would be free. For months no one
in the Kimberley family had thought or talked of anything but Fiona's wedding. It was definitely the wedding
of the year in Porthcudden; not exactly the entire county

of Cornwall, but important enough in this corner of the peninsula.

Adele lay back on the pillow for two more minutes of quiet, girding her strength. She knew that once the day began it was going to be tense and fraught, despite all her careful forward planning. So much was last minute, so much depended on other people doing their part. If no one let them down, the whole event should go like clockwork.

On a hanger on the back of the door was her outfit in her favourite colours, blue and lilac. A silk dress, Twenties style, created for her by an expensive dressmaker in London that Aunt Elvina had recommended. Lady Elvina knew all the right people in London. She had spent her life moving in diplomatic circles, always dressed to perfection and flitting discreetly, Adele suspected, from one affair to another.

Thank goodness she did not have to go to the hairdresser's, Adele thought, yawning. Her short, nut-brown hair always looked its best the day after. Cutters was rather trendy for Porthcudden and Adele still couldn't get used to seeing men having their hair cut. She was small, dainty, a good-looking forty-five. People would be saying all day that she did not look old enough to be the mother of the bride.

Graham was sound asleep beside her, taking up more than his fair share of their king-size bed. He was going bald and had started this ridiculous habit of combing his hair sideways. Adele wished he wouldn't, especially in the mornings when the extra-long strands lay on the pillow before being lacquered over the bald patch. She had this terrible urge to snip them off while he was asleep. One day she would.

She slipped her bare feet out of the warm bed and padded across the thick carpet to fetch her wrap. On her way to the bathroom, she called out to the two girls.

'Fiona. Carolyn. Time to get up. I'm just going to put the kettle on.'

There was nothing but a grunt from Carolyn's room. Carolyn was always grumpy in the mornings. Her first civil

2

words were timed for about eleven o'clock. Before then she wandered round bleary-eyed and hair tousled, mumbling monosyllables and being as prickly as a hedgehog. Adele had given up on her. She hoped this was not going to be one of Carolyn's extreme mornings. She couldn't cope with both of her daughters being difficult.

Not that Fiona was difficult, but it would only be natural if the bride did throw a few tantrums. Though she had not shown any nerves yet. She had been extraordinarily calm about the whole event. She had shown a calculated interest in the guest list and gift list, but the choice of hymns and the floral decorations for the church were irrelevant. It was not surprising, since she and Hal had been living together for the last six months and were not short of a cruet.

'Don't I get breakfast in bed?' Fiona called from her bedroom. 'Bride's prerogative and all that?'

'When did you last eat breakfast?' said Adele. 'You were taking your O Levels. You said breakfast made you feel sick. Well, there's no point in making yourself sick today. Your hair appointment is for nine.'

'I'll make do with a cuppa then,' said Fiona, stretching. 'It does seem strange being at home. Hal's always up first; he makes the tea.'

'For heaven's sake don't mention anything like that today, especially in front of your father. You know how it upsets him.'

'I'm not ashamed of living with Hal. It's a sensible step before marriage. How well did you know Dad before you married him?'

Not at all, Adele told herself. She had hardly known Graham at all. She did not know what had prompted her to marry him. Panic, perhaps. She had thought herself to be in love with him, she supposed. He had been quite good-looking and amusing. It seemed the right thing to do at the time. Dates at the cinema, several prom concerts, long walks and drives . . . None of which prepared her for years

3

of living with the same person. They had never been to a prom concert since.

Carolyn brushed past Adele on the landing in the skimpy printed T-shirt she wore in bed. She did not say a word. She was obviously in one of those moods. She went into the bathroom and slammed the door.

'Morning, sunshine,' said Adele, not expecting an answer. She peeped into her son's room. Timmy was upside-down in bed, his head where his feet ought to be. He always began tucked up the right way round, but turned turtle in the night. He'd been a restless embryo, kicking and pommelling her womb for a good five months.

His seven-year-old face was rosy with sleep; this late child of an ebbing love. Flaxen hair framed his angelic features, though he was not quite so perfect when awake. A white sailor suit hung on the door. This was in keeping with the vaguely nautical connections of the Vaughans. Norman Vaughan had a cabin cruiser and Hal liked sailing and fishing. Adele wondered if he brought home dead fish for Fiona to gut. If Fiona knew *how* to gut fish . . .

The Vaughans were rich, one of the richest families in that part of Cornwall. They lived at Rosemullion House, a rambling manor house built of Cornish stone, full of character, that stood in acres of gardens and grounds with its own river and fishing rights. They were giving Fiona and Hal a bungalow as a wedding present. An entire bungalow. It made Adele's lovingly chosen silver cutlery and Graham's cheque look like mail order gifts.

No one had given them a house, thought Adele as she filled the kettle and got out the bone china mugs they used for early morning tea. They had begun married life in a poky flat over an estate agent's, then moved to a semi-detached house with one tree and a rabbit-hutch garden.

When Graham became manager of the south-west regional office in Truro, they had sold up and moved to Cornwall. Because of the difference in property prices, they had been able to afford Tregony, a detached house in two acres of wilderness. It had been extended and modernized since they bought it. Adele had the kitchen and utility room of her dreams, a sun lounge, a flower-filled porch, two garages, and there were more trees than she could count. She liked gardening and spent hours raising seedlings to transplant into the flower beds.

This summer she had filled the garden with yellow and white flowers to match the bridal colours. The idea pleased Adele. She wanted everything to be perfect for Fiona's wedding. A symphony of colour. It was the least she could do for her.

She carried the tea tray carefully upstairs. This was not the morning for tripping on the hem of her nightdress. Didn't more accidents happen in the home than anywhere else? She knew that one day she would slip on the polished oak stair treads and break her neck. Graham would probably be pleased. He'd look suitably sad for a few weeks and then assume the role of the merry widower.

Fiona was sitting up in bed, thumbing through a magazine as if there was nothing more important on her mind than a few drinks with friends at lunchtime. She was a pretty young woman who took her looks for granted and did nothing much about them. Her hair, fair with golden highlights, hung straight to her bare shoulders. Her face was heart-shaped, her eyes a startling blue fringed with sandy lashes that barely showed.

'Thanks, Mother. I'm gasping. That party last night has left me dehydrated. I must drink gallons to get rid of the poison.'

'I simply don't understand it,' said Adele, opening the flower-sprigged curtains and letting the sun pour in. She checked that the marquee was still upright. So much depended on those acres of canvas. 'The bride isn't supposed to have a stag party. It's the groom who drinks himself stupid the night before.'

'Why should Hal have all the fun?' Fiona grinned. 'We didn't drink that much. It was nice to be all girls together down at the sailing club. I don't often see my friends these days. Hal groans if I go out on my own.'

'Men can be so possessive,' said Adele lightly. 'We are mere chattels. Drink your tea and I'll run a bath for you if Carolyn is out of the bathroom yet. She's probably changing the colour of her hair.'

'I sincerely hope not. Fuschia-pink punk would ruin her outfit.'

Adele turned to look at Fiona's wedding dress for the hundredth time. Since it had arrived at Tregony earlier in the week, special delivery, she had been unable to keep her eyes off the creation.

It was the most exquisite dress Adele had ever seen. The layers and frills of ivory silk taffeta would have outshone Cinderella at any ball. The bodice was fitted and plain with tiny pearl buttons, but the picture neckline was looped with creamy-yellow roses, matching the deeply frilled hem with more loops and roses. Heaven alone knew what it had cost. More than Fiona earned annually with her boutique and gift shop. Adele wondered who had paid for it. Two stiff petticoats hung over a chair. A pair of matching slippers were still in their box.

Adele remembered her own wedding dress. It had seemed wonderful and glamorous at the time, but the photographs showed that the dull white satin had not flattered her. And the satin had creased like the devil. All through the service she had been tormented by the thought of everyone looking at her creased bottom. Perhaps that was why she was so particular now. She never looked less than perfect.

The veil was on the dressing table on a wig stand. It was short and simple, a puff of filmy net to be held by a coronet of real creamy-yellow roses that would be delivered with the bouquet. Fiona had turned down Olive Vaughan's offer of the family Bruges lace veiling. She had said it was too overwhelming for the dress and the wrong colour anyway, and Adele had to agree with her.

Mrs Vaughan had hidden her disappointment. Two sons and no daughters meant she was never likely to see the beautiful veil worn again in her lifetime.

'It's truly magnificent,' said Adele, touching the cool, smooth silkiness of the fabric with the tips of her fingers. 'You'll have to store it away carefully after the wedding.'

'Oh, I'm going to sell it,' said Fiona carelessly. 'No point in keeping the dress. After all, I'm not likely to wear it again, am I?'

Adele tried not to be shocked. She had kept her wedding dress and she hadn't even liked it. But then Fiona had a streak of ruthlessness, of practicality that was totally different to Carolyn's wayward stubbornness and moods.

'Daisy hasn't arrived yet,' said Adele, more to herself. 'I hope she isn't going to let me down. I really need her this morning. There's the downstairs cloakroom and the bathroom to clean, and the kitchen before the caterers descend on us.'

'She's probably had one of her turns,' said Fiona, leafing over a page. 'Get Carolyn to help.'

'She's never cleaned a loo in her life. Anyway she'll be far too busy getting herself ready.'

Carolyn was the real beauty of the family. She was petite and slim, with long hair like molten silver. Her eyes were blue like her sister's, but a deep amethyst-blue, and she dyed her lashes navy so that her eyes looked huge. Everything about her appearance was perfect, from high, chiselled cheekbones to small pearly teeth. She looked like a mermaid.

'I wonder if Jonathan will turn up,' said Fiona.

'I doubt it. The Vaughans don't even know where he is. They haven't heard from him for months.'

'But his own brother's wedding. You'd think he'd make the effort. It's unforgivable.' Fiona yawned.

The pace of the morning began to quicken. Adele did not know where the time went. Her head began to ache. The

7

caterers arrived laden with huge bowls of salads, platters of fresh salmon, sliced turkey and ham covered in cling film, tureens of mixed seafood. For afters, if anyone had any room, there were strawberry and raspberry pavlovas and jugs of cream. They began setting the hired furniture in the marquee, shaking out white damask cloths from linen hampers. The champagne was cooling in barrels of ice on the shady side of the house.

Grace, the flower lady, arrived. She had completed the church flowers first, following Adele's detailed yellow and white plan. Now there was the marquee to decorate with hanging baskets and garlands of flowers along the edge of the tables. Her van was loaded with white daisies, white candy-tuft, forget-me-nots and salvias, yellow zinnias, marigolds and chrysanthemums. It had been a nightmare getting the right colours. Most mothers left the choice to Grace and were thankful to have one less task to do. Adele was different.

'The cake has arrived and Mrs Carter wants paying now,' said Adele breathlessly. 'Can you write a cheque, Graham?'

'Write a cheque, Graham. Write a cheque, Graham. That's all I've been hearing for days.' Her husband was picking at a slice of turkey. A waitress glared at him. No one had made him any breakfast and he was peckish. 'I'm going to be totally broke after this wedding. Why couldn't she have eloped? Much cheaper.'

'You know you really want your daughter to have the wedding of the year,' said Adele, putting on a soothing voice. 'It's going to be a wonderful day. Just look at the weather and the garden.'

'That marquee is going to ruin my lawn. It'll never recover, probably have to be resown. We should have said no stilettos on the invitations.'

'Go and put your morning suit on and have a glass of champagne. It'll make you feel better,' said Adele, shooing him out of the kitchen before he started on a pavlova. She took the cheque from him and ran out to the marquee. Mrs

8

Carter was fussing about the position of the cake table and the selection of tablecloths Adele had offered. Nothing was right. The cake-maker wanted an old lace cloth that toned with the touches of gold on the cake.

'We can't have that hanging basket here,' said Mrs Carter curtly. 'It'll drip on my cake.'

'My baskets don't drip,' said Grace. 'But if you're worried, move your cake.'

'The cake looks absolutely gorgeous, Mrs Carter,' said Adele, thrusting the cheque into her hand. 'What a work of art. I'm sure it'll taste just as good too.'

'Of course it will,' said Mrs Carter. 'I'm not just a decorator.'

The inflexion on that last word was for Grace's benefit. Adele fled before the two women came to blows. She hoped they had more sense. Something must have upset them.

'There's going to be a fight in the marquee,' she announced to anyone who was listening. 'Mrs Carter and Grace are rolling up their sleeves.'

Timmy was leaning out of his bedroom window, absorbed by all the activity below.

'Oh good, can I go and watch?' he asked, itching to be doing something.

'No, be a good boy and stay here. Sandy will be round any minute now to help dress you.'

Timmy scratched his nose, not really listening.

'I'm already here.' A pale, serene face appeared from round the bathroom door. It was Sandy, her dark hair pulled back into a low ponytail, ballet style. 'Daisy hasn't turned up so I'm having a quick go at the grime. You don't mind, do you? I shan't come across any secrets, shall I? Any hidden drugs behind the loo?'

'Sandy, you're an angel, and let me know if you come across anything remotely scandalous. You wouldn't have time to do the downstairs cloakroom as well, would you?

They'll both be put to good use. All these people coming.
There'll be a constant queue.'

'As long as you don't mind me coming to church in tatty
jeans and this T-shirt.'

The two women laughed at each other. They both knew that
Sandy's appearance could be transformed in five minutes flat.
Adele had seen it happen many times. It was Sandy's stage
training that cut corners.

'Come along, young man,' Sandy went on. 'Let's get you
into that smart sailor suit. Are you clean? Yes, you look
well scrubbed. Once you've got that outfit on you won't be
able to eat.'

'I'm not hungry,' said Timmy, hardly audible.

'Not nervous, are you?' said Sandy, taking his small hand.
It felt clammy. 'It'll be all right, you know. Weddings are
a piece of cake. All over in a few minutes. Just like the
dentist.'

'Thank you for those encouraging words,' said Adele.
'We've had to bribe Timmy into being a pageboy. It's taken
weeks to get him into the spirit of things.'

'You rascal,' said Sandy. 'What are you getting?'

'A new pair of football boots,' said Timmy, his eyes
lighting up.

Adele's glance darted to the clock. She had allowed herself
twenty minutes to change and do her face. Everything was
ready and laid out. She had even put what she would need
into her handbag the night before. She was so organized.

The girls were back from the hairdresser's. The top stylist
at Cutters had transformed Fiona's straight locks into a cas-
cade of ringlets with careless tendrils softening her face and
neck. Carolyn's look was medieval: hair pulled back from her
face and secured into an arrangement of fine plaits entwined
with narrow yellow ribbon. She went upstairs without saying
a word, so Adele could not tell if she was pleased.

There seemed to be some kind of disturbance in the road.
People were coming out of their houses and standing on the

grass verges. Adele ran on to her bedroom balcony in a lilac satin slip, not caring if the neighbours saw her undressed.

A tremor of excitement clutched her. The wedding car had arrived. A vintage Rolls, circa 1928. A huge, magnificent vehicle with polished walnut doors, gleaming headlamps, leather roof rolled back, the driver in a silver-buttoned uniform, gauntlets and peaked cap. It was a carriage fit for a princess. The Rolls set the scene for the fabulous dress, all part of Fiona's dream wedding.

Fiona was downstairs already, the big skirt of her dress rustling, veil thrown back, looking quite unconcerned and drinking a Buck's Fizz with her father. Timmy was stiff and self-conscious in his sailor's outfit. Adele knew she looked elegant in the blue and lilac silk dress and cloche hat, but no one said anything. She did not expect any compliments. She never had.

'Carolyn is fussing about her shoes,' said Fiona. 'She says they slip and they are not what she chose.'

'Of course they are,' said Adele. 'She wasn't paying attention in the shop, so if she's got the wrong size, it's her own fault. I'll find some foam insoles and see if they help.'

'Have a drink,' said Graham, pouring out half a glass of champagne. 'No point in saving it all for the guests. Guzzlers.'

'I don't think I dare,' said Adele. 'Someone's got to keep a level head. What will Father Lawrence think if we breathe alcoholic fumes over him?'

Carolyn was sitting rebelliously on her bed, not caring if she creased the yellow organza dress which Adele had carefully ironed the night before. There were shoes all over the floor.

'I can't go,' she said. 'I've no shoes to wear.'

Adele kept her patience. 'Where are the yellow satin slippers? The ones that match the dress?'

'Fiona knows I hate yellow. That's why she chose it. It makes my skin look sallow and my hair white. I suppose

11

she wants me to look a freak at her wedding so that she and her friends can laugh. I won't be in any of the photographs, Mother, I won't. I absolutely refuse.'

'It's a very pale yellow,' said Adele, finding the slippers tossed in a corner. 'And a very pretty colour. Not harsh at all. Look, I've put foam soles inside. See if they are more comfortable now.'

'I suppose they are,' said Carolyn, her glum expression quite ruining her lovely face. She knew how to put on make-up. She painted her face like an artist.

'Come along, Carolyn. Your flowers are here and so is the Rolls. It's taking us to the church first with Timmy, then coming back for Fiona and your father.'

'If he can still stand up straight by then,' said Carolyn, catching the sound of clinking glasses.

'Everyone is nervous,' said Adele, giving her second daughter a quick hug. 'It's only natural.'

'Fiona isn't nervous. But then she isn't natural,' Carolyn added, snatching up her posy of tiny Victorian roses. 'Yellow again. I might have guessed.'

Adele turned away. She could not cope with Carolyn's malicious streak today. Perhaps she would be happier at the reception when more attention was being focused on her, and people were complimenting her on her appearance. Perhaps she would be chatted up by the best man, Ralph, an old friend of Hal's from Vaughan Precision, his father's company.

The church was packed. Had they really asked all these people? Was there going to be enough food, enough champagne? Supposing it suddenly rained and they all had to pack into the marquee? The guests would be tramping round the house, looking into rooms she had not had time to tidy . . .

There was Lady Elvina, looking marvellous for nearly eighty, in a soft lavender colour that was kind to her ravaged skin. Sandy had managed to change into a dramatic outfit, with a big hat hiding her face. Hal was sitting in the front row, turning round at every footstep. She had almost forgotten about Hal in the rush of preparations, yet he was the reason for all of this. A friendly young man, darkly handsome and clever, as well as prosperous. He would be a very satisfactory son-in-law.

Adele knew the bride had arrived even without turning round. It was the rustling sound of all those yards of silk taffeta. She hoped Carolyn would put a smile on her face.

The flowers in the church were lovely. Grace had made a really good job of it, though Adele noticed the archway she had designed was missing. She wondered if she could save some of the pew posies for afterwards. She hated the thought of all these flowers being thrown away before they were dead.

The organist broke into a triumphant march as Fiona began the journey down the aisle on her father's arm. There was no doubt she made the most beautiful bride. The years rolled back and memories of Fiona as a baby, pink and helpless, came into mind. Adele felt her nose prickle with emotion. She hoped she wasn't going to cry. Her mascara would run and she would look a mess.

'Dearly beloved,' began Father Lawrence in a priestly voice.

Adele was not really listening; she was taking in other impressions. She wanted to remember everything. The coolness of the old church; the carved memorials; the riot of flowers, their scent; the bride so beautiful and remote; the bridesmaid outshone for once; Graham's side-slick a little out of place from wearing a top hat. Then, the music, glorious, every note chosen by herself.

'I only know one hymn – "All Things Bright and Bashful",' Fiona had laughed. 'You choose the music, Mother. I'm sure it'll be fine.'

Father Lawrence paused and caught Adele's glance. He was a dear but a fake, Adele thought. The service was so theatrical. He liked being the star in his ecclesiastical robes,

13

but at this wedding his billing was far down. He was merely a supporting actor.

He cleared his throat. 'Those whom God hath joined together, let no man put asunder. Amen.'

Adele did not remember much of the signing in the vestry. It was a kaleidoscope of colours and voices. Strangely enough, one voice did not ring true, but Adele could not understand why, nor could she place it. She smiled, chatted to Olive and Norman Vaughan, straightened Fiona's flounces, Carolyn's ribbons. Graham never spoke to her.

The organist crashed chords into the Wedding March. It was not an original choice, but Adele did not think it could be beaten for a really stirring march. There was music with more class, but useless for processions.

Outside a young man was waiting with a video camera perched on his shoulder. This was Hal's idea. It was another of his friends, someone called Izzy, who was an expert, apparently. After the endless group photographs, the bride and groom got into the Rolls amid a shower of confetti and cheers.

The drive back was unreal. Adele prayed that everything was ready at Tregony. A great tide of guests began descending on the house and garden, and the bridal receiving line was only just set in time, both pairs of parents hiding their tulip glasses of champagne behind Grace's tubs of potted plants. There was more smiling and shaking hands, saying what a lovely bride Fiona made and how lucky they both were.

Adele noticed that Graham took a glass of champagne from almost every tray that passed. She hoped he was not going to get drunk. He couldn't be that nervous. It was nearly all over. The food lasted, though Adele missed out on any fruit pavlova. They vanished in minutes. She was sure people had seconds. Everyone seemed to be enjoying themselves. The sun shone brilliantly and the garden looked superb, with people wandering around the flowering borders in groups, glasses in hand. The Vaughans were talking to people they didn't know, which was a good sign. Only the waitresses were flagging.

The speeches and cutting the cake went smoothly. Adele rather liked Ralph, the best man. A good choice. He had managed quite neatly to halt Graham's dreadful speech. His own speech was dry, witty, and brief. He had warm brown eyes behind his spectacles and seemed captivated by Aunt Elvina.

'Aunt Elvina has a new admirer,' said Graham, his face red from heat and alcohol, side-slick flapping, moustache beaded.

'She is a very charming old lady,' said Adele. 'And the stories she has to tell can be amusing.'

'All lies,' said Graham. 'She doesn't know fact from fiction these days. It's got confused in that raddled old mind.'

'Nonsense. She's as bright as a button, and her memory is flawless.'

Adele had been disappointed in the cake. It was very ordinary indeed. The sun was dazzling her eyes. She felt faintly sick, very tired, and was wondering if the caterers would consider she was asking too much if she requested a cup of tea from her own kitchen. They would probably charge for it. Graham was going to have a shock when he saw their bill.

'I think it's time for Hal and me to go,' said Fiona, still not a hair out of place. She had been a perfect bride, talking to everyone, mixing with all the relations, floating around like a fairy-tale princess on a few glasses of bubbly. She had hardly eaten anything.

'Of course, dear. Don't be too long. Izzy will want to take pictures of you leaving before he goes.'

'Jonathan will be sorry he missed all this, but at least he'll see the video,' said Mrs Vaughan, being quite friendly. Adele was pleased. They had only met once before the wedding, at Hal's flat, and it had not been a successful occasion.

She saw Carolyn deep in conversation with Hal by the

hydrangea bushes and that pleased Adele too. At least Carolyn had behaved herself at the wedding, and it seemed she was going to get on with her new brother-in-law. Perhaps one day they would all be good friends. Adele smiled to herself, relieved that the day had gone so well. It would be nice to sit down and let people revolve round her without having to think.

Fiona was taking a long time changing. She had been upstairs for half an hour and the guests were getting restless; the drink was running out and the marquee looked as if a riot had hit it. The looped flower chains had broken, petals everywhere among bits of cress and crumbs of meringue.

Adele went upstairs to hurry Fiona along. She pulled off her hat, shaking out her hair. It couldn't take such an age to change into her going-away outfit. Surely Hal hadn't gone up with her? It shocked Adele to think that perhaps they couldn't wait to make love; that the strained look on Hal's face during the service had been caused by lust.

She went into Fiona's bedroom. Her first thought was that it was a ridiculous time for the bride to take a nap.

Fiona was sprawled across her bed, still in the fairy-tale dress. One hand was limp across her face. Then Adele saw a thin glint of silver, though she did not recognize what it was as two-thirds of the instrument was buried in Fiona's quiescent breast.

She was not aware of the silent scream that came from her mouth. It turned into a piercing, primeval howl from the depths of her soul that stunned the guests in the garden below. Adele staggered from the room and ran down the stairs, half slipping and falling, past the startled caterers, out into the sunshine of the garden, her hands outstretched in horror.

She did not see Timmy hiding in the bushes, his face white with shock, crying little dry sobs, three spots of fresh red blood on his sailor suit.

# One

S he never tired of the sea. She went daily to stand on the cliff edge of her garden and watch the surfing waves below. She loved it most when it was a high tide and the giant waves thrashed the granite rocks and sent up high spumes of spray. Sometimes the spray was caught in the wind and flung upwards into her face and she could taste the salt on her mouth.

Grace was sure that she was descended from the Druids. Even more than the sea, she loved the sun with a pagan ferocity. Her skin was always tanned and she did not care if she got skin cancer. She looked better brown, and that was more important than a few extra years of life.

And she loved the sun because it grew flowers. She had greenhouses and flower beds full of plants practically all year round. Her garden was in a secluded dip between headlands, a pocket of microclimate that was like gold dust.

It was a hobby which had grown into a business. Calendula, scabious, clarkia, sweet william; they grew like weeds. When her husband left her for a pert child who worked in a boutique in Helston, she despaired of finding work. He had systematically filtered off their savings into a secret account and when he disappeared in the car one Sunday evening, Grace found there was less than £160 in their joint account. He had left her the cottage, so she supposed it was a fair division of twenty years of marriage.

She lost a stone in weight during those first weeks. She worked in the garden on her knees till the light faded and she could hardly see her way back along the paths. How could she possibly find work? No one would employ her. She had nothing to offer.

'Titus, what's going to happen to us?' she said to her smooth black and white cat, as they shared the last tin of sardines. 'What am I going to do? We can't live on air.'

Titus promised to catch more mice and rats, even the odd seabird, but knew that his mistress would not take them from him. She was always fair about his prey, only scolding him if it was a baby bird that hadn't stood a chance of escaping his jaws.

'I've got to get a job. There must be something I can do, but what?'

There was always the possibility that her husband might return. The girl in the boutique had a murky dark-green aura, which told Grace that she was overemotional and not to be trusted. He would find out one day, to his regret. But she was not sure if she wanted him back now, even if he came.

Grace often saw auras around people. It was their radiating light energy; a fascinating phenomenon. Titus had a beautiful healing indigo, but not when he was out hunting. Then it disappeared altogether.

Later Grace realized she should be grateful that her husband's infatuation had reached its height in summer and not winter. The garden became a jungle of blooms, thriving on the sun and sea and warm Cornish rain. She ran out of vases. She put the sagging chrysanthemum heads into milk bottles and cracked mugs. Finally she put a pailful of cut flowers out on the grass verge in the lane, with a printed sign saying PLEASE TAKE.

They were all gone in an hour. That someone also took the pail only sharpened a newly awakened glimmer of an idea. But not for Grace buckets of blooms for sale outside her cottage. She was not going to become a pail lady. Instead she designed and took, by bus, a flower arrangement suitable for a hotel foyer. She carried it round the big hotels in Falmouth until her arms ached. But she returned to the cottage that evening with firm orders from three hotels and a one-off commission to do the table flowers for a Rotary lunch. It was a beginning.

'This is going to grow,' she told Titus as she cooked some fresh pilchards for them both. 'Not too big, but big enough. We won't starve for a while.'

They did not starve at all. In a year Grace had bought an old second-hand van, was paying a lad to do some digging after school, and often had to buy in blooms from bigger market gardens in order to meet all her commitments.

She liked doing weddings best of all. She enjoyed decorating the churches, reception halls and marquees. Her business came from word-of-mouth recommendations. There was no name. It was just 'Grace's flowers'.

'We could have Grace's flowers,' Adele said to Graham early on in the planning stage. 'She did the flowers at the fashion show beautifully. It made all the difference. The catwalk looked so professional. And afterwards we auctioned all the flowers; she didn't mind as long as we gave her the containers back. What do you think, Graham?'

'Do what you please,' said Graham, making a fresh batch of tonic in the Sodastream. 'It's your wedding.'

'No, it's not. It's Fiona's wedding.'

'Same thing, it seems.'

Grace was not quite sure if she was pleased when she got a phone call from Adele Kimberley about her daughter's wedding. Although she knew her by sight – Porthcudden was a small harbour town – the fashion show had been their first encounter professionally.

Mrs Kimberley had been charming but determined. She knew her own mind and nothing would deter her. Grace had felt the clash of wills right from the beginning over the red colour scheme, the height of the flowers, the timing. There was no way Grace could have them all in place by ten o'clock for the photographer from the local paper. It was a marathon task to be ready by midday.

The last straw was when Adele Kimberley sold off all the flowers at the end of the show. The arrangement had been that the flowers were hired, at a very economical price. But when Grace arrived in her van to remove everything and salvage what was reusable, she found only her containers and a lot of spilt water.

'We knew you wouldn't mind, as it's for charity,' Adele had said, busily counting the money. 'They were half-dead anyway from the heat of the lights.'

Grace had swallowed any retort; after all it was for charity. She could afford a few flowers, but she would have liked to have been asked. And Adele's aura was magenta. Yellow creeping into a mix of blue and red. Very unusual. Her strength was an ability to organize and a love of beauty. It was pointless to argue in the face of magenta.

'My eldest daughter is getting married in July and we would like you to do the flowers for the church and the marquee in our garden,' said Adele when she phoned, straight to the point. 'The marquee will be a hundred square feet and I'd like trees in tubs at the entrance, hanging baskets inside and all the tables edged with garlands.'

'Sounds lovely,' Grace murmured, making notes on the back of an old envelope.

'The church has got to look absolutely stunning. I don't mind if you cut corners in the marquee; people will be drinking and eating and they won't notice the flowers after a few drinks. But the church is different. The setting must be perfection.'

'Perfection,' said Grace, longing to say she never cut corners.

'In yellow and white. Everything must be yellow and white. And, of course, touches of green. We have to have green, don't we?' Adele laughed. 'Stems and leaves.'

'Are you sure about the colour scheme, Mrs Kimberley?

Yellow and white is very much a spring wedding. Daffodils and tulips.' Grace was thinking fast. She had rows of blue cornflowers and pink candytuft planted, lobelia and astors. 'Why not pink and white or blue and white? More summery.'

'No, I don't think so. The church needs the warmth of sunny colours, yellow and gold. And Fiona is blonde, so is her sister. No, yellow is right. With white, of course.'

Grace understood the slight hesitation over the last comment. She had heard that Hal Vaughan had been living with the Kimberley girl for several months. So now they had decided to marry. It seemed a strange way of going about things, but it was the way people did it these days.

'I'll send you an estimate of the cost and a contract for you to sign,' said Grace. 'It'll take me a few days to work out where I shall get all the yellow flowers. If you could confirm as soon as possible. I get very booked up in July.'

'A contract? That's very formal. Is it really necessary? For a few flowers?'

'A few thousand flowers, Mrs Kimberley. This is a business like any other. If the wedding is suddenly called off, I could be left with a lot of flowers on my hands.'

'Oh, it won't be called off,' said Adele confidently. 'They are both very serious about this.'

'That's good,' said Grace, wishing she felt more enthusiasm for the young couple's wedding. She must do her best with these decorations or she would feel guilty.

She went out into the garden after the call, Titus following at her heel. Sometimes he was more like a dog than a cat. She lifted her face to the afternoon's watery sun and longed for summer warmth. Sometimes she was so tired of working. This year she promised herself a few hours of leisure on the seashore, on a sun-baked rock, perhaps down by Ladies' Pool, absorbing the sun's rays into her veins.

'A little sunbathing isn't too awful, is it, Titus? People make out it's a sin these days.'

The cat rubbed his soft head round her ankles. He liked the sun too, but in the garden. He had his own secret places among the lupins and the herbs. He wouldn't go anywhere near the sea nor that plant.

A strange plant had appeared, an almost flat rosette that was rooted deep in the earth. It grew right down by the cliff's edge as if it needed the sea spray for nourishment. It had short-stemmed, bluish, sweet-smelling flowers. Grace was always meaning to find out more about it, but there was never the time or opportunity. Titus would not even sniff it and that seemed to speak volumes.

The Kimberley wedding presented a lot of problems, apart from getting enough yellow flowers. The timing, again, was tight. She had to get the flowers cut and collected, the set pieces arranged, the pew posies in place and the special floral altar decoration; it was going to take hours of work. She would have to be up at dawn, and have some help. Fortunately she had a few trusty helpers she could call on who were good with flowers under her direction.

A few days before the wedding, Adele Kimberley phoned. She had had a brilliant idea. She wanted a floral archway outside the church. She thought that would be wonderful.

'I'm sorry, Mrs Kimberley, but I can't do an archway. Flowers have to be supported by something. They don't just hang in mid-air by themselves.'

'Surely it only requires a bit of wire? Can't you think of something? You're so clever, Grace.'

Grace stifled a sigh. She was a fool. Why didn't she say no and be done with it?

'I'll think about it, but I make no promises.'

'We'll pay for anything extra.'

'Of course you will,' said Grace. 'But cost isn't the issue. It's whether it's a possibility.'

She almost slammed down the telephone. Adele Kimberley had everything in the world: a successful husband, a big house and garden, money, a social position, ample leisure. Now she wanted an archway as well. It was asking too much.

Mentally, Grace went on strike. She flung out of the cottage with a towel and a book and took the coastal path that led to a secluded cove called Ladies' Pool. It was small and rugged with wild gorse and heather carpeting the slopes. A narrow zigzag path and precipitous steps were only for the sure-footed. Hardly anyone knew of its existence.

She put out her towel and took off her shirt, slipping down the straps of her bra. There was no one to see if she sunbathed in her undies, only the squawking gulls and they did not care. The book was a dusty gardening manual she had borrowed from the library. Its last date stamp was 1973 . . . That was sad; no one wanted to read the old book. Grace liked old books; there was often a handy tip or scrap of wisdom she could make use of in her cultivation of flowers.

She pottered through the book, her arm shielding the sun from her eyes. It was gloriously warm and her sun-starved shoulders were soaking up the essence of heat with pleasure. A line drawing caught her attention and she looked more closely. She recognized the big rosette of long leaves close to the ground. *Mandragora officinarum* var *vernalis* – the mandrake root. That was it! That's what she had growing in her garden. The plant that Titus hated and avoided at all cost.

How on earth had the plant got there? Its natural habitat was the Mediterranean and Greece, North Africa and Spain. Perhaps a bird had brought the seed and this sunny spot was enough to succour it. She read on, interested in its mythical properties and ancient lore. She remembered the fruits that followed the flowers, little yellow tomato-shaped things, clustered in the middle of the rosette. Chillingly, she read that their seeds, when sucked, caused dilation of the eyes and severe headaches, but if swallowed could cause temporary madness and a deep sleep. The seeds and powdered root were an opiate, and if used in excess could be poisonous.

23

Grace closed the book, keeping her finger in the place. It was not pleasant to think that she had such an evil-intentioned plant in her garden. Yet it was only evil in the hands of man. It did no harm sharing the earth and the rain. Perhaps a cold, frosty winter would finish it off. She did not fancy moving it.

She lay back, putting aside all thoughts of the mandrake root. What was more puzzling was what had happened to her tray of Giant Suncrested pansies. She had grown these superior pansies from seed, nurturing them along at every stage. Now they had suddenly vanished. She knew she was getting absent-minded in her old age, but to forget where she had put them . . . No, that was not possible. Titus often sat on a tray of tiny seedlings, ruining them, but these had been flowering well and were ready to put out.

She listened to the rhythmic wash of the waves on the pebbles, the seabirds crying, the wind riffling through the gorse. It was very therapeutic. She was almost asleep.

A small motor cruiser came chugging into the cove, the sound of its engine vibrating against the close walls of rock. Grace sat up, disturbed. It was putting down anchor right in the middle of Ladies' Pool, where she had planned to swim. A stocky young man in shorts was busy on deck; he was setting fishing lines, a ghetto blaster thumping out pop music at his feet.

He wouldn't catch anything with that racket going on, thought Grace. She tried to slide out of view, pulling up her straps, but he had seen her, whistled and waved. She was slim and brown so probably, at a distance, her age did not show. He cupped his hands and bellowed at her.

'Come on over,' he called. 'Come and say hello.'

She shook her head and held up her book, hoping he understood her intention of reading.

'Reading's boring,' he bellowed back. 'Come and have some fun.'

Grace began to feel annoyed. All she wanted was a little

peace and privacy, not fun. The cruiser swung on its anchor and she caught sight of the name *Sea Sprite* painted on the bows. She knew who the *Sea Sprite* belonged to. It was the Vaughans' boat. Surely the young man, whistling and inviting her over, was not the groom-to-be? Last wild oats, perhaps, but that was not quite the Vaughan style. Or could it be the other son, Jonathan, the one who was always away?

She might as well leave. Her swim was ruined. The young man was going to hang around until he caught something or came over. She was not going to stay to find out which came first. There was work to do and she had not yet decided if she could make an archway out of nothing.

'Don't go, sweetheart,' the young man bellowed again through cupped hands. 'I'm getting lonely.'

She was not surprised. He was altogether too brash and forward, a rather blotchy-faced young man with spiky hair. A quiver of alarm ran down her spine. She was alone in the cove. It wasn't safe.

Grace waited until his attention was drawn to the farthest side of the boat, then swiftly she caught up her belongings and made a hasty retreat along the rocks. She heard him call out to her again. She gave him a cheerful wave and scrambled up the zigzag path and steps, glad to be out of earshot, and not pausing in her climb until she reached the top of the cliff.

She stood at the top leaning into the strong wind, gasping, clutching a stitch in her side, panicking at the pain. That had been a mad, foolish climb. She was not a young chicken any more. If she was taken ill on the cliffs, no one would find her for hours, days even. What would happen to Titus? Who would look after him?

Gradually her breathing quietened. She calmed down and walked slowly towards home.

Pre-dawn on the wedding morning was bleak and chilly. Grace dragged on an extra jersey as she stumbled downstairs to make a pot of tea. Titus stirred in Grace's old shopping basket but decided to tuck his nose under a white paw and hang out a do-not-disturb sign.

The profit from this wedding is going to buy a new wheelbarrow, Grace decided as she cupped her stiff fingers round the hot mug of tea. She gave her rickety old contraption about ten days before the bottom fell out.

'So there's no phoning up the Kimberleys and saying you've got a headache,' she told herself aloud.

Titus gave a small snort of protest at the noise.

'Lazybones,' said Grace, curling her hand over his furry head. 'I hope I'm going to be a cat in my next life.'

The containers, baskets and posy rings had all been prepared with wire, Florapak and well-soaked moss the night before. Grace trudged down the path in semi-darkness to start cutting the flowers and putting them in pails of water. She did not have time to appreciate the glorious dawn tinging the horizon with pink and orange and streaking the far hills.

She switched on the van's headlights for the fifteen-mile drive to the outskirts of Helston, where she was to pick up a special order from a big market garden. It was nearly eight o'clock by the time she returned with a vanload of yellow chrysanthemums, cream freesia and tiger lilies. Her two girl helpers had arrived and soon the greenhouses and kitchen were a mass of blooms being cut and wired. Grace had still not had any breakfast, nor had Titus. He went out to catch his own.

Before they left for the church, Grace did a quick change into a more presentable shirt and jeans, made some instant coffee for them all and ran a comb through her short wiry hair. There was no time for anything more.

The fine old granite church was already a bustle of activity. The verger was vacuuming the carpet. A mechanic was wiring the altar steps for a recording of the service. Another young man with spectacles was unwrapping a parcel of printed service sheets. Fiona and Hal . . . Their names were emblazoned across the cover in gold.

Grace's team worked hard. Bursts of sunshine came through the narrow east windows, alighting on the mass of flowers, turning the yellow to gold, and the white to cream. The blooms brought the church to life, softening the Cornish stone, masking the slightly damp smell with their own fragrance.

Father Lawrence came down the aisle, his gown swishing round his ankles. He genuflected at the altar steps. He was not yet fully robed for the service; his starched lace and red brocade was laid out for him in his private robing room. He was a thin scarecrow of a man, his face unpriest-like in its lack of piety. Everyone spoke well of him, and he was always courteous and kind, but Grace saw no aura. Nothing at all. It was strange. He should have been bathed in a healing light, white or pale blue.

'Good morning, Grace,' he said. 'A busy morning.'

'Good morning, Father. Absolutely frantic. I've the marquee to do as well back at Tregony. And it's a big one. I'll be glad when today's over, I can tell you.'

'So shall I. I find these very fashionable receptions a little overwhelming. But Mrs Kimberley has organized everything so well, down to the last printed napkin.'

'I'm sure she hasn't missed anything. I hear the car is a vintage Rolls, out of a museum.'

He gave a short laugh. It sounded faintly derisory.

'Excuse me, but are you the flower lady?' a voice asked.

Grace would have liked to come back with a snappy retort, but the young man had a nice open face and warm brown eyes. He did not look too happy.

'I'm sorry. That was a stupid thing to say. You're hardly here to tarmac the drive. I'm Ralph, the best man of sorts. Of sorts, because I'm a total beginner at this. I only hope I get it all right.'

'Of course you will,' said Grace encouragingly. 'Make sure you've got the ring, and that your speech is short when they cut the cake.' The mention of food made her feel weak with

hunger. Her stomach rumbled. She should have had a biscuit.
'Now, if you don't mind I've still a lot to do . . .'

'I wouldn't dream of delaying you. It all looks marvellous.
You obviously have a gift, a very special way with flowers.
Adele – Mrs Kimberley – gave me a message for you. She
says the archway is round at the side of the church. Graham
knocked it up yesterday.'

Grace gasped aloud. 'Archway? Heavens, no. I said I
couldn't do one.'

Ralph shuffled with slight embarrassment. 'I'm sorry. I'm
only giving you a message. I don't know anything about it.'

'No, no, it's nothing to do with you. Don't worry. I'll sort
it out. It's not your headache.'

'I ought to go. The groom, you know. I phoned him and
he's a bit on edge,' Ralph said.

'You'd better be off, then. Can't have the groom fluffing
his lines.'

Grace left her helpers clearing up the church; not a petal
or a leaf must be left on the floor. She would inspect their
work later, putting the last final touches with the deft hand
that could twitch a bloom into a better position. But first she
had to find the archway. She almost fell over it outside. It
was dreadful, a bodged-up affair of bamboo sticks, plywood
and wire, leaning drunkenly against the wall of the church.
It would need a hundred flower heads, as well as moss and
fern, to cover it over. Hours of work, even if she had enough
flowers – even if she could get it to stand up. It would have
to be secured firmly to the front steps somehow. No, it was
impossible in the short time left.

A surge of anger nearly choked her. The gall of some
people, to expect miracles at the last moment. She hid the
archway out of sight and hurried round to the front entrance,
ashamed of her anger.

'Have we any flowers left?'

'Just a few, Grace. Bits and pieces.'

'Let me have them. I'll try to do something with the porch.

Perhaps I can put a few in the little niches at the side and on the handrail. What about ribbon?'

'Yards of ribbon. There's another roll in the van. I'll get it for you.'

They arrived a little late at Tregony to decorate the marquee. The caterers were everywhere, putting out furniture and linen. There was hardly room to move. Grace unloaded the van and put the flowering tubs immediately in place at the entrance. It was a kind of signature.

Mrs Carter was fussing about her cake, wanting the table first in the middle of the marquee and then by the entrance with the guest book. Grace ignored her, carrying in the four hanging baskets that would decorate the fluted edge of the doorway in the canvas.

'We can't have that hanging basket there,' said Mrs Carter, hot and flustered in a totally unsuitable tweed suit. 'It'll drip on my cake.'

Grace half hoped it would. Mrs Carter produced rock-hard icing that defied cutting. 'My baskets don't drip,' she said. 'But if you're worried, move your cake.'

Adele Kimberley shot her a look of dismay. She was trying to smooth Mrs Carter's ruffled feelings. Adele looked her usual immaculate self in a silky white tracksuit, not a hair out of place. Grace nodded to her but Adele was more concerned with paying for the cake. Grace saw a cheque change hands and hoped she would be paid as promptly.

It was hot in the marquee and Grace went to the garden tap to fill a fine spray can. She wondered if there was the slightest possibility of a cup of coffee from the caterers. As she rounded one of Adele's carefully planted flower beds, she caught sight of a splendid display of pansies in a rockery. She bent down on one knee to inspect their smiling faces, but as she did so, her heart fell. She would know them anywhere. They were her Giant Suncrested. The big yellow heads with hearts of blazing old gold.

She sat back on her heels, fighting down indignation.

They were her pansies, every one of them! How did Adele Kimberley come to have them in her garden? Surely she hadn't stolen them. Grace shook her head in disbelief; that was impossible . . . A woman like Adele would not stoop to stealing. Or would she? There was something fanatical about her arrangements for this wedding and reception.

'Are you all right?' A young woman in tattered jeans and a faded T-shirt was peering over her. 'It is getting hot.'

'I could do with a drink,' said Grace, moistening her lips. 'Perhaps some water. Everyone is so busy . . .'

'I can do better than that. Would you like a coffee? It won't take a tick. I know where everything is kept, and Adele won't mind.'

'If you're sure . . .'

'Sit down here in the shade and I'll be back.'

It didn't help that her view was of her giant pansies growing bigger by the minute, but it was nice to be treated like a person and not an invisible nobody. When the coffee arrived, it was blissfully strong and the good Samaritan (her aura was a lovely shade of violet) had also produced some sweet biscuits.

'You are kind,' said Grace, stretching out for the little tray. 'It's my own fault. I didn't have time for any breakfast.'

'I don't think many of us did! It's been all go from the start. Fiona's big day and all that.'

'Thank you again.'

'Just leave the tray by the back door when you've finished. Must fly. I'm Sandy. Got another loo to do.'

Grace went back to the marquee with renewed vigour. When everything was finished, she had to admit it looked perfect, cool and white, all the spotless tablecloths edged with garlands, the gleaming glasses, the glacial cake. Pity so many people had to come in and spoil the picture.

'Looks lovely,' said a passing waitress.

Adele was not around to pass comment. There was a flurry going on at the front of the house. The vintage car had arrived to take the wedding party to the church. Grace cleared up slowly. The rush was over and suddenly the garden was empty. Thank goodness she had nothing booked for this afternoon, but she still had her normal work in the greenhouses to do . . . watering and weeding. She paid off her helpers. They never had to wait for their money.

It was so quiet and peaceful in the garden that Grace could almost have forgiven Adele for pinching her pansies. She wandered around, thinking how nice it would be to own such a lovely house and garden, to have people to do things for you.

She was good at judging the length of a wedding service; she had done enough of them. She would disappear from Tregony before the party returned, go back to the church and remove the pew posies, which would soon suffer from a lack of water. The big set pieces she would leave in place for the Sunday service, though that meant another journey to collect the containers and dead flowers during the week.

Her timing was so good that she drove past the elegant vintage Rolls taking the bride and groom leisurely back to the house. It was her first glimpse of the bride, a radiant, ethereal creature in a bouffant ivory dress, leaning towards the man sitting at her side, her blonde curls bouncing in the breeze. It was all for this fragrant girl, this totally unknown girl, all this effort and back-breaking work.

As she drove past, Grace also glimpsed something disturbing. The bride's red aura was normal for a spirited, passionate young woman, but it was tinged with grey. Grey meant illness. Somewhere in her body were already the genes of disease. Grace thrust the thought from her mind.

Guests were still leaving the church and Grace had to wait while the traffic jam sorted itself out. Then she was able to ease the van into the car park as the last stragglers left. They were probably people who had only been invited to the church and so had no need to rush back to Tregony in case they missed the food and drink.

Food again, Grace groaned. It was becoming an obsession with her empty stomach. She planned a really nice supper for herself and Titus. They deserved it. And perhaps there would be a good film on television that they could watch together and relax.

The stone steps were littered with confetti and fake rose petals. No wonder some churches banned them; a brief fall of rain and it would be a sodden mess. At least the birds soon finished up rice.

As Grace walked down the aisle, she wondered for a moment if she had come to the wrong church. She stood stock-still, her heart suddenly thudding in her chest with unaccustomed fierceness. Fear crept up her spine again as if she was in the presence of something terribly evil.

It was a scene of devastation.

The flowers had been totally vandalized. They lay all over the place, trampled and broken, their glorious heads crushed, stems twisted, water trickling over the carpet in ominous stains. The big altar piece had been overturned, the container smashed; the hanging baskets hung drunkenly on broken chains, their contents spilling out; the pew posies had been torn down and stamped on beyond recognition.

'Oh . . . no . . . no,' she said, shaking her head. Grace trod carefully round the dying flowers, murmuring to herself, stepping over the ruined blooms, their perfume in death even more fragrant. 'Why . . . why?'

She did not attempt to clear up. There was nothing to salvage. She would have to tell Adele Kimberley immediately; unfortunate though it was. The police should be informed and the proper steps taken.

One small cream rose had escaped the plunder and lay forlornly in the shadows. Grace picked it up. It would finish the day in a single-stem vase on her window sill, but out of sight. She could not bear any reminder of this havoc.

Shakily she drove back to Tregony. There were so many cars in the leafy road that she had to park quite a distance away. She would have to pick her moment carefully, perhaps when the bride and groom had left. She could not break in with the awful news.

The garden and marquee were crowded with people strolling in the sunshine, tall champagne glasses in hand, lovely dresses and hats competing with the flowers. A small boy in a white sailor suit was jumping about by himself, at a loose end with no one to play with.

Grace watched Adele coming out of the back door. She almost tripped over the little tray which Grace had left there earlier. The tray slid down the step, the cup and saucer rolling down the paving stones with a noisy clatter.

'Who on earth left that there?' she said. 'What a stupid place to leave a tray.'

Grace darted forward to pick up the cup, hoping it was not chipped or broken, or valuable bone china. She retrieved the spoon from a lavender bush.

'I'm so sorry, that was me,' she said. 'A lady very kindly gave me a coffee when I was here earlier.'

Adele swung round on her. Her features were cool with annoyance. 'Grace, just the person I want to see. I've a bone to pick with you. What happened to the archway? The archway that I specially asked for. My husband spent hours making it. I suppose we shall get some outrageous bill for all the extra hours you'll say these decorations have taken you to do, when in fact you were lazing about here, drinking coffee and not bothering one whit about my daughter's wedding.'

Grace took a deep breath. She did not really know what to say. She was no good at defending herself. It had been the same when her husband left her. She had accepted all the blame for the breakdown of their marriage. It had seemed easier at the time.

'I'm sorry about the tray and the coffee,' she began. 'There will be no outrageous bill, only the agreed estimated cost. I couldn't do the archway. I told you on the telephone it was impossible. There was no way I could suddenly conjure up

33

all the flowers necessary to cover the archway your husband made. Flowers don't grow on trees, you know.'

Suddenly the absurdity of that remark hit Grace and her face creased into a bleak smile. But it did not last long. Adele was incensed by what she thought was Grace's insolence, and began anew.

'I'm not at all sure that we're going to pay your bill,' she argued. 'I wanted banks of flowers at the church. Where were they? A few miserable displays here and there. I wanted Fiona to walk into a church absolutely amass with glory. I was really disappointed, and so was Graham.'

'I'm sorry you were disappointed,' said Grace, her face stiff. 'I can't think what you expected. If you wanted massed banks of flowers then perhaps you should have employed the Bailiff of the Royal Parks to do your daughter's wedding.'

Grace almost added that there would be no charge whatsoever in the circumstances, but thoughts of her old wheelbarrow and the stolen pansies stopped her in time.

'I've no time to talk to you now,' Adele said. She turned to one of the waitresses. 'Please take my daughter a cup of tea. She's changing in her room.'

Adele swept away, lilac and blue silk fluttering in the afternoon breeze. Grace stared after her. She hadn't told her about the vandalized flowers. After this fuss, she would not be believed. They would say she had done it herself, out of spite. There had been no witnesses to her discovery. Trouble clouds were gathering over her like a summer storm.

'I'll wash and wipe the tray for you,' she said to the waitress making the tea.

'Thanks a lot,' said the girl. 'We're rushed off our feet.'

Grace found she was still holding the single cream rose. Whatever had possessed her to bring it in?

'Hold it! I want a shot of the workers. Elbow grease and sweaty brows. That's it, a bit of local colour, you know.

Smile please. Look as if you are enjoying it even if your feet are killing you.'

A video camera was humped on the young man's shoulder like a grotesque Quasimodo, his spiky hair not unlike the unkempt locks of Charles Laughton. Grace recognized him immediately. It was the cheeky young fisherman on the *Sea Sprite.* She pulled her crumpled shirt closer as if to disguise herself, but she need not have worried. This tired and dishevelled woman did not resemble in any way the almost-naked water nymph on the rocks.

She turned away from his probing camera. She did not want to be on record as one of the workers. She did not want Adele to be able to say, every time the video was run, 'and that's the awful woman who made such a mess of the flowers'.

Grace was alarmed by the bright solar disc around the young man. It was the overcharged yellow of a schizophrenic. She'd had a lucky escape.

She backed into the kitchen. A cup of tea stood on the counter, ready to be taken up to Fiona. Grace wiped the tray, then felt in her pocket for a handkerchief to dry her hands. Her fingers closed round seeds clinging to the seam and the lining of her pocket. She had picked them some days earlier, drying them off in the greenhouse, planning to try an experimental planting.

The mandrake seeds came easily out of her pocket, a few stuck under her nails, some clinging to her wet fingers. A charge of power came over her. It was a glorious, cleansing feeling, primeval and vindicating. She had the means, she had the opportunity, and for a moment she lost all sense of reason.

A really nasty headache, a little temporary madness, a deep but not fatal sleep. It was no less than the bride deserved, a kind of justice. After all, she was the cause of all this trouble. The cause of everything horrid that had happened today. Grace only had to stir the seeds into the cup.

'Shall I take the tray up?' Grace said, moving the cup of tea precisely into the centre of the tray.

She put the single surviving rose beside the cup of tea. It seemed an appropriate gesture.

# Two

O live Vaughan knew it was unreasonable, but at the same time perfectly justified, to carry the hurt and bitterness from a careless remark in her heart for six years. There were a lot of circumstances to take into consideration . . . Her pride, her insecurity and the queasy feeling that she felt every time she set foot on their new boat, *Sea Sprite*.

She never used to feel seasick; she had spent many hours pottering round the rocky Cornish coast with Norman, rarely sailing out of sight of land. But *Sea Sprite* was bigger. It had the most modern equipment, even stabilizers, but somehow she and the boat never synchronized. It was uncanny. It seemed like another way for Norman to cut her out of his life with a new purchase.

She stood unhappily on the deck, wondering how she was going to get into the galley to prepare lunch. She hung on to the rail, looking down into the green depths, mesmerized by the waves lapping against the white bows.

'Lunch?' Norman called. 'Is it ready?'

'No, sorry, not yet. It won't be long.'

She crept unsteadily down the narrow steps into the cabin and galley. It would have to be salad, though she doubted if she would be able to mix the French dressing. Norman's bottle of good Napoleon brandy stood on the side. It would help settle her stomach. She poured herself a small quantity and diluted the taste with some orange juice, pulling a face as she sipped at the concoction.

'Urgh,' she said, but did feel some relief as the fiery liquid slipped down her gullet. She poured herself a second glass, watching the brandy discolour the orange juice as she swirled it round.

'Purely medicinal,' she told herself.

The brandy warmed and relaxed her, enabling the task of preparing lunch to go ahead without mishap. There were cold salmon fillets sent down from Scotland to accompany the salad, with a fresh strawberry flan and cream afterwards. Olive always served a good meal, even on-board ship.

She went up on deck to tell Norman that it was ready, but also to get some fresh air. She had a feeling he would not approve of the brandies, and wanted to rid her breath of any fumes. A trim sailing dinghy was passing, crewed by bright young things in brief shorts and bikini tops, the men muscular and bare-chested. They waved cheerfully, and Olive waved back, distant and aloof. Norman's sleek new motor cruiser was a cut above a dinghy.

'Hey, get the latest fashion, girls.'

'Baggy pants!'

'Droopy drawers!'

The girls shrieked with laughter at their remarks. A slim teenager with straight blonde hair pulled out the sides of her skinny shorts and wiggled her hips.

'Elephant's pyjamas!' she hollered.

Olive heard a confusion of words as the dinghy skimmed by. She went red with humiliation. She knew they were laughing at her. *Elephant's pyjamas* . . . They were jeering at an overweight, middle-aged woman wearing a pair of voluminous navy and white striped cotton trousers. She gripped the rail, wishing that the entire dinghy would sink, hit a mine, rip out its bows on a submerged rock; that the mocking young blonde would soon be gasping for breath as the waves sucked her under.

She saw Norman wave as the dinghy cut out to sea. He came over, wiping his hands on a rag.

'Nice to see youngsters enjoying themselves,' he said.

'Your lunch is ready,' she said.

Olive was not quite sure when she had begun to put on weight. She had been a normal size fourteen after the birth of Hal, although she had always been solid round the hips. Somehow the weight had crept on when she was not looking. Being a good cook had not helped. Building up Norman's business connections had meant giving dinner parties for eight or ten people, or eating out at expensive restaurants with contacts. In the early days she had no more than a cleaning woman to help in the house, so she did all the catering. Cooking meant tasting, and the following day, finishing up. She hated to see good food wasted; it was a hangover from the Second World War, when food had been rationed and to waste half a banana was practically criminal.

She chased a slice of beetroot across her plate, the unkind remark still echoing in her mind. The outfit had been carefully chosen for its slimming effect: a plain navy tunic top concealing a heavy bust, and the striped trousers to minimize the inch war round the hips. She was not so much pear-shaped as pyramid-shaped, with a small neat head, her tinted hair coiffured and waved weekly by a hairdresser in Helston.

'I shall be in London on Wednesday and Thursday,' said Norman. 'Some Americans coming over. I'll be staying at the Grosvenor as usual.'

'Very well, dear,' said Olive, with relief. She liked the unfettered freedom that his business trips to London gave her. She could eat what she liked; wear what she liked; sit in front of the television with her feet up and a big box of chocolates at her side. And she could finish off the lot without a single pang of guilt. Whereas when Norman was around, she had to pretend that she ate abstemiously.

It was not fair. Norman had hardly put on any weight over the years. Perhaps he was a little more solid, but he carried it well. His brown hair was a brindled grey, but it suited him. In fact, he was better-looking now than in his youth.

Maturity looked well on him. So did his expensive suits and bulging wallet.

Norman Vaughan had worked hard, building up his father's business of making marine navigation instruments with customers in all parts of the world. His latest range of computerized instruments was able to tackle the increasingly demanding accuracy required. He was proud of his success. Olive took no interest in Vaughan Precision. She had never understood a word.

But she was grateful for the rewards it brought. In particular, Rosemullion House. Their love for the old manor house was one thing that she and Norman had left in common.

Olive's heart filled with pride when driving back to Rosemullion House of an evening. It was then, when the sun was sinking, that the greyish stone turned to a warm pink tinge, the mullioned windows gleamed with light and even the creeper on the walls glowed a reddish gold, the slate roof reflecting the sun like ingots of silver.

The house had once belonged to a Cornish tin-mine owner. He had made and lost money; the mine had long since been closed, but the house survived. It was set in twenty acres of park and woodland. It had seven bedrooms, three of them en suite; four reception rooms; a billiards room, tennis court and croquet lawn. The stables had been converted to garage three cars. Norman drove a Mercedes-Benz, Olive had a sedate Rover. Hal changed his car every year. At present he was running in a new Aston Martin. Jonathan was never home long enough to own a car.

There were panoramic views of moorland and distant views of the sea dashing against the rocks. Olive loved these views as much as the house, and so did Norman. But they never strolled the grounds together any more. Norman always seemed too preoccupied for Olive to intrude with her company, so she left him alone, sometimes watching from behind a long curtain, wondering where the earnest young man she married had gone.

The two drinks before lunch were a habit, even though she now employed a cook/housekeeper. She experimented among the bottles in Norman's cocktail cabinet and developed a liking for a dry martini or a cream sherry on the rocks. Sometimes she had a third sherry just to use up the ice in the glass, an economy which never failed to amuse her.

It was essential to keep her growing attachment to alcohol from Norman and the boys, so in their company, entertaining guests or dining out, her intake was modest.

'Just a teeny glass of wine for me,' she would say. 'It goes straight to my head, you know.' Or she would stick to orange juice, sometimes spiking it with vodka from the small flask she kept in her handbag.

Her day had a pattern of drinking. She liked a couple of dry martinis before lunch, some sweet sherry mid-afternoon with a slice of fruit cake, more dry martinis before dinner, some wine with the meal, then, if Norman was not home, she took two large brandies or whisky and dry ginger during the evening. She thought it was a reasonable amount. It never seemed to affect her. She knew nothing about unit intake. She was never drunk, and she was careful not to drive if she had been drinking alcohol. There had to be twelve hours without alcohol before she got into her car.

'Do you know where my twelve-year-old malt has gone?' Norman asked, coming through from his study with an almost-empty bottle.

'Heavens, how should I know?' Olive exclaimed. 'I don't even know what twelve-year-old malt is.'

'We shall have to watch any new staff,' Norman growled. 'I thought my drinks were disappearing.'

'I'll have a quiet word with Mrs Flynn,' said Olive.

From then onwards, she made sure she replaced what she drank, or kept her supply elsewhere in the house. Life took on a hazy quality in which Olive existed without feeling very much. It suited her. She did not want to feel anything.

One weekend Hal brought home a new girlfriend for a

game of tennis. Olive heard their laughter from the court, and strolled over to meet the girl. She liked to play the role of lady of the manor. She was wearing a flowing caftan in shot silk that swirled almost to her ankles, but was just short enough to reveal her feet in dainty sandals.

The girl was in the usual mould of Hal's girlfriends. Slim, lithe, blonde, reasonably pretty. Her long brown legs flashed round the court, her bouncy pleated white skirt showing glimpses of trim white panties. Hal broke off the game to bring the girl over to meet his mother. He had nice manners.

'Mother, this is Fiona Kimberley. She lives at Porthcudden, just along the coast.'

'I do know where Porthcudden is, Hal,' she said with a mouth as dry as dust.

'How do you do, Mrs Vaughan,' said Fiona, smiling prettily. 'What a lovely home you have.'

'How do you do, Miss Kimberley,' said Olive. 'Yes, it is a beautiful house. It's a Grade Two listed building, you know. Perhaps Hal will show you round after your game.'

'Oh, I'd like that,' said Fiona. 'We have a big house, but this makes ours look like a matchbox.'

'Fiona lives in Trewartha Close,' said Hal. 'On the old estate.'

'It's called Tregony,' said Fiona. 'A lovely Cornish word. The name came with the house. It has a good-sized garden, but nothing as gorgeous as this. My mother enjoys gardening.'

'How nice,' said Olive, bringing the conversation to a distinct end with an inclination of her head. She could not be civil for one moment longer. It had required the utmost effort to contain her indignation and hurt to say those few polite phrases.

*Elephant's pyjamas* . . . The young, brittle voice rang in her ears. And by the cruellest of fates, Hal had brought the same girl to his home, reminding his mother of an insult she had never forgotten. Everything about the jeering teenager on the dinghy was etched into Olive's mind – the short blonde hair blowing in the wind, the red lips, the boyish figure, the loud, insensible voice.

Olive strolled back towards the house, trying not to look as if she was hurrying. But she was. She was racing towards the only comfort she knew: the bottle of whisky hidden in the flower pantry behind the store of vases. She took a gulp of Scotch straight from the bottle, not waiting to pour it into a glass.

Why that girl? she thought, trembling. Of all the young women in Cornwall, Hal had to bring that one home. Olive supposed he had met her at the sailing club. It was where he picked up his girlfriends. Perhaps it would not last long, thought Olive, taking a slower sip as the alcohol did its work, soothing her.

But Hal continued to go out with Fiona. She was the bright, vivacious kind of girl he liked to escort around. Pretty too, but not beautiful. Still Olive could not forgive, though common sense told her that six years was a long time and Fiona had changed from a brash teenager to a pleasant young woman.

It was to take her mind off the growing seriousness between Hal and Fiona that Olive decided to take a shopping trip to London. Norman was already in London, seeing some Japanese customers. It was only five hours on the train from Truro. She would surprise Norman at the Grosvenor and perhaps they would see a show together and she could stay the night. It was a long time since she had been to the theatre.

She sat in a first-class carriage, watching the countryside flashing by, a flask of brandy tucked in her handbag. A few drops improved the coffee from the trolley.

London had changed and there were so many tourists about that it took Olive some minutes to get over her disorientation. She queued for a taxi to the West End and spent the afternoon shopping in Bond Street. She bought things she did not really want, but saying no to persuasive sales assistants was beyond her ability these days.

When her feet began to hurt, she took another taxi to the Grosvenor Hotel in Park Lane, over-tipping because of the status and size of the hotel. As she stood on the forecourt, reassembling her carrier bags, Norman came through the revolving doors of the hotel. She paused to adjust her hat, knowing he did not like her to look flustered or untidy. But as she did so, he turned and slowed down the glass door to allow a woman to emerge with less haste. It was the kind of courteous action that came natural to Norman. Olive went to greet him.

Norman had not seen her. He took the woman's arm and helped her into a waiting limousine. He spoke to the driver before getting into the back himself.

'The palace,' Olive heard him say quite clearly.

Olive stood on the pavement, dumbfounded. Her mind would not work. The palace? Buckingham Palace? And who was that woman? She did not look Japanese, although all Olive had seen was a woman wearing a slim cream trouser suit and a shady red hat.

She did not know what to do. She stood helplessly, surrounded by all her shopping, trying to decide. Eventually she went inside the hotel and up to Reception.

'Is there somewhere I can wait for my husband?' she asked. 'I seem to have missed him.'

'Would you like to wait in the coffee lounge? I could have him paged for you when he returns.'

'No, thank you. That won't be neceesary. I'm sure he won't be long.'

Olive deposited her coat and shopping in the cloakroom and ordered coffee and cream cakes in the lounge. She was thankful to be able to sit down and think.

She sat in the lounge for a long time, getting stiff and numb. She repeated her story about missing her husband to the curious waiter and ordered more coffee and cakes. She badly wanted to visit the ladies' room but dare not move in case Norman returned in her absence. It was all so stupid. Why didn't she simply go to Reception and ask for the key to his room? He would have a bathroom. She had every right, but something stopped her.

She was almost rigid with bladder discomfort and fatigue when she caught a glimpse of a red hat in the foyer. Norman was taking his coat from the woman's shoulders and shaking rain off it. They were both laughing. It was a special, intimate sort of laughter, not ordinary laughter at all. Olive withdrew deeper into the chair that had imprisoned her for hours, watching them through the fronds of a tall Swiss cheese plant. She was mesmerized by the scene. The woman was standing with her back to the lounge. She touched Norman's face briefly, a silent thank you for the loan of the coat. The warmth in his eyes was a knife in Olive's heart.

They went towards the lift together, holding hands like youngsters. Olive saw a folded pamphlet sticking out of Norman's jacket pocket. It was a theatre programme . . . Of course, the Palace Theatre. They had been to the theatre.

As the lift doors closed on them, Olive felt the first of the shock waves hit her. She closed her eyes to shut out the image of them together, but their outline was imprinted on her eyelids. They both had a maturity and confidence, a way of holding their bodies that showed they were at ease with the world, at ease with each other.

'Is Madame all right?' The curious waiter appeared to clear the table in front of her. 'Can I fetch you a drink?'

'I am feeling a little faint,' she said. 'Perhaps a brandy . . . Thank you.'

She could not stay under the same roof. After downing the drink, she paid her bill and waddled swiftly to the ladies' room, almost passing out with the relief. She collected her shopping and stood on the pavement in a daze, wondering where to go. She was lost and desperately unhappy. The last train back to Cornwall had long since departed. She would have to stay in town, but she dared not use her credit card. Norman always settled that account and he would notice a hotel debit and question it. She would have to pay with whatever cash she had on her.

It was the most miserable night of Olive's life. She stayed in a backstreet Asian-run hotel near Paddington station, all she could afford. She did not undress but slept in her creased petticoat. She slept because she emptied her flask and put herself out for the count.

In the morning she could not face the ketchup-stained tablecloths of the small basement breakfast room, and caught an early train to the south-west. She sat in the buffet car and drank coffee after coffee, hardly seeing the verdant countryside rolling past. It was a meaningless journey. She longed desperately for Rosemullion House to close its walls round her. She would never leave it again.

When Norman returned the next day, he was his usual self: quiet, courteous, distant. Nothing in his manner showed any sign of guilt or deceit. It could have been going on for years, thought Olive, and she would never have known.

'Were they nice? The Japanese?' she asked. 'Your business contacts?'

'Very polite,' he said with a slight smile.

'What did you do in the evening? I should imagine the Japanese must be difficult to entertain.'

'I took them to the theatre,' he said, taking a folded programme out of his briefcase. 'The Palace. I don't suppose they understood a word.'

He said it so smoothly. She wanted to shout at him, rage, shake the lapels of his expensive suit, throw the asparagus soup in his face. But Olive did nothing. And she was convinced she would never do anything about it. She was too much of a coward.

At first it was only curiosity, but gradually a new compulsion crept into her life. It became almost a lifeline to cling to. She began to live for the days and nights Norman spent in London, making her own plans with detailed precision.

It was a game, a game she played with all the skill she could muster. She became extremely clever and devious. She developed a cunning she did not know she was capable of, going to lengths that would have been labelled insane by anyone who did not understand.

She probably had gone insane.

Olive found what she wanted in an Oxfam shop: a shabby navy coat and nondescript felt hat. They were her disguise. As the train neared Paddington, she would go into the toilet and in that cramped compartment change her appearance. Even Norman would not have recognized the dowdy shopper who got off the train from Truro each time he stayed in town.

She became quite adept at following her husband around London. It was not in the least boring. In fact, she was more fully occupied than she had been for many years. She did not mind the hours she sometimes had to wait, as long as she could sit down. There was always so much to watch: people, tourists, traffic, then, with a mounting excitement, she would spot Norman and his svelte companion.

Occasionally she took herself to the same theatre or concert as Norman and the woman. She was really proud of herself when she managed this. She sat at some distance, keeping them within sight. She never really saw the woman close to or face to face. Her features were often in shadow under the brim of a big hat, or she wore her hair tucked into a silky turban with big glasses shielding her eyes.

Once Norman made a sharp turn in a theatre bar and almost collided with his wife. Olive had stood, frozen, wondering how on earth she could explain her presence. But he did not even notice her, his eyes being on the woman waiting by a window table.

'Sorry,' he said, doing a balancing act with two brimming glasses of white wine.

Olive merely nodded, keeping her head down. It was a

close thing. She almost turned on her heel to escape from the bar, but her need for a dry martini was stronger. She stayed in the bar till the curtain went up on Act Two and had to be asked to leave.

She no longer stayed in a fourth-rate hotel, but made sure her cash flow enabled her to spend the night at small, discreet, but comfortable hotels. She ate well too, often at the same restaurant as Norman. If the waiters thought her outfit a little shabby for an expensive eating place, she made sure they caught sight of her rings.

The evidence she collected was all itemized in a small notebook from Woolworths: dates, times, places. She also took a whole film of photographs of them together. She did not know what she was going to do with all the information. There was no thought of divorcing Norman.

She kept everything in a capacious handbag, though somehow she lost the packet of photographs. She had a feeling she took them out whilst hunting for some seasickness pills. A quick search of the cruiser found nothing, so she feared they had gone overboard with the rubbish.

Twice she spoke to the woman on the phone. She knew instantly that it was her when a husky female voice asked for Mr Norman Vaughan. Olive felt very calm, although she was momentarily at a loss for something to say.

'I'm so sorry,' she said, assuming the Scots accent of Mrs Flynn, their housekeeper. 'Mr and Mrs Vaughan are dining out with old friends.'

There was a pause. Olive felt pleased with her ingenuity. That would give the woman something to think about. The Vaughans were regarded as a married couple and out with friends. It was the part of Norman's conventional life from which she was excluded.

The second time the woman phoned, Olive had an even better ploy.

'Mr Vaughan is in London on business. Can I give him a message when he returns?'

'Er . . . no thank you. It's not important.'

Olive put down the receiver with a satisfied grin. She could see Norman outside in the garden talking to their gardener. Now the woman would think Norman was in town without contacting her. It was a nice touch. Perhaps she would start to wonder if Norman was seeing someone else or had grown tired of her . . .

Norman was careful. There was never any clue as to the woman's identity. He never called Olive by a different name by mistake. Olive was no nearer to a name than the day she first saw them outside the Grosvenor.

One lunchtime there was a subtle change to the pattern. Norman and the woman were eating at a small riverside pub that was one of their favourite places. But instead of eating, they let the food grow cold in front of them. Their hands were linked across the table and Olive sensed a tenseness. Norman's face was serious and he seemed to be doing a lot of talking. The woman kept shaking her head. She stood up to go, buttoning her slim black jacket. Norman's face was pale beneath his customary healthy Cornish tan.

As the woman threaded her way through the pub's customers, Olive realized that this was her chance to find out the identity of the woman. She gulped down a glass of Chablis and hurried out after her. The woman was hailing a taxi and Olive was near enough to hear her ask for Paddington station.

Another taxi came cruising by, red light on, and Olive flagged it down, blood pounding in her veins.

'Paddington, please.' She nearly added 'follow that cab', but there was no need because they were doing exactly that.

She nearly lost sight of the woman among the travellers at the station. Olive pushed through the bustling crowds, craning for sight of that big-brimmed red hat. Then she saw her quarry hurrying on to platform four, walking quickly, her shoulder bag bumping against her hip. Olive's gaze flew to the indicator board and the destination leapt out: TRURO.

Truro. Cornwall. At first it made no sense. It was as if it was a foreign place. Olive began to move, awkwardly, not knowing what she was going to do.

'Do you want this train, missus?' asked the porter at the barrier. 'If so, you'd better hurry. It's signalled to go.'

Olive jumped on to the train with more agility than she had shown for years. The woman was from Truro. It made the affair seem far, far worse than Norman picking up some London tart. All through the journey, Olive tried to unscramble the facts. At each stop, she checked carefully that no red hat alighted. But she knew already. They were both going to Truro.

Suddenly Olive was very tired. Following Norman round London had been exciting, a challenge to her ingenuity, and she had lived for practically nothing else. It had become an obsession. But it would be impossible to continue locally. She was too well known, a name at the sailing club and in the social round. Besides there would be no frisson of excitement in going round Helston in an old coat and hat. She would look ridiculous. And someone would be sure to recognize her.

At Truro, the woman in the red hat went straight to a phone booth and apparently phoned for a taxi. Olive hurriedly retrieved the Rover from the car park and waited at a discreet distance.

Olive followed the taxi through the streets of Truro. She had an unreal feeling of suspense as they left the shops behind and drove out into the countryside. They went through small grey villages towards an area of affluence, of white villas, guest houses, retirement bungalows. The dark saloon ahead slowed down and turned into a leafy road . . . Trewartha Close. Where had she heard that name before?

The car stopped outside a large, white stone house. The woman got out, paid the driver, and hurried down the drive, almost at a run. By the time Olive reached the house, she had disappeared indoors and the front door was closing.

Olive slowed down almost to a standstill, the engine still running. She stared at the rustic name of the house. Tregony. Tregony . . . Hal's new girlfriend, Fiona, lived at Tregony, Trewartha Close.

She sat back, trembling with shock. That's why everything about the woman seemed so familiar. It was Fiona. Norman was having an affair with his son's girlfriend. It was obscene. Hal was an elaborate smokescreen and they were both using him. They could meet openly at Rosemullion House without anyone being suspicious. It was so clever and devious. Olive was shattered. It would be a long time before she discovered she was mistaken.

Somehow she drove home, negotiating the steep, winding lanes and endless blind corners almost automatically. It was not until she reached the sanctuary of her bedroom that she realized she was still wearing the Oxfam clothes. She flung them into a corner of the room and began to sob, the great tears rolling down her plump cheeks as if they would never stop.

'Mother, I hope you don't mind but I'm moving out,' said Hal some days later.

'Moving out? I don't understand.'

'I'm going to live in a place of my own. I've found a small flat.'

'But what's wrong with your home? Don't you like it here any more?'

'It's not that, of course not. But I want to be independent and manage for myself. Don't you think it's about time?'

Olive knew in a flash. It was in Hal's eyes. She had always been able to read Hal, knew when he was lying. He was not telling the whole truth now; he was half lying.

'You're going to live with that girl, that Fiona Kimberley,' she accused, spluttering with indignation. 'That brash, rude girl. You're going off with her. Don't lie to me, Hal. How could you?'

'Don't make a big thing of it, Mother. Lots of people live together before they get married. It's better than making a mistake.'

'Get married? You're not going to marry her, surely? You hardly know the girl. Oh, Hal, when there are so many nice young women around. Who are they anyway, the Kimberleys? They come from London.'

'You talk as if we're something special, an ancient local family. We're not, Mother. We only live in a bigger house and have more money. I love Fiona, and if everything works out, we may get married.'

'I don't want to hear any more of this ridiculous notion,' said Olive. 'You are not going to live with this girl, and you are not going to marry her.'

Hal's dark eyes glinted dangerously, and for a moment he looked very much like Norman when he was angry. 'Don't make me say something I might be sorry for, Mother,' he said. 'You can't stop me.'

Olive thought there might be some reaction from Norman, but he took the news quite calmly, as if he expected it. But then it all fell into place. This was the news Fiona would have been telling him at that riverside lunch, that it was all over, that she preferred to be a young wife than a young mistress.

'Aren't you going to stop him?' she demanded of Norman.

'No, why should I? It seems quite a sensible thing to do, these days.'

'But our friends . . . the sailing club . . . what will they think?'

'Since half of the sailing club seems to be living with the other half, I doubt if it matters much what they think,' he said with a wry smile.

'Then it's up to me to do something about it,' she cried. 'I won't stand by and let our son ruin his life with this cheap floozie.'

'What an odd description,' said Norman, filling his pipe slowly. 'I thought she was rather a nice girl.'

Olive found there was nothing she could do to stop Hal's plans. He and Fiona moved into a very small flat overlooking the estuary, and seemed to be happy. Olive and Norman were invited to Sunday lunch one weekend to meet Fiona's parents. It was a disastrous occasion. Olive took an instant dislike to Adele Kimberley when she saw how slim and dainty she was. It simply was not fair.

'We want you all to know that Hal and I are going to be married in the summer,' said Fiona, her eyes shining. 'So keep the first Saturday in July free. It's going to be our big day.'

'Darling, how wonderful,' said Adele, giving her daughter a big hug. 'So you've decided to make it legal.'

'It's a shotgun wedding.' Hal grinned, then realized his mistake. 'No, I didn't mean anything like that! I mean that Fiona is bullying me into it. She thinks I'll do more of the chores if I'm a legal husband.'

'You're always sailing or fishing,' Fiona pouted.

'Aren't you pleased, Mrs Vaughan?' said Adele, turning to Olive. 'They'll make a lovely couple.'

Olive was hardly listening. She was watching her husband's face for signs of distress. His thoughts seemed miles away, then he visibly made an effort to return to the room.

'We're very pleased,' said Norman. 'Hal's a lucky fellow.'

'July? Heavens, I'm going to have a rush, arranging everything,' said Adele in mock despair.

'Mother is going into overdrive,' said Fiona, taking Hal's hand. 'She loves organizing things. I ought to have warned you about this.'

'I'd better start saving up,' said Graham. 'If I know Fiona, she'll want a big wedding.'

'I'm going to invite absolutely everybody,' she exclaimed happily.

Olive tried to put a pleased look on her face, but all the time she was asking herself how she could let her son marry his father's ex-mistress. And a big wedding . . .

there was no outfit in the world that would make her look presentable for a fashionable wedding. She might as well say she would not go.

'You will come, won't you, Mother?' Hal asked gently, seeing the dismay cross her face.

'Of course,' she said stiffly. 'I could wear elephant's pyjamas,' she added.

Everyone looked at her blankly, not sure if it was a joke. Fiona came over and sat beside her.

'You wear what you like,' she said pleasantly. 'We want you to be there.'

'There's the family Bruges lace veil,' said Olive as they left. 'You may borrow it if you wish.'

Norman bought the couple a bungalow for a wedding present. Olive thought it was completely over the top, but then he would want Fiona to have a comfortable lifestyle. A good dressmaker in Truro made her an outfit in turquoise chiffon, a dress and three-quarter coat. It was cool and summery and Queen Mother-ish, but it was concealing and quite elegant with toning shoes and a curiously odd straw hat.

They had a fishing party on board the *Sea Sprite* the weekend before the wedding. It was a glorious day, the kind that Cornwall sometimes produces after a week of mist and rain, the sea glittering, the air so light. Olive was in a perpetual brandy haze now that she did not have to drive to Truro or go up to London. She had instructed Mrs Flynn to prepare a luncheon hamper. She sat on deck on a lounger, nodding in the sunshine, hardly aware of her surroundings or anyone else, or even whether it was night or day.

She hurt so much inside. She felt bloated and ugly. She was a battered wife but not a bruise showed.

While Norman unpacked the hamper, she cleared away some of the smelly fishing tackle left on the deck, moving unsteadily, her fingers responding automatically. She put a small, silvery harpoon dart in her handbag without really knowing why. It seemed a tidy idea.

The wedding was a lavish affair. She had to admit, grudgingly, that Adele had organized everything to perfection, and the food and drink were generous. Fiona looked like a princess, and if it had not been for the pain in Norman's eyes, Olive could almost have accepted her as a suitable daughter-in-law.

Olive stood in the receiving line in the garden of Tregony smiling graciously, but at the same time managing to convey that this was all very much beneath her, and that the reception should have been held at Rosemullion House. She found that Fiona's relatives were quite pleasant, and that the thin elderly woman in a classic lavender ensemble that shrieked Paris actually had a title. That surprised her. The waitresses were coming round with laden trays and the Buck's Fizz was strong and plentiful. She managed to down three fast glasses.

She tried not to watch Adele drifting about like a beautiful gossamer butterfly while Norman stood searching the garden with his eyes, obviously under some strain. Some idiot friend of Hal's called Izzy kept trying to take a video picture of her, but she refused bluntly. She knew the hat was wrong. She wanted no record that she was even at this wedding.

Hal installed her in a comfortable cushioned cane chair in the shade of the marquee. He was being very kind and considerate. The garden was a picture. People kept coming over to talk to her as if she was royalty.

'Only a very little, please. Oh, that's far too much,' she protested as Graham brought her a plate of cold turkey and salad. 'Thank you, so kind. Your garden is really lovely.'

'Adele does most of it. She enjoys gardening.'

The speeches went right over Olive's head. She heard people laughing and clapping. Graham's was long-winded but Olive did not hear a word. Everyone was watching the cake-cutting ceremony and Olive wondered if this was a good moment to tip some of her flask into the empty champagne glass. Her hand was reasonably steady as she unfastened the flask and poured out the dark golden liquid.

She heard a rustling nearby and someone put a plate on the table beside her. On it was a slice of wedding cake. It looked sweet and sugary, glossy with chopped cherries and her taste buds wept with desire.

'For you, Mother-in-law,' said Fiona, smiling as she handed Olive the plate. 'To wish us luck.'

Then Fiona saw or smelt the brandy in the champagne glass. She did the unforgivable. She winked at her new mother-in-law. It was a familiarity that Olive could not tolerate for a second. The anger and humiliation of the last months and years surged to the surface in an uncontrollable and violent paroxysm of rage.

'Elephant's pyjamas,' she choked. 'You tart. You think I don't know. I know everything!' Then, wrapping shreds of dignity round her like a cloak, she asked, 'Would you show me where the cloakroom is?'

As she followed Fiona unsteadily into the house, bladder bursting, the cream wedding dress rustling and flowing in waves of hazy light from that slim waist, Olive's fingers closed on something long and sharp and unfamiliar in her handbag. It was a harpoon dart, dried fish scales still clinging to the shaft. It was like an omen.

Olive locked herself into the lavatory, perspiration breaking through the thick make-up. She did not recognize the clown's face in the mirror, distorted with violence.

# Three

The garden at Tregony had belonged to Bert long before the Kimberleys bought the property. It had once been part of a big estate, a piece of Cornish rural history that had been dismantled and divided, the old manor house crumbling into a ruin and pulled down when it became dangerous.

As a boy, Bert played in the grounds, hiding in bushes, climbing trees, roaming wherever he wanted. His father had been employed as a gardener so there was no question of trespassing. The whole place was his to explore. He knew every tree as a friend, every slope like his own limbs, the scent of the earth as intimately as his inner skin.

The dissolution of the estate began when he was at school, so at first he did not notice when his playground began to shrink. Land was sold off, the house boarded up and abandoned. Bert played among the nettles, hardly aware that soon his father would be out of work.

'Aye lad, things are changing,' said his father. 'Soon there won't be anyone wanting gardeners. We're a dying breed. You'd better learn a trade.'

'I don't want to learn a trade,' said the young Bert. 'I'm a gardener.'

They did not foresee a new generation of home-owners who were far too busy earning money to do more than a little weekend pottering in a greenhouse. As the new roads cut through the estate and houses were built on prime sites, Bert had no difficulty in getting work. He watched with despair as the developers cut down familiar trees and levelled the ground, but still there were features of the old estate that only he could recognize.

Some of the hurt healed as the big gardens matured, and saplings grew and became friends, and bushes took shape under his pruning. Birdsong returned and tranquillity descended in the calm of the evenings. Tregony was one of his favourite gardens and he landscaped it successfully through several owners. It had two of the original silver birch trees and a massive rhododendron walk that had somehow escaped the bulldozers' ruthless swathe.

Bert never married; he lodged with Daisy, a widow, in the village. His only love was the earth of Cornwall. People did not matter. There was nothing permanent about them.

'The lifespan of a tree, now that's really something,' he told Daisy, bringing her a cabbage like a green globe from one his gardens.

'If you say so,' said Daisy. 'Your tea's ready, Bert. On the table.'

'Right.'

He was not unlike a tree himself. He was big and burly, weathered and gnarled. Sometimes he even dreamt he was a tree. No one remembered a young Bert. He had grown up gnarled, with a thatch of grizzled hair and eyes perpetually screwed up against the elements, even when indoors.

'Bloaters,' he said, sitting down.

'Nice and fresh.'

When the Kimberleys bought Tregony, he had continued to tend the garden in his usual dogmatic manner. He brooked no interference. He decided what should go where, what flowers should be bedded, what vegetables grown. Most people did not mind. They were only too pleased to leave it to someone who knew what he was doing. Adele was busy with her children and, apart from a climbing frame and a sandpit, the Tregony garden stayed much the same as Bert had always had it.

When the children started school, Adele found herself with

time on her hands. Daisy came three times a week to help in the house, and everything ran like clockwork. Adele began to take an interest in the garden, much to Bert's dismay.

It became a battle of wills. Adele had ideas and liked to experiment. She also held the purse strings and the clout, but she did not have the know-how. When a plant died, or some exotic vegetable refused to germinate, she tended to be suspicious of Bert's administrations rather than her own ignorance.

'Wrong soil,' Bert grunted, digging up a shrivelled root of fennel.

'Oh, nonsense, I've seen it growing in Cornwall.'

'Needs chalk,' he said stubbornly.

Adele did not like to argue with Bert. Graham was not interested in gardening, and where else would they get anyone willing to put in so much time? He had done everything his way for years, simply ignoring Adele's requests and instructions.

'Let's grow mangetout this year,' said Adele. 'I've bought the seeds. We'll start them off in the greenhouse.'

Bert grunted and stared at the ground. Cabbage he liked, and cabbage he would grow, not them flat foreign peas.

Adele put off telling Bert about the wedding for weeks. She knew he would not take kindly to her suggestions for a colour scheme, nor the marquee. Graham had no patience with her.

'For goodness sake, tell the old bugger. You're the boss. It's our lawn. If we want a marquee on it, we'll have one,' he said.

'But he's so proud of that lawn.'

'I'm proud of that lawn. If it gets damaged, I'll buy a new one.'

'You don't understand. It's sort of personal to Bert.'

'Rubbish. Grass can't be personal. I'll speak to him if you won't.'

'No, I'll do it. I'll have to pick the right moment, and go bearing a large slice of his favourite cherry cake.'

Bert heard about the wedding from Daisy. She prattled on and on about the arrangements till Bert had to take some notice. He was only vaguely aware that Fiona existed. She had been at school, then out to work, only making weekend use of the Tregony garden when Bert wasn't around anyway. He doubted if he would recognize her if he saw her.

'A marquee? I'm not having no stupid tent messing up my lawn. What's wrong with a hotel or the village hall?'

'People like the Kimberleys don't hire the village hall,' said Daisy, hiding a superior laugh. 'And a hotel won't be big enough. There's going to be hundreds of guests.'

'Not on my lawn, there isn't.'

When Adele broached the subject, armed with a mug of strong coffee and a generous slice of his favourite cake on a plate, Bert had his arguments ready.

'Ruin the lawn. Never recover. That grass has been there twenty years.'

'Then it won't hurt if we have to have it re-sown,' said Adele with artificial cheerfulness. She took a deep breath and went on. 'All the flower beds will be planted with yellow and white flowers. A sort of colour scheme, so that everything is matching.'

'What about them carnations, the biennials I started off last year?' he grunted, ignoring her remarks. 'They're ready to go out.'

'Oh, those carnations? What colour are they they?'

'Pink and red and white.'

'We can't use anything pink or red. They'll have to go unless you can separate the white blooms. No, I shan't want them. But the white will be lovely.'

A shutter came down over Bert's eyes. 'What about my phlox, my blue phlox?'

'It'll have to be moved or cut back.'

'That herbaceous border has been there twenty-five years,' he roared indignantly.

60

'Then it's time we had a new one!' Adele glared back, turning on her heel. The man was impossible.

When Adele reported her lack of success, Graham was merely amused. He was not interested in the garden. Adele could fill the flower beds with rhubarb for all he cared.

'You'll either have to put your foot down, or do the work yourself,' he said, pouring out his first vodka of the evening.

'That's impossible,' Adele said. 'I've got hundreds of things to do for this wedding. I can't do the garden as well. Tomorrow, I'm going to see Mrs Carter about the cake. Now, there's another difficult person.'

'Then don't have her.'

'But she makes the best fruitcake for miles. And her icing is very professional. Besides, I thought up a special design and you can't get that from a High Street baker's.'

'You're making a rod for your own back with all these special arrangements. Fiona won't notice the garden or the cake; she'll be too preoccupied with Hal.'

Adele started to defrost their ready-meal supper in the microwave. 'I don't agree with you. People *do* notice these little touches. Our guests will notice, especially the Vaughans. I want to impress them. I want everything to be perfect for Fiona's wedding.'

'Wedding cakes are either round or square.'

'Boring ones are. I want something different.'

'How about a model of the church, or their boat, the *Sea Sprite*? Now the Vaughans would be really impressed by that.'

'Don't be silly, Graham,' said Adele, serving out their meal on plates to heat up. 'You're not taking this wedding seriously.'

'As long as I take the bills seriously,' he said, opening his newspaper at the stock exchange page, 'that's what you ought to be worrying about.'

Bert planted out the carnations, ostentatiously following

61

Adele's instructions for only the white blooms. He also planted white daisies and asters to show willing. He liked asters and daisies. It was weeks before Adele discovered that he had planted all the carnations, and that a riot of red and pink were coming into bloom indiscriminately. She was appalled. She felt like pulling up the lot and tossing them on the compost heap. It was one more example of Bert's insubordination.

Adele hurried round the garden, wondering what else Bert had planted against her wishes. She poked through the flower beds with a stick, wishing she knew more, that she could recognize varieties when they were tiny. No doubt Grace, the flower lady, could recognize them all. Perhaps she would ask her to call in.

Bert sat in his shed, drinking strong tea from the flask Daisy filled for him. Mrs Kimberley always gave him coffee, which he disliked. But she could bake a good cake, he gave her that, even if she knew nothing about gardening. He distrusted anyone who looked neat and tidy for outdoor work. Work clothes was work clothes and a bit of dirt did no harm.

He watched her planting out a tray of French marigolds and African marigolds. She had a proper little mat to kneel on and wore gardening gloves. It were a ridiculous carry-on. He didn't reckon this wedding much. But Daisy was full of it. She talked of nothing else.

'The food that's been ordered! Enough to feed an army. Turkey and ham and prawns and salmon and dozens of different salads. And meringue cases filled with raspberries and strawberries. It fair makes my mouth water,' said Daisy.

'Mine, too,' said Doreen, her daughter. 'Mrs Carter was in the salon this morning for her usual perm. The cake is going to be four tiers, can you believe it? Four tiers! It'll fall down, Mrs Carter says. No one has four tiers, except royalty. And she wants the cakes shaped like a clover leaf, each one bigger than the other. Mrs Carter says it'll be a nightmare to bake, but Mrs Kimberley won't listen.'

'Clover leaf? That's a rum idea.'

'It's based on the clover design of the castles around here.'

'Well, I never. I never knew that. There'll be a lot left over,' said Daisy, knowingly. 'It won't cut. I'll be getting it for elevenses for weeks.'

Doreen rubbed her aching legs. Hairdressing was tiring work but Cutters was the best salon around that part of Cornwall and she was making good money. 'Mum . . . you know my party, my engagement party? Well, why don't we have it the same day as the Kimberley wedding?'

'Heavens girl, don't be daft. I shall be worked off my feet that day. I couldn't do a party as well. You're expecting a bit much, aren't you? I don't suppose you'll be around to give me a hand.'

'We're doing the hair for the wedding. The bride and the bridesmaid both have appointments. I think Mrs Kimberley is coming in the day before.'

'Then your party is definitely out.'

'But think, Mum. There's bound to be a lot of food left over, and you know how generous Mrs Kimberley is. Remember their last dinner party when she gave us enough chocolate gateau for a week? You're bound to bring home all the leftovers. Perhaps even a few bottles of bubbly!'

'Doreen, you've got something there. Now, I wouldn't mind doing a party for you if the food all came ready prepared. It's standing in this kitchen making all them sausage rolls and cutting sandwiches that get's me down.'

'First Saturday in July, then,' said Doreen happily. 'I'll start inviting people. Thanks, Mum, it'll be really smashing.'

'Just pray the wedding guests don't come hungry!'

'Perhaps the wedding'll be cancelled,' said Bert, who had been only half listening. 'Wreck my lawn, indeed. Maybe she'll change her mind.'

'Fiona Kimberley change her mind? That'd be a laugh,' said Doreen. 'She's had her eye on Hal Vaughan for years, but he doesn't know it, poor soul. That girl's determined to be mistress of Rosemullion House.'

'But isn't there another brother?'

'He's not interested in anything except travelling the world and trying to save animals. Perhaps he ought to come back and save Hal Vaughan from his fate.'

Bert munched thoughtfully through a plate of custard cream biscuits and gulped down a mug of tea. He liked the Vaughans. They had a lovely garden, and didn't keep changing things. Once, Mr Vaughan had invited him to come and take cuttings, but he had never gone. It had seemed like an imposition, taking cuttings from somewhere like Rosemullion House, but it would have been very pleasant, like being a proper guest.

But if Fiona Kimberley was anything like her mother, what would she do to the garden there? It didn't bear thinking about. She'd have them Frenchie peas growing everywhere in no time. The more he thought about it, the more he was convinced the wedding was a big mistake. It was going to ruin his lawn, disturb his herbaceous border and goodness knows what it was going to do to Rosemullion. It was a disaster all round.

Bert watched the marquee going up on the Thursday with the same feeling of grief that had consumed him during the felling of his beloved trees. The noise was appalling, all the hammering and banging of metal stakes being driven into his beautiful velvet lawn and the heavy boots of the workmen tramping over fragile blades of verdant summer grass. He ground his teeth, grimed nails clenching into the hardened pad of his hand. He felt so helpless; there was nothing he could do.

He paced the perimeter of the garden like a big bear, ready to pounce on any foot that trespassed on to a flower bed. Any blossom that was accidentally damaged by a clumsy arm, any infringement of the garden that was his domain and they would hear about it.

'They'll hear about it,' he growled. 'They'll hear about it. My word, I won't have none of it. Not at Tregony.'

The next morning, the Friday, he arrived early, anxious to repair any damage to the lawn. The monstrous tent flapped wetly in the dew-hung breeze, a Goliath of canvas, damp-white and slumbering. It didn't look like his garden at all.

Something else was wrong. Bert sniffed the air, screwing his eyes to slits. There was a subtle difference in the familiar outlines and colours. At first he could not pinpoint the change. He tramped the flower beds, puzzled, bewildered. Then he realized . . . Where were his phlox, his delphiniums, the round clumps of blue lobelia, the pink and red carnations? A hard lump formed in his throat. Dewy heads of flowers nodded at him, but they were all stiff strangers, yellow and white. Where were his old friends, his companions? They had all gone.

A mounting roar choked on the lump as a hazy red fury swam across his eyes. He staggered into his shed, stumbling and swearing, groping about in the darkness.

Fiona's first scream came at seven thirty a.m. on the morning before her wedding day. She was spending some pre-wedding nights at Tregony. Hal was abroad, so the flat was empty and she knew Adele liked the convention of having the bride at home.

She was in the bath, up to the armpits in rose-scented bubbles, when she glanced up. Staring at her through the window was the most enormous black-faced gorilla with staring eyes, bared fangs and teeth, growling ferociously. She screamed and screamed with terror, transfixed, her mouth locked into the piercing sound.

There was an uproar, a commotion. No one knew for sure what was happening. Adele banged on the locked bathroom door. Graham looked out of the window, then threw on a dressing gown and ran downstairs. Someone had moved the ladder from their double garage.

'What the hell's going on? I'll get the idiot, the fool,'

Graham shouted, holding his bad back as he hurried round to the back of the house.

'Open the door, Fiona,' Adele called, trying to sound calm. 'Let me in, please.'

'What's the matter with Fiona? Why is she screaming?' asked Timmy, wide-eyed. 'Is she ill?'

'We don't know. Daddy's gone downstairs to find out. Go back to bed, there's a good boy,' said Adele.

'But it's time to get up.'

Graham found Bert lumbering down the ladder, still wearing the gorilla mask over his sweating face. Graham sacked him on the spot. He refused to listen to Bert's explanation about clearing the gutter of leaves.

'Clear out and stay out. You've scared my daughter. I don't ever want to see you here again,' ordered Graham, furious. 'I'll send your money round.'

It took Adele a while to calm Fiona and Graham, who was incoherent with rage. Bert disappeared somewhere but Adele was much too busy to care. Aunt Elvina and Carolyn were due to arrive after lunch and there was still the guest room to prepare, Timmy to ferry to and from school, a visit to the hairdresser's and meals to cook.

She and Daisy cleaned and polished all morning. Once it was done Adele did not intend to even lift a duster. She hoped none of the wedding guests would wander through the house expecting a guided tour.

'I'll stay as long as you need me tomorrow,' said Daisy, rinsing out the polishing cloths in an excess of suds. She was always heavy-handed with other people's detergent.

'Just an hour in the morning would be lovely,' said Adele. 'I'd like you to come and wash up the breakfast things, then give the bathroom and downstairs loo a last-minute go.'

Daisy was not sure that she had heard clearly. 'But I can stay all day and help with the clearing up,' she faltered. Plates of leftover sliced turkey and bowls of pink seafood started to recede into the distance, leaving a strong, lingering smell of good food wasted.

'There's no need, Daisy. The catering firm are bringing all their own staff. They'll do the clearing up. It's part of their service. So you can go home and put your feet up for the weekend.'

Daisy's face fell. She saw cartons of cream going home unopened with the waitresses, punnets of strawberries in their carrier bags. She would have nothing at all for Doreen's party, and she had only bought a few packets of crisps. Panic set in. Now she would have to rush to the shops and see what she could buy. The expense would be unthinkable. Doreen had asked far too many people for their small cottage.

'Well, if that's what you want, Mrs Kimberley,' she said stiffly, folding up the cloths with a contained precision. 'I had hoped to be here for Miss Fiona's wedding, seeing I've known her years.'

'But you're very welcome to come to the church, Daisy, of course. Do come. We'd love to see you there.'

'Mebbe,' said Daisy, struggling into her coat. 'Or mebbe I won't.'

Adele could not understand what she had said or done. A sourness clouded the atmosphere. She had thought Daisy would be pleased to be let off the clearing up, but quite the reverse. Daisy seemed positively annoyed. Sometimes Adele simply did not understand the mechanics of people's minds, especially the people who worked for her.

Adele suddenly remembered the flowers and hurried out to the garage, bringing back an armful of carnations, all shades of red and pink.

'A few flowers for you,' said Adele. 'Just a little thank you for all the extra work.'

'Very kind,' said Daisy even more stiffly, taking them with a curt nod. Flowers. Fat lot of use. No one could eat flowers.

Daisy's face was more than Adele could stand. She hurried

next door with another armful of blooms. Sandy opened the door, taken aback by the sight of her flower-laden neighbour.

'Heavens, what's this? A deputation? There must be something you want me to do.' Sandy grinned.

'Now you've spoilt everything. The flowers are a present, but I have got a favour to ask.'

'They are lovely,' said Sandy, taking the large bunch of delphiniums and stocks and sniffing their perfume. 'There you are up to your eyebrows, getting ready for tomorrow, and somehow you find time to bring me some flowers.'

'Watch my halo.'

'How can I help?'

'Could you be a dear and come over tomorrow morning to help Timmy get dressed? His outfit is all white and I don't want any sticky fingers on it. You know what he's like. He'll start eating chocolate. Do you think you'll have time?'

'Of course, plenty of time.'

Adele looked at Sandy suspiciously. 'You are coming to the wedding, aren't you? No more of this nonsense about not coming.'

'I'm not sure, Adele, really. Don't press me. I may not be able to come.' Sandy's eyes clouded over with pain.

'You must come. You're my best friend. I want you to be there. No one will notice your limp.'

'It's not my limp, silly.'

'And you've masses of glamorous clothes. You'll outshine us all. Now I don't want to hear any more. You're coming.'

Daisy made no effort to go to Tregony on the morning of the wedding. Let them wash up their own breakfast things and clean the loos, she thought; she had enough to do. She couldn't think why Doreen had to have an engagement party. It wasn't done these days. People didn't even get properly engaged any more. Well, she wasn't making a fancy cake, that was for sure. She opened a tin of luncheon meat and a tin of corned beef and began creating a mountain of sandwiches, slapping in unwashed leaves of Tregony lettuce between each slice.

'You'll have to get your own breakfast,' she said sharply to Bert as he appeared rubbing his rough stubble. He hadn't bothered to shave and he had not slept well. He never said a word about being sacked. Somehow he was not sure if it had really happened. Afterwards he had wandered about, not knowing where to go, not going home nor to the other gardens he looked after. He still had some odd-job work he could do, but Tregony was his biggest and favourite garden. It was his life.

'I'll have a bite and get on down to Tregony,' he mumbled, mouth full of digestive biscuit. 'Busy day.'

'Very busy,' Daisy snapped. 'For some.'

He waited for her to fill his flask but she did not make a move. He hobbled over to the stove and put on the kettle. He knew to keep out of her way when Daisy was in one of her moods. He made some strong dark tea and drank it noisily, then filled the flask.

'I'll be off then,' he said.

'All right for some,' she said. 'Hope it doesn't rain for the wedding.'

He peered at the cloudless blue sky, a perfect arc of azure, not a puff of white anywhere. He caught a whiff of the sea and it stirred a shamble of forgotten memories. He had not seen the sea for years. 'It ain't gonna rain.'

He took his time getting to Tregony. When he got there, a great deal of activity was going on, waitresses in high heels making more holes in his lawn. No one noticed him amble down to his shed. He went into the gloom and settled himself on the dirt floor. Returning to Tregony had intensified the agony. All his beautiful flowers gone. Beheaded. Cut down in their prime. He couldn't believe it of Adele. She had destroyed every single flower. It was a savage mutilation of his garden.

He sat down to wait, shaking his head. What he was waiting for, he was not sure.

At that moment Mrs Carter was driving carefully along the narrow lanes in her wooden-doored shooting brake, the big cardboard boxes in the boot. It wouldn't do to ruin hours of work going over a pothole.

She had, in the end, gone along with Adele's idea of a clover leaf, although it had meant having a new set of baking tins made specially. However, she had experimented by making a simple economy fruitcake as a trial, and fortunately it came out of the tin reasonably well. She also had to practise using the gold paint on a forest of hand-made sugar-icing roses. She got quite good at it eventually, and the last few dozen were perfection. They went on the fourth and largest base cake to complement the gold ribbon. The four coats of white royal icing on the sides had taken hours.

Parking was no problem, but she was taken aback by the lack of welcome from Daisy when she went into the widow's cottage in the village.

'Your Doreen asked me to make her an engagement cake,' said Mrs Carter, bustling into the kitchen with a large square cardboard box. 'It was very last-minute, and I must say I prefer more notice. A good cake isn't made in five minutes. However, I'm sure Doreen will be pleased with this. It's a simple fruit and cherry cake, but a new design.'

She dumped the box on the table among the debris of sandwiches. It was her trial-run cake using the new clover-shaped tin. No point in wasting it. 'Nothing to pay. Doreen paid me in advance. Not like some I might mention. Still, I suppose it's easy for her with tips and such. Some people forget I've got ingredients to buy. And the price of dried fruit! It costs a fortune these days. Not to mention the brandy.'

'Very nice, I'm sure,' said Daisy, hardly glancing at the box. She had no time for the hard-faced woman, perspiring already in her tweed suit, her feet like meat plates in sensible brogue shoes.

'I'll be off now to Tregony,' said Mrs Carter, sweeping a professional eye over the thick white sandwiches. 'You ought to cut the crusts off, if it's a party.'

Daisy sniffed. 'I'm not wasting bread,' she said, cramming a pile of filled slices back into the plastic baker's bag ready for cutting into quarters later. 'We're not made of money.'

'Not needed at Tregony this morning then?'

'Busy. I've my Doreen's party to see to.'

Daisy did not even attempt to go to the church. She was not going to waste time putting on a decent dress and tidying her hair. She gulped down some sweet cooking sherry, thinking of the champagne she might have been drinking. That stuck-up Miss Fiona wouldn't notice whether she was there or not. Nor would Mrs Kimberley, far too busy chatting up her posh friends. They didn't want their cleaning woman around at the wedding, but she would be welcome on Monday morning to put straight the weekend mess. It would be chaos. Old faithful Daisy would be welcome then all right.

She poured out another tumbler of sherry and put up a deckchair in the back garden. She'd have her own reception, right here. A tear squeezed out of her eye. She'd really been looking forward to it. As she dozed off in the sun, her last thought was that she had not opened the cake box.

Later, when she did open the box, she was pleasantly surprised. It was a magnificent cake, funny shape but superbly decorated with gold roses and ribbon. Doreen had been extravagant, spending all that money.

Bert woke with a start. He wondered where on earth he was in the gloom and the unaccustomed noise. The barrage of voices was an assault on his ears. He peered out through a crack in the door. He'd never seen so many people, not even at Helston cattle market. Hundreds of strange people were walking about, treading on his lawn, throwing cigarette ends on the flower beds, polluting the air with their smoke. It was horrible.

And it was overly warm, a swamping heat that drained his juices. Several dozen of the gilt-legged chairs had been moved out of the marquee, legs sinking into the soft turf like bullet holes. The air was heavy with the scent of flowers, *her* flowers, not his precious blooms.

'Ruined, ruined,' he moaned softly to himself, rocking.

He caught sight of Fiona, the centre of all this pandemonium. She was laughing and smiling, dancing about, all done up in a big frock, pretending she was somebody special, a right poppy show. That girl had lost him his job, his life, his Tregony. This garden was his whole reason for living. He might as well cut off his right hand. His clumsy fingers went through his tool box, searching, till he found what he wanted: a pruning knife, honed to a thin sliver of steel.

He stumbled out of the shed, blinded by the sudden sunlight. No one noticed him. They were all too busy eating and drinking and talking in loud voices. He sidled past the marquee, hung about by the shrubbery, sweating and shaking, stalking his prey like a grizzled old bear. He peered in at the kitchen window and one of the waitresses shrieked.

The noise startled him. That weren't the right girl. He was looking for the one in the overgrown frock, the one with the yellow-pansy hair and a laugh that went through his head like a spike.

He were going to give her a really good fright this time, right now, a really good fright. My God, he were going to give that girl a right good fright.

# Four

Sandy knew that dancing was to be her life from the moment that she discovered music. Her childhood, living on the dormitory fringe of Surrey, was spent at one dancing school after another, each developing her talent for ballet, tap, modern, and Greek classical dance. Her first love was always ballet and, when she was accepted by the Royal Ballet School in London, she felt that all her dreams were coming true. Her parents, already in their late middle-age, were overjoyed.

Sandy moved to music as if she were part of it. She did not have to be told what to do with her hands, her neck, the tilt of her chin. She seemed to know instinctively the fluid line of body that went with a dance step. 'Sandy is a natural dancer,' said her teachers.

Her training cost her parents a fortune, but they did not begrudge her a penny. She was a delightful girl, a sweet daughter, and her joy in dancing was all the reward they wanted. When she joined the corps de ballet of a well-known theatre company, they came to watch every performance they could afford.

'Mum, Dad, how lovely to see you,' said Sandy, finding them hesitating at the stage door after the show. 'Come in and meet everyone. I didn't know you were coming or I would have got you some tickets. Did you have good seats?'

'A bit high up, but then we didn't have much choice.'

'Your mother felt dizzy.'

'Then tell me next time you're coming. No more sitting up

73

in the gods. It's not good for your blood pressure, all those stairs to climb.'

Sandy had begun to worry about them. They were both getting old. She saw the years etching patterns on their faces, bringing a fragility to their paper-thin skin. She was a child of their autumn years and her training had cost their savings. She longed to be successful, to become a star and earn good money so that they would not have to make any more sacrifices. She wanted to take care of them, to repay everything they had done for her.

'I've managed to wangle a week's holiday,' said Sandy. 'I'm going to take you both away. Is there anywhere you'd particularly like to go?'

'Cornwall,' they both said.

The Walkers had spent their honeymoon in Cornwall, a fact that Sandy had not known. In those days, they had been walkers indeed, a family joke which came out for a new airing. They had walked many of the coastal paths at Trevellas Porth and Bassett's Cove, Land's End and The Lizard, long before vast tracts became the property of the National Trust, and these romantic sea vistas had stayed in their minds throughout their long Surrey incarceration.

'We'd love to see it again,' said Mrs Walker.

'Remember those walks, Mother?' said Mr Walker. 'I doubt if we'd get that far these days.'

'But the views will be the same,' she consoled him.

They spent a pleasant week at a small farmhouse hotel outside the market town of Helston, and it did not take Sandy long to realize what her parents really wanted. They wanted to move to Cornwall, to live out their last years together in the place that had so many strong romantic memories for them. The Surrey they knew had changed, and they did not like it much any more. And why not, Sandy thought? They had devoted their life to her. They deserved their own wish-fulfilment. Now she knew how she could repay them.

She left them contentedly shopping in the steeply cobbled

Coinagehall Street while she toured the estate agents. A bungalow would be the answer; something easy to run with no stairs. But they were like gold dust; so many retired couples wanted a bungalow.

'I've several fisherman's cottages,' said the last agent. 'They need modernizing, of course. No gardens to worry about, just a back yard.'

'No, I don't think so,' said Sandy. 'My parents would like a bit of garden. Not too big, but enough to keep my father pottering about. And they'd like one good-sized sitting room, with a big sunny window for my mother.'

'Why don't you build? Have you thought about that as an alternative? We've a very nice plot just come on the market. Part of the garden of a large house in Trewartha Close. The owner wants to make a bit extra by selling off some of his garden. It's an odd wedge shape. They've got building permission.'

'Can we go and see it?'

'Of course.' He searched through a filing cabinet. 'Here are the particulars.'

Sandy knew that her parents loved Trewartha Close as soon as they drove along it. The houses were old and substantial, each set back from the road, each one curtained by hedges or shrubs. They were big family houses, some with a pram in the garden or a toddler's tricycle on the lawn. It looked a friendly road, and one could almost smell the sea, even though it was some way distant.

The plot had been roughly wired off with netting. It was an odd shape, tapering to nothing, but that did not deter the enthusiasm of the Walkers. It was the scrap end of the big garden, with a rockery, some raspberry canes and a bed of mint and sage.

'It's a lovely place, Sandy, just lovely,' said her mother, rubbing a minty leaf between her fingers. 'But do you think we'll be able to afford it?'

'I can afford it. I can get a mortgage on my salary. Lots

of the dancers are buying places. It's an insurance against the day when one is too old to dance.'

'And there's a good train service from Truro,' said Mr Walker. 'We'll still be able to come and see you dance when you're in London.'

Sandy laughed. The garden was sunny and aromatic. Of course, they were seeing it on a good day. Shrouded in rain and mist, it might not look so attractive. 'That's the last thing you should be taking into consideration. Our European tour starts next month. Heaven knows when we'll be booked into a London theatre again.'

Things moved quickly. Sandy couldn't believe it was so easy. She had thought house-hunting was a long-winded, drawn-out affair, an agonizing search with setbacks called chains and gazumping.

She put a deposit on the plot, employed a firm of local solicitors to put the sale through, and found a building firm willing to build a simple one-bedroomed bungalow. They had several standard plans which only needed a little alteration to suit her parents' requirements and the peculiarities of the site.

'Three months,' said Sandy happily as she drove her parents back to their suburban semi. 'They reckon you'll be moving in three months. You'd better put this house on the market.'

'We'll bide awhile,' said Mr Walker. 'We'd like to see a roof on first.'

'Your father's right. Better see a roof on first.'

Sandy was in Hamburg when the letter caught up with her. The building plot had been withdrawn. The owner had changed his mind. Sandy's cheque for the deposit was enclosed, and the agents regretted any inconvenience caused, etcetera . . .

Her parents were disappointed but not surprised. It had all seemed too easy. Sandy was annoyed, but she could do nothing from Hamburg. The builders did not charge her a cancellation fee, but she had to settle with the solicitors for work already prepared. She felt like sending the bill to the owners of Tregony.

It was not easy to house-hunt from a distance. The agents continued to send particulars of useless properties from mansions to flatlets. Mr and Mrs Walker continued to stick newspaper cuttings in their scrapbook as the ballet company toured Europe and were greeted with rave notices in every capital.

'I could have made your favourite raspberry jam,' said Mrs Walker to her husband, thinking of the raspberry canes.

'And that rockery would have been a perfect windbreak if you had wanted to sit out in the garden.'

Sandy began to get small roles to dance in *Giselle* and *Coppelia*. Ballet had a new spice and vitality these days, to keep pace with other forms of entertainment, and she was happy to be part of it. She loved the travelling and the excitement of each new production. She was sorry that she had not been able to do anything for her parents.

When she came home from the long European tour, she was exhausted. She looked thinner than ever, her bird-like bones emphasizing her fragility. Her high cheekbones were more pronounced than ever, and her smooth, dark hair hung like a dark cloud.

'You're nothing but skin and bones,' said her mother, immediately planning nourishing soups and stews. 'Don't you ever eat properly? Dad, put the kettle on. Lucky I made some scones this morning, and don't say you're on a diet.'

Sandy could only laugh. She was too tired to argue and it was lovely to be home and spoilt again. But the spoiling was only going to last a short time. She had noticed her mother's breathlessness and the effort it took to do everything.

A few days later, she was spring-cleaning their living room, sorting through piles of correspondence, circulars and old magazines. 'These leaflets from estate agents, do you want to keep them?' she called out.

'Throw them out. They sent us nothing but rubbish. We didn't bother to look at them in the end.'

The word *Tregony* flashed up from a crumpled page. Sandy spread it out on the floor, pushing back her hair as it fell forward. Her heart leapt, hardly able to believe what she was reading. The plot was on the market again. The same plot, the same size, a higher price.

Her hand hesitated as she dialled the telephone number of the agents. She did not want to raise her parents' hopes if it had already gone.

'Well, we have got an offer for the plot, Miss Walker. But it's not what Mr Kimberley is asking, and he is holding out for the full price.'

'Why is Mr Kimberley selling now? I thought he went against the idea of a new property being built next to his Tregony?' Sandy could not stop herself from asking.

'I understand Mr Kimberley needs to raise some capital to put into a business. That's why he's changed his mind.'

'I'll pay the full asking price,' said Sandy. 'But I'll sue him if he changes his mind again,' she added, her voice suddenly much harder and determined.

It was like an instant replay. Sandy went through the same moves. Her parents were clearly thrilled and began to plan which pieces of furniture they would keep and which they would sell. Sandy did not allow herself to be caught up in their enthusiasm. She would start cheering the day they moved in.

The ballet company had a four-week engagement to dance in New York. Sandy did not like being so far away, although she was thrilled to be going to America. It was her first visit. But her parents looked so old; it hurt her to leave them. Sandy was pinning her hopes on the Cornish air and climate to improve their health.

She made one last desperate call to the builder before taking the Piccadilly line out to Heathrow Airport.

'Is there any way of hurrying things up?' she asked. 'I would like to see my parents move in before the winter.'

'Unfortunately, there's been a bit of a hold-up,' said the builder. 'It's certainly something we did not anticipate. There was no doubt about the building permission, but some of the residents of Trewartha Close have pointed out that there's an old by-law prohibiting a bungalow being built.'

'What? Why? I don't believe it.'

'Well, as you know, the houses are quite big on that road, and they feel their properties would lose value if little bungalows started being built on garden plots. They do have a point, Miss Walker.'

Sandy could barely contain her impatience. 'How far have you got?' she asked.

'The foundations are dug and the outside walls are three-quarters up. Then we stopped because of this objection. We were going to write to you,' he added apologetically.

'Carry on building,' she said, a circle of steel enclosing her heart. 'Make a room in the roof with a window looking out towards the sea, even if you can't see it. Add a spiral staircase going up from a corner of the living room. Change "bungalow" to "chalet" on the plans, and if there is any more of this nonsense, write to every one of those interfering neighbours and tell them I shall personally sue them on my return from America. Got it?'

'Ah . . . yes, got it. Chalet instead of bungalow. Right, Miss Walker.'

Sandy slammed down the receiver, knocking her knee as she struggled out of the phone box with her travelling bag. She cursed all those stuffy house-owners worried about the value of their big houses if one small bungalow appeared in their midst. And she had thought it looked a friendly road. It was about as friendly as a nest of vipers.

They were opening in New York with the great classic, *Sleeping Beauty*. The queues started forming early outside the Broadway theatre, and the dressing rooms were high on excitement as the ballerinas changed into their costumes and fixed their make-up. Sandy began her warm-up as carefully as an athlete, emptying her mind of everything except the dance ahead. She loved Tchaikovsky's music, and was trying to use it to calm her nerves. She was to dance the most responsible role of her career: that of the Bad Fairy. It was character dancing, which demanded more than pure technique. Her first costume was ethereal, white and silver with touches of violet. Her old-woman disguise was swirling yards of hooded cloak, black as midnight.

The first act was superb. The christening scene was enchanting, with each of the fairies dressed like flowers, bestowing their gifts, their characters clearly defined. The confrontation between the Bad Fairy and the King was electric. Sandy could not believe the applause when their *pas de deux* came to a dramatic climax. She ran off the stage, her face glowing. There were congratulations, kisses, hugs. She went back to the dressing room, knowing she would not be able to relax. She did not go on again until the spinning wheel scene.

She stood in the wings, waiting to go on, wrapped in the voluminous cloak. The applause was still ringing in her ears; it seemed like a special lucky sign. Everything would be all right now. Her parents would soon be in their new home, happy, their health improving.

Her first dance in the scene was difficult; she had to convey to the audience the dual character, repeating some of the intricate steps of the christening scene, but now shrouded in the great swirling cloak. She began a series of elaborate pirouettes, increasing the tempo, suddenly aware that something was wrong with her knee. It was not responding. Her arms were lost in the folds, unable to move the hood which had tipped forward, obscuring her vision.

She crashed into the rocking chair, a bone in her ankle snapping with an audible crack. Pain shot through her calf with a ferocity that took her breath away. She gasped in agony, attempting to regain her poise. She continued the dance glazed with pain, faltering, changing the choreography to fit her limited movements. She could barely put her foot to the floor. Sweat poured off her face. The audience thought that her crippled, staggering gait was a development of the old woman's character and applauded loudly.

Sandy did not remember much of the rest of the scene. She collapsed afterwards into the arms of an astonished stagehand, her foot swollen beyond recognition, the pain shooting up her calf into her knee.

An ambulance took her to a private hospital in Manhattan where her foot was put in plaster. The diagnosis was three broken bones, a pulled calf muscle and torn knee ligaments. She knew with certainty as she came out of the anaesthetic that her professional dancing career was over.

She was convalescing when her mother had a heart attack. Sandy flew home in time to find her mother in intensive care, her failing heart a flickering and erratic thread monitored on a screen. Four days later she died. During the winter there was an epidemic of legionnaires' disease, which Sandy's father had not the strength or willpower to withstand.

'I never had time to do anything for them,' she whispered to herself at his funeral. 'I left it too late . . . But it was that man, the Kimberley man. He spoilt everything.'

It was spring before Sandy went down again to Cornwall. The new chalet was finished now. It stood empty and desolate in the neglected and bedraggled garden. She stood among the weeds and wept. But the air was wonderful. It brought life back to her.

She stood like a statue, unaware of the rain trickling down her neck. It was such a waste. The effort and heartbreak that had gone into the buying and building of this house for her parents, and now they were both gone.

'Can I lend you an umbrella or something?' a cheerful voice called out. 'You're getting soaked.'

Sandy came back from the wilderness slowly and looked

round. A woman was coming across from Tregony, a neat and dainty woman in a lilac tracksuit. She was waving a big multi-coloured golf umbrella.

'I'm sorry, but I've been watching you from my house. You looked so forlorn standing there, and my goodness, you are wet! You'd better come in and dry off. Don't say no, I'm longing for an excuse to stop work and have a cup of tea.'

The woman's face was genuinely concerned, nothing like the predatory ogre Sandy had been imagining for months. It was a difficult adjustment to make. Sandy was wary.

'Come along. You'll catch pneumonia. This Cornish rain can be relentless. By the way, I'm Adele Kimberley.'

'Sandy Walker. This is my house,' said Sandy.

'I thought so. We've been wondering when someone would turn up. It's a shame to see such a nice place lying empty. It's so pretty. If you put up wooden shutters, some carved pine ones, and a few window boxes, it would look like a Swiss chalet.'

'Yes, I suppose it would,' said Sandy indifferently.

Sandy followed the enemy into Tregony. It was a big house, full of the evidence of children and hobbies. Adele had been ironing a pile of shirts. She cleared a space on the kitchen table and began to put out bone-china mugs and a cake tin full of chocolate cupcakes. Sandy could not remember when she had last eaten a cake; she could hardly remember when she had last eaten anything.

'You're limping,' said Adele, filling the kettle. 'Have you hurt your leg?'

'I had an accident,' said Sandy, the pain of it evident in her voice. 'Last year.'

'You should be doing therapy and exercises,' said Adele. 'You mustn't let the muscles lose their tone.'

A wry smile touched Sandy's face. She knew all about physiotherapy and muscle tone. 'That's true, but why bother? It won't ever get any better. I'm going to limp for the rest of my life.'

'But you're only limping with one leg,' said Adele. 'Why sentence the other leg to a lopsided existence!'

Sandy could not help but laugh. It was such a ridiculous remark. She met Adele's eyes and saw only sympathy and friendliness. Some of the hostility receded from deep in her heart. 'Can I hang my jacket somewhere? I'm afraid it's dripping all over your floor.'

'Here, by the boiler,' said Adele. 'But don't let's talk about the past, which is obviously painful to you. The future is the thing. Are you going to come and live in your new chalet? Please do. Porthcudden is a really nice place, and your garden could look lovely. I know, you can borrow Bert. He'd love to get things straight for you. He keeps peering over the fence and shaking his head.'

'Bert?'

'He's our gardener. He thinks he owns the place and that we are here to do his bidding. He wouldn't mind helping you out, as long as you don't want to change anything.'

'Oh no,' said Sandy, who had been planning to sell the chalet. 'I've no changes in mind. He could do what he liked.'

'That would suit our Bert.'

'But I don't know my plans. I'm not sure what I'm going to do. I may sell the chalet. It's no use to me down here in Cornwall. My work is . . .' She faltered. 'Well, my work was centred in London, but there's no saying what I'll do now.'

'Whatever has happened to you has obviously been very traumatic,' said Adele, pouring out the tea. 'It's written all over your face. Do help yourself to a cake. Why don't you give yourself a breather? Come and live in Porthcudden for a while and see how you like it. It would give you time to get over your accident and build up your strength. Then you could pick up your career again.'

'You don't understand,' said Sandy, unable to keep the bitterness out of her voice. 'My career is over. Finished. I'm a has-been. There's nothing left for me to do.'

Adele was disturbed by this passionate outburst from the young woman. 'Well, you can tell me off for being an interfering busybody, but I don't believe that. There must be hundreds of things you could do. Perhaps you haven't given yourself time to think about them yet.'

'Oh, I suppose I could serve cream teas in a tea shop, or sell souvenirs in a post office. That's about all I'm fit for,' said Sandy.

Adele laughed. 'Oh dear, what a plague of the blues. And a very pretty waitress you'd make. The takings would soar, I'm sure of that. But there are so many more sides of life, you'll see. Be patient. Something will come your way. Have some more tea. There's some colour in your cheeks at last.'

Three weeks later Sandy moved into the chalet. It was practically camping out at first, with a few pieces of her parents' furniture and nothing in the larder but fruit and cheese. But it gave her an interest in life, and she enjoyed shopping with Adele, choosing curtains and carpets, even mundane pots and pans. They became friends without effort on either side, almost as if they were sisters.

Sandy kept her distance from Graham Kimberley. She could not forget what his selfishness had cost her, that it had denied her parents those few final years of comfort and happiness.

One evening she took the car down to a remote part of the cliffs. She needed to think. The small rough car park was deserted, and so was the headland. It was a windswept expanse of yellow gorse, the clumps of heather moaning and rustling as if in competition with the pounding seas below. She took her walking stick out of the car and began to climb the path, pacing it steadily, feeling the pull on her calf muscles, the ache in her ankle. She stood on the edge of the cliff, looking down at the black rocks below and the power of the waves breaking over them.

It would be so easy to walk forward a few feet fur-ther. Then it would be all over. She would have no more problems, no more decisions to make, no more painful memories.

Something knocked against her good ankle, a wet bundle, an animal of some kind. She started, startled. She looked down and saw a small hairy dog, eyes lost amongst wet hair, sniffing around her feet. It was a long-haired Scottie, brindled and white, so short-legged that it could hardly straddle the heather.

'Hello, little fellow,' she smiled. 'Are you lost, like me? Are we both lost on this wild cliff?' She went down on her good knee to stroke his wet hair. As she pushed the long strands out of his eyes, she realized from his blank, opaque stare that he was blind.

'No, Jock isn't lost, he's with me. Sometimes he remembers more of his youth than his old age, and decides to go off on his own.'

A man was standing not far away. He was tall, grey-haired, casually dressed in a windcheater and cords. He had a leather lead in his hand. When she did not speak, he moved forward, slowly, hesitantly.

'When I saw you by the cliff, I confess I was momentarily worried. I thought you did not realize how close you were to the edge. I even forgot my poor old Jock for a moment. Not that I need have worried about him. He has a sixth sense for danger.'

Sandy looked away. She was embarrassed that this man had sensed her thoughts. 'Please don't be concerned on my behalf,' she said.

She turned away from him, letting the wind blow her hair across her face, hiding her expression. Her hand went out to stroke the wet head still nuzzling her ankle.

'Jock likes you. Be flattered. He's very particular. I suppose you've noticed that he's blind, but he still loves a good old ramble along the cliffs. I can't deny him some freedom. It would be too cruel to keep him to the garden.'

'Is he very old?'

'Thirteen years old. That's a good age for a small dog. I shall miss him when he goes. He's a good companion.'

'I've never had a dog.'

'What a shame.' The man had deep-set eyes beneath hairy eyebrows, eyes that were dark brown and kindly. 'You have a pleasure in store, believe me.'

'A dog? Me?' She gave a short laugh. 'Never.'

She got up. The conversation was too disturbing. She wanted to get away, to be alone; this man's friendly conversation was an intrusion on her grief. She gave him a brief nod and moved off, stumbling over clumps of thick grass in her haste.

'Don't go away. I mean no harm. You'll hurt your leg trying to hurry.'

She turned on him, panting, eyes raging with indignation. 'I've already hurt my leg. Hurrying won't make any difference, so please leave me alone. I don't want company. You've been very kind, but I'm in no mood for pleasantries, can't you see that?'

'I can see that you are in pain, not only from your leg. You don't know me. I'm a stranger. Would it help to talk?'

'No,' she said bluntly.

'Is the injury to your leg permanent?'

'It is,' she said bitterly. 'And it's ruined my life. Ruined everything. Those people, those selfish people. They have no idea what they have done to my life, and to my parents. It's entirely their fault, my neighbours. They are to blame for everything.'

'Everything?'

Hot tears stabbed her eyes. 'If they hadn't been greedy, withdrawing the land then putting it back on the market again at a higher price . . . You should see the size of the garden they've got. If it had not been for their avarice, we would have had the plot nearly two years ago. The house would have been built and my parents would have been living here, in Cornwall, alive and well. Instead they are both dead.'

'I don't pretend to understand all this,' said the man carefully, putting Jock back on the lead. 'Do you feel like explaining a little more clearly? Sometimes it helps to talk to a complete stranger, someone you'll never see again.'

The wind was strengthening, buffeting them both with relentless power. Sandy leaned into it, for once finding a challenge in a battle with the elements.

She walked along the narrow path, aware that he was following her, Jock yapping at his heels. She was also aware that the man was steering her away from the rugged edge by taking the outer side of the path, next to the steep drop to the rocks. She began to feel more at ease in his company, although she could not keep the bitterness out of her voice.

Month by month, she forced herself to tell the man the saga of the plot of land, and its effect on herself and her parents.

'You can't really blame your neighbours for not wanting a lovely garden to be sliced up,' he said evenly but without criticism. 'Nor for then selling when they needed capital for a business venture. That's only common sense.'

'Common sense, when it killed my parents?' she said coldly.

'Did the circumstances kill your parents?'

Sandy was trembling. 'Yes, they did!' she cried out. 'They were old and ill. It was selfish.'

'Ah, I see. Neighbours are supposed to run a charity.'

She turned on him, outraged. 'Don't talk to me like that. You don't know anything about what happened.'

'That's true. I'm trying to make you see another point of view. Forgive me, I know it's an impertinence, but it seems to me that you are managing to blame these people for everything, perhaps your leg injury too.'

'It was their fault, indirectly,' said Sandy. The air was full of the fragrance of heather, the salt of the sea. But she hardly heard the call of the seabirds or the thundering seas below. 'My concentration was ruined. Instead my mind was full of building problems, their objections to the original plan, hundreds of little irritating details. They were all buzzing around when I should have been thinking of my dancing and nothing else.'

'Are you sure they are to blame for everything?' the man said casually, evenly. Sandy would not look at him. His face was obscured in shadow. He was merely a tall man, grey and brown, who was saying sane things he had no right to say. 'Even for the death of your parents? You did say they were an elderly couple and in poor health.'

'Are you trying to blame me? It wasn't my fault. Though the shock of my accident might have caused my mother's heart attack.'

'How do you know? Were you there? Do you know the actual sequence of events? A heart attack can be triggered by anything. And your father . . . was that your neighbour's fault too? I'm sorry. I know I sound cruel, but you gave me quite a fright standing so close to the cliff's edge. It seems to me that it is essential for you to get everything sorted out. You can't blame these people for a string of events that happened elsewhere.'

Sandy was incensed, but a glimmer of truth was getting through the self-imposed barrier. She knelt down and stroked Jock's head, trying to steady herself, to calm her feelings. 'You make me sound very stupid,' she said, her breath coming in gasps. 'Perhaps I'm a fool. I am what I am, and I can't help it.'

'No, you're not a fool, young lady. You've been having a tough time and I know what that means. Believe that you will come through. Give yourself enough space to recover mentally and physically. You owe it to yourself. Live in this house of yours for twelve months, see all the Cornish seasons – if you can tell the difference,' he added with a chuckle.

'Perhaps, maybe,' she said. 'I don't know.'

He stopped and searched the sky. 'The light's fading. I must get back. Goodbye,' the man said, holding out his hand. 'Good luck and be careful. Remember, Jock may not be around another time.'

He shook her hand; it was a warm, pleasant handshake, firm and momentarily comforting.

She watched him stride downhill, the shaggy little dog at his heels. It had been a shattering encounter. Who the man was, she would never know, but he had saved her reason.

Sandy stayed more than a year at Porthcudden. A new career opened in choreography with a group of talented young dancers for TV variety shows, commercials and cruise ships. She travelled all over the country, but always looked forward to returning to the chalet. In fact, she had lived there over four years by the morning of Fiona's wedding. She was not bitter, but she had never forgotten, not completely.

Everything was perfect for the Kimberley family; nothing spoilt their blue horizon. Adele was her friend, but not Graham. He was the enemy. Sandy longed for some disaster to happen that would hurt his pride and puncture his gross vanity. He was often rude to her.

'I can't thank you enough for cleaning the loos,' said Adele halfway through the reception. 'And looking after Timmy. He's been so good.'

'Yes, he has. He deserves his bribe. And he even managed to look interested during the service.'

The flower lady had disappeared, probably exhausted by her early start and no breakfast. Sandy watched Graham downing champagne as if a drought was imminent. If anything happened to his showpiece wedding, he would be shattered. It would ruin his pride at being able to pay for this expensive exhibition.

Fiona floated by, her ivory skirts like an extravagant tutu. 'Hello Hopalong,' she grinned, the thoughtless words stabbing Sandy to the heart. 'How's the gammy leg? Glad I didn't ask you to be a bridesmaid.'

'We're hardly on bridesmaid terms,' said Sandy.

'No way. You're a has-been. A had-it. A failed dancer. There's nothing failed about me. I'm on my way up, whereas you're on your way down.'

Sandy needed a drink . . . water. She went into the kitchen. Adele had made a favourite chocolate cake for Timmy, thinking he would eat little of the wedding food.

The baking tin, egg whisk and mixing bowl had not been washed up in the morning rush. In the bowl lay a steel skewer that Adele had used to test if the sponge was cooked.

Sandy's hand closed on the skewer. *Hopalong. A failed dancer. On her way down.* How could Fiona be so cruel on her wedding day? Father and daughter, they were both heartless. They would deserve whatever happened . . .

# Five

It was like a rehearsal for death. She had let him go and the parting was a daily agony. She was dying by inches, not from an illness but from a state of mind, and could not see any release into a new life.

She thrashed the growing wheat with a bent branch, violently and angrily, stomping over the field with no care for the farmer's crop. The field went right down to the gorse-fringed cove, and Carolyn struggled towards the edge of the cliff. The wind flattened her dyed magenta hair, whipped the black widow garments against her skinny greyhound body, blew the chaff off her muddied grannie boots.

'Hal . . . Hal . . .' she cried, scaring the gulls into frantic white-tipped flight. 'Hal . . . Why? Why me?'

She scrambled down the slippery path to the small cove, her boots sinking into the wet sand. Ripples of water washed into the impressions, disturbing the rim of sand, shifting the particles into the anonymous centre. Carolyn stood at the water's edge, contemplating the misty horizon, the scudding clouds of rain sweeping over the headland.

'Hal . . . Oh, Hal . . . I can't live without you,' she wept. She sank on to her knees, oblivious of the wavelets tugging at her black skirts, unaware of the cold and encroaching wetness.

Her feverish brow touched the wet sand and she crouched into a huddle of misery, closing her arms over her head. They thought that because she was only sixteen she could not feel real emotion. How could they know what she felt? They

91

were so involved with their own lives. Mother was totally absorbed in an energetic small boy, the longed-for son and heir, Timmy. Father was busy making money to pay for all the improvements to their house and new cars. Fiona was far too single-minded in her growing business career to notice what was happening to her younger sister.

How could anyone understand? Carolyn had said goodbye to Hal this afternoon and it had been like cutting a vein. For months she had lived only to see him. Each day was planned around chance meetings at the sailing club or outside the office of his father's business.

Carolyn's sixteenth-birthday present had been junior membership of the sailing club. She had been thrilled, even more thrilled when someone introduced her to Hal Vaughan and he suggested that she could crew for him.

'That's a date then, Carolyn,' he had said. 'It's been great meeting you. Happy birthday.'

Carolyn walked on puppy air. Hal was ten years older, tall and attractive, with thick, dark hair that fell over deep-set dark-blue eyes. He was everything she had ever dreamt about, worldly and sophisticated. He drove a fabulous sports car, low-slung E-Type, bright red.

'Hey, what's going on?' one of his friends had ragged. 'Baby snatching at your age? Isn't it an offence?'

'Pipe down. I was only being pleasant. It's the girl's birthday.'

Carolyn did not care what anyone said. She followed Hal round like a pet dog. She was always first on hand to pull his boat ashore, wading knee-deep in the sea. She swilled it out, packed away the sails, and for two glorious weeks helped him repaint the keel. She was an adoring, uncomplaining slave.

'Carolyn's looking for you,' someone shouted from the shore one afternoon.

'Who?' said Hal, looking up, frowning.

'You know. Your little handmaiden.'

'Which one?' He grinned.

Carolyn heard. It was a shock, and the first push down a slippery launching into tempestuous seas. Carolyn went straight home and dyed her fair hair an outrageous magenta. 'I'll give you "which one".' She glared into the bathroom mirror. 'You'll remember me now.'

She bought dreadful clothes with her allowance: old, black, shapeless cast-offs at jumble sales. Hal noticed her all right; so did everyone else. Her appearance attracted the worst element in the club and in the surrounding area. She started going round with a wild bunch, staying out late, gatecrashing dubious parties. Several times Graham was hauled out of bed in the small hours to rescue her from some all-night party that had got out of hand. He was not pleased.

'What a time of night to get me up. You shouldn't be at such parties. Where were the parents, I'd like to know,' he grumbled, driving home at two in the morning through sleeting rain. 'Look at you. Half-naked, your face painted like a clown. No wonder your mother is worried out of her mind.'

'Worried, is she? A pity she doesn't show it,' said Carolyn, sulking in a corner of the car. 'Far too busy with our little baby angel. Timmy this and Timmy that. It's a wonder she even knows my name.'

'I'm warning you, Carolyn, I'm not coming out to fetch you again. Come home at a reasonable time with one of your girlfriends, or share a taxi. You're only sixteen. At your age I had to be in by ten o'clock.'

'Oh, "at your age" . . . Get lost. Are we talking about the Middle Ages?'

'You're asking for trouble, young woman, dressed up like that. And your hair, for God's sake. I've never seen anything so ridiculous.'

'At least I've got hair,' she taunted.

Graham swallowed hard. His temper was very frayed. Visibility was poor and this was no time of night to have to concentrate on driving and listen to such cheek.

'Another smart-alec remark like that, Carolyn, and I'll stop the car and make you walk home.'

'Do that! Do just that!' said Carolyn, tugging at the door handle. 'Stop the car. I want to get out. All you've done is criticize and tell me off and tell me what a nuisance I am. I'd be better off walking. Perhaps I won't come back!'

'Pack it in, can't you? You're hysterical. And leave that door handle alone. Stop behaving like a silly child and sit still. It's hard enough driving without you trying to wreck us . . .'

Carolyn glared at her father. At that moment she hated him. She hated him for everything he stood for. Respectability, discipline, conforming. She did not want any of those things in her life. Her growing, ripening body only wanted Hal, to feel his hands, his weight, and most of the time he did not even notice her.

As the car turned into Tregony, Carolyn felt as if she was returning to a prison. She stood in the rain, letting it soak her to the skin, not caring.

'Come in and wash that muck off your face,' Graham shouted. 'And don't wake Timmy. He's fast asleep.'

'Stop shouting then,' she retorted. 'You're making more noise than I am.'

She heard Graham swearing, and for a moment she was quite frightened. Her father was a burly man and he had an unstable temper. He had never actually hit her, but he had come close to it several times. There was a mean streak in him that was only thinly covered by respectability. He had no charm. She could not understand why her mother had married him. Perhaps he had been different as a young man.

It was a bombshell when Graham and Adele informed Carolyn that she was going to France. They had arranged for her to go to a French school for two years, a convent-run finishing school a hundred kilometres south of Paris.

Carolyn went white. 'I'm not going.'

'But, darling, it's a wonderful opportunity for you. A French finishing school! Most girls would love to go. And you are so good at French. You'll become bilingual, get a brilliant job.'

'I'm not going,' Carolyn repeated mutinously.

'There's nothing you can do about it and it doesn't matter what you say. It's all settled,' said Graham. 'I'm taking you there myself. You'll find it hard to run away in a foreign country. The nuns will make sure of that.'

'Nuns? You're both crazy.' She glared. 'What are you trying to do? Make a saint out of me?'

'We're giving you a chance to finish your education in a very civilized country, to become a really elegant young woman,' said Adele, shaking.

Carolyn shouted a rude word and flung herself out of the house, slamming the door. For days she refused to speak to anyone. The time came for her to go and there was nothing she could do about it. She went down to the sailing club to say goodbye to Hal.

It was an unsatisfactory meeting in the crowded coffee bar where Hal was holding court, recounting the hazards of his last race to some cronies. Her stiff, formal farewell hardly registered. She wondered if he was even listening.

'That's great. You're a lucky girl. Have a good time, kiddo,' he said. 'Come and see us when you get back.'

'I don't know when that'll be. I may go skiing, or tour Europe with a French family to improve my French.'

Hal chuckled and leaned forward to kiss her cheek. 'What a clever, *petite enfant. Je t'adore, mon amie.*'

Carolyn ran all the way to the sea, tears on her cheeks. He hadn't been serious. He'd been teasing, making fun of her in front of his friends. But he had kissed her, and whatever the circumstances, no one could take that moment away from her.

It was on Carolyn's last day in England that Sandy found her in the little cove, huddled on the wet sand, letting the sea wash over her and her widow's clothes. Her magenta hair was swirling in curious ripples like a sad river of blood.

'Carolyn? It is Carolyn, isn't it?'

Sandy fell on her knees, touching the girl's shoulder tentatively. Carolyn looked blankly at the woman.

'I'm Sandy. I live next door to Tregony, in the new chalet, though I don't suppose you've noticed me. I hear you're going to school in France.'

'Yes. Tomorrow. Isn't it awful?'

Sandy took in the young, tear-stained face. 'Is it awful? Are you saying goodbye to the sea?'

Carolyn thought about it. 'Yes, I suppose I am.' She looked down at her soaked clothes and shrugged. 'Somewhat over the top, but why not?'

'Why not, indeed? I'm all for the dramatic gesture. Now the watery farewell is over, would you like to walk back with me?'

Carolyn scrambled to her feet, bedraggled and red-eyed, the wind whipping her wet clothes around her. At least Sandy was not making fun of her. Clouds were gathering, dark and grey; the gulls shrieking in flight. 'It's going to rain.' Carolyn shivered, getting cold.

'Then we'd better hurry,' said Sandy. She stooped down to pick up a smooth pebble. 'This one might do.'

Carolyn squelched over the sand, her boots full of water. 'A pebble? What's so special about that one?'

'I injured my foot and some days it really hurts. The only thing I can do to relieve the pain is put a small pebble in my shoe, under the instep.'

Carolyn wiped the wet hair out of her face. 'How very odd. But doesn't that hurt too?'

Sandy smiled. 'Sometimes the only way to get rid of one pain is to counteract it with another. But perhaps you already know that?'

Carolyn nodded, a sudden contraction of her heart reminding her. The pain of parting was smothering the equal pain of rejection. Hal hadn't wanted her. She had been only one of a mob of youngsters hanging around the club, but she had refused to see it.

'Yes, I think I know. But a pebble seems a bit tough on yourself. What about physiotherapy? Can't they do anything?'

Sandy laughed. 'I've had more physio than hot dinners. They've tried everything. I'll stick to my pebble.'

'How did you hurt your foot?'

'Dancing. I was a professional dancer. Stupid, wasn't it? Two seconds of lost concentration and snap, crunch, pop, my career was over.'

'How awful. Was it very painful?'

'Very. Excruciating. I teach now and do some choreography. Television shows and cruise ships.'

Sandy had parked her car at the end of the lane that led to the cliff path. It was an old Renault, battered but reliable.

'Would you like a lift home? You could come in and dry off in my kitchen. No need for Adele to know you've been doing pagan sea rituals.'

'Thanks. You're being very kind.'

'Not at all. I'm glad of the company. I live on my own.' They smiled at each other and at once cemented friendship. It was nearly three years before Carolyn came back home to Tregony, apart from fleeting visits. The nuns clucked over her magenta hair and made her grow it out. At first Carolyn thought about Hal all the time, imagining what their first meeting might be like, fantasizing different scenarios and passionate love-making.

But gradually the pain receded. After two years at the French school, she stayed an extra year in Paris working as an apprentice with a fashion house. They made hats. High-fashion creations that were ordered by rival couturiers for their collections. Carolyn learned to stitch and block and steam, make flowers out of velvet, net and straw. But more often she was required to model the hats in the salon, where

97

her long silver hair was much admired and her English complexion was the envy of the more olive-skinned French girls. She was not tall enough to be a model, but hats were another story.

There was no doubt that the duckling had turned into a swan. Adele could not take her eyes off her second daughter. At nineteen, Carolyn was quite breathtakingly beautiful, putting the simply pretty Fiona in the shade. Not that Fiona was aware of it. Unbeknown to Carolyn, she had started going out with Hal and, apart from her work, there was little else on her mind.

'Are you going to stay in England now that you are home?' Adele asked, wondering if she dare hug such a porcelain beauty.

'I don't know. I'm looking for a job. It might be anywhere. London, New York, Rome, wherever they wear hats.'

'They wear hats in Penzance,' said Adele.

Carolyn pulled a face. 'I've seen them. Frumpy, Mother. Not exactly *à la mode*. The kind I make have outrageous price tags.'

'I bet Mrs Vaughan could afford your hats,' said Adele. She was ironing Timmy's school shirts. He was a jumpy six-year-old now, never still, always running about, not an ounce of spare flesh on him.

'Mrs Vaughan?'

'Yes, you remember the Vaughans, down at the sailing club. They're pretty well off, lovely old house, their own boat. There are two sons, Jonathan and Hal. Fiona is pretty keen on one of them. She spends more time at Rosemullion House than here at home.'

'Oh. Rosemullion House. Really?' Carolyn could not believe the sudden dizziness that made her catch hold of the back of a chair. After all this time. It couldn't be possible. 'How interesting. Which son is it?'

'Hal, of course. No one knows where that Jonathan is. He's always away.'

It was only with the utmost effort that Carolyn kept upright. The room swam around her. She could not focus on her mother's face. She heard herself saying, 'Could I have some water? I'm feeling a little faint.'

'You do look pale. It's the long journey and probably no food. I'll make you a cup of tea. Timmy, leave your sister alone. You can talk to her later.'

It was a week before Carolyn found the courage to go down to the sailing club. She changed her mind a dozen times as to which outfit to wear. Ridiculous when Hal probably wouldn't even be there. But nothing had changed. It was still the same dingy coffee bar and unpolished tables, the trophies on the wall, the curled snapshots. There were the same weather-beaten faces, the same jokes. The one person who was startlingly different was Carolyn.

She looked like a mermaid from the deep. Slim hip-hugging white-sheen jeans; skinny emerald silk top, her long silver hair hanging down her back. Her skin was dewy and luminous with an expert touch of expensive Parisian cosmetics. Hal blinked. He came over cautiously.

'Hello,' he said. 'Don't I know you?'

'No, I don't think so. I'm Carolyn Kimberley,' she said, holding out a slim hand. 'Hi.'

'Are you Fiona's sister? The one who has been away?'

'That's right. I've been in France.'

'Didn't you often come down to the club when you were a little girl?'

'I don't remember,' Carolyn lied. 'Perhaps you're confusing me with someone else.'

He grinned. 'You're right. I could never have forgotten those looks. Stunning. Can I buy you a coffee?'

It was strange to return and find that Hal was almost part of the household. He was often at Tregony, either calling for Fiona or bringing her home. Carolyn found herself included in invitations to Rosemullion House. It took some getting used to. His behaviour towards Carolyn was exemplary. She could not fault him. She almost wished he would flirt with her, or say something uncomplimentary about Fiona so that she could be angry and hate him.

But he didn't. He was charming and attentive, an attitude now laced with a friendly teasing towards the younger sister. Despite the years abroad and her Parisienne panache, Carolyn came to realize that her feelings had not changed. They had in fact deepened into a mature and unselfish love. A love that stood back and watched the relationship between Hal and Fiona grow more serious. But when they moved in together, it was more than she could bear.

She went to work in Knightsbridge, making and modelling hats, sharing a flat with an old school friend. She rarely came home. It was no surprise one weekend to find that her sister's engagement had been announced. Fiona was conventional at heart, with a strong practical vein, and Hal was a catch. He was the most eligible bachelor in the neighbourhood. He would probably inherit both his father's business and Rosemullion House, as Jonathan showed no interest in either.

'I'll make your going-away hat,' said Carolyn generously, hiding her pain. 'It'll be absolutely gorgeous. And your hat, Mother, for the wedding. Just let me have some of the material from your dress and we'll play around with it.'

'Are you going to make me a hat?' Timmy asked.

'Of course, you rascal. I'll make you an admiral's hat with loads of gold braid.'

'Is that a promise?'

'No dear,' said Adele. 'You can't have an admiral's hat. Your hat will come with your outfit. It'll be hired.'

Carolyn bent down and brushed the long hair from the small boy's ear. 'I'll still make you a splendid admiral's hat,' she whispered. 'To wear in secret.'

'Heaven knows what I'm going to wear,' Adele sighed. 'My favourite colours, blue and lilac, of course. But I don't want the stereotypical bride's mother's outfit, the matching dress and jacket. I'm sure Mrs Vaughan will turn up in that.'

'Poor Mrs Vaughan,' said Fiona. 'Whatever she wears, she'll look dreadful. I'm sure she knows it. However much money she spends on clothes, it makes no difference.'

'Why not try the Twenties look?' Carolyn suggested. 'You're slim enough. A dropped waistline, droopy hem, handkerchief points . . . It would be fun. I'll make you a cloche to match and a trailing scarf to float about in.'

'That sounds nice, but there's so much to organize,' said Adele. 'I can't think about my clothes yet. There's Fiona's dress to get first, and your bridesmaid's dress.'

Carolyn pretended she had not heard. She went over to the window and looked out at the big garden her mother spent so much time on. The gardener, Bert, was mowing the lawn, a dour Cornishman who barely spoke to anyone. Adele made many attempts to win a smile from him with coffee and slabs of home-made cake, but all she ever got was a grunt.

'I may not be here,' she said in a high, unreal voice. How could she be a bridesmaid? 'I may be in New York. There's going to be a fashion fair at one of the big Fifth Avenue stores and I've been asked to go over.'

'Nonsense, you can't go. Tell them it's your sister's wedding.'

'You've got to be my bridesmaid,' said Fiona, laconically eating grapes. 'Or I shall have a tantrum.'

'That's settled then,' said Adele, mentally ticking it off. 'One bridesmaid, one pageboy.'

Carolyn never said she would be a bridesmaid, but it was assumed, and everything seemed to go ahead without her being consulted further. She made three hats: an elegant cream straw boater decorated with glossy cherries for Fiona, a magical pleated silk cloche that was immediately copied for the Knightsbridge shop, and a pint-sized Nelson cocked hat, heavily embellished with every fake medal she could buy in Portobello Road.

She came home a few days before the wedding. Hal was also due home the same day. He had escaped most of the more frenetic wedding preparations by going on a Far East promotional tour for his father's business.

As the day neared, she remembered the waking death feeling from before she went to France. It was happening all over again. How many times would she have to go through this? On their anniversaries? Celebrations? Christenings? She was going to have to watch forever, from the sidelines, as her sister lived out her life with Hal.

Carolyn could barely look at Fiona's dress. It was so beautiful. It must have cost a fortune. Graham had not bought it. He was grumbling at all the money he was spending, but he did not mention the extravagant dress. She disliked her bridesmaid's dress intensely, but what did it matter? She never wore yellow. The colour did nothing for her skin. It made her look washed-out and anaemic.

'You'll look lovely in it,' said Adele, seeing the dress but not her daughter's face.

It was pure chance that Carolyn followed Fiona rather too quickly into the bathroom early on the morning of the wedding. She had not been able to sleep, tossing and turning most of the night, wishing it was all over and she could disappear.

'Morning, sister dear,' said Carolyn. 'How is the virgin bride?'

Fiona shot her a sharp look before scurrying back into her bedroom. It was an odd look, one that Carolyn could not make out. Perhaps Fiona had thought the remark inappropriate. Perhaps it was nerves. A few nerves would not be out of place.

Carolyn locked the door, turned on the hot tap and poured in some of the expensive bath oil she had brought her mother from Paris. Everywhere steamed up in a satisfactory fog. She remembered how as a little girl she had played at being lost in the mist in a steamy bathroom, writing SOS messages on the mirror. Her father used to tell her off for wasting hot water.

She turned to the mirror and wrote HELP I AM LOST with her forefinger on the steamed-up surface. Her pale face appeared, fragmented in the letters. Droplets gathered, beckoned by gravity, to make the great run to the edge before dropping on to the glass shelf.

Carolyn looked at the shelf and the unfamiliar apparatus standing there. She picked up a glass phial, an applicator, and another container. She was puzzled. She had never seen anything like it before. It had the look of immediacy, as if it had only been there a few moments.

The blue liquid in the phial meant nothing. On the floor was a narrowly folded printed sheet. Carolyn picked it up and opened it out. It was instructions for an early pregnancy testing device.

*Why wait when you can know in days?* ran the first line. *Accurate results guaranteed in minutes . . .* Carolyn had to read the instructions twice before the significance of the blue-tinted liquid registered. Fiona was pregnant. So what? She had been living with Hal. This was her wedding day, so why the stricken look?

Then Carolyn knew. It was an early pregnancy test, which worked two days after a missed period. Hal had been away in the Far East for nearly a month. It wasn't Hal. It was someone else. Fiona was pregnant by another man.

Carolyn climbed into the bath, trembling, and sat in the scented water unable to think straight. Fiona lived with Hal . . . Hal had been away . . . Fiona with someone else. What was happening? Was Fiona going to go through with the wedding, or was she going to call it off at the last minute? Or, my God, was she going to let Hal think the child was his? Fiona had a mercenary streak. It was almost too late for any change . . . for any kind of action.

And who was the father anyway? Would he be at the wedding? Perhaps he would stand up at that moment in the service when Father Lawrence would ask if there was any known impediment to the marriage. Would this man come rushing down the aisle, shouting and demanding that Fiona marry him instead? Or would she be the one to halt the wedding? thought Carolyn. Would she, out of her deep, everlasting love for Hal, be unable to stop herself?

Carolyn took some painkillers before going back to her own room. She was getting a headache. She put the apparatus behind the bathroom curtain. There was no point in Timmy asking awkward questions, or upsetting Adele. It was up to Fiona now.

She climbed back into bed and pulled the duvet over her head. It was all some horrible nightmare. She had dreamt about going to the bathroom; she would wake up soon and the morning would start all over again, fresh and uncomplicated.

'Fiona. Carolyn. Time to get up. I'm just going to put the kettle on.'

Suddenly Carolyn felt sick. She rushed past her mother on the landing and went into the bathroom again, hanging over the basin, her hair tumbling over her face.

'Morning, sunshine,' Adele called.

She heard her mother go downstairs, fill the kettle; the refrigerator door opening, a rattle of china. Such reassuring domestic sounds. How could Adele be so normal when the world was going collapse around them any moment now? When would Fiona tell her it was all off, the great day cancelled? Perhaps when Adele went in with her tea.

Carolyn could not face any tea, or breakfast. She sat on the edge of the bath, sponging her face with cold water until she felt better. Where would they all be tomorrow? Who would eat the wedding cake? They could take it up to the cottage hospital and let the geriatrics have a piece with their tea. At least she would not have to wear that dress. It could go back to the shop.

She looked out at the marquee, flapping and empty. What

a waste. They ought to have a party. People had divorce parties. Perhaps they would be the first family to have a left-in-the-lurch, stood-up-at-the-church, got-pregnant-first party.

'Have you drowned in there?' squeaked Timmy, banging on the door. 'Mummy says I've got to have another bath, even though I'm absolutely very clean, every bit of me. I haven't even breathed on my skin.'

'Just a minute,' Carolyn choked. 'I'm coming out.'

'Put some clothes on,' Fiona called. 'We're due at the hairdresser's in half an hour.'

'Nothing is going to be done to my hair,' said Carolyn. 'I'm not having anyone touch it.'

'Don't be difficult,' Fiona sang out. 'They'll do just what you say. Trust me.'

Trust her . . . that was a laugh. It looked as if Fiona was going through with it, that she was going to let the unsuspecting Hal think he was the father. Surely he would be able to count dates? He would know. But by then, Carolyn supposed, it would be too late. The Vaughans would not want a scandal sullying their good name.

Carolyn could hardly speak to anyone. They thought she was in one of her adolescent moods. The blue phial disappeared from the bathroom window sill, but Carolyn had kept the printed sheet of instructions. Proof that she had seen it for real; that it was not an invention of her tormented mind; that jealousy had not warped her good sense.

Fiona chattered away at the hairdresser's, had her nails painted a glossy coral. She did not look in the least bit perturbed about anything.

'I'm getting engaged this evening,' said Doreen, the stylist, setting Fiona's hair on jumbo rollers. 'We're having a bit of a party. My mum is doing it all. You know my mum, she helps out at Tregony.'

'Oh, Daisy? Yes, of course, I know her. Well, I hope you have a wonderful party. It's lovely, getting married.'

'We haven't got anywhere to live,' said Doreen, shaking out a tangled hairnet. 'So it won't be lovely yet.'

So much had happened by the time they got back to Tregony. It was like an invasion. The caterers had arrived with mountains of food; the marquee was a hive of activity with chairs and damask tablecloths; a woman in a lumpy tweed suit was wandering around asking everyone and anyone for a cheque.

Carolyn fled upstairs, only to meet Sandy coming out of the bathroom with a can of cleaner and a J-cloth in hand. She was limping badly.

'You're cleaning the bathroom,' said Carolyn, surprised. 'Why?'

'My role for the day. Daisy hasn't turned up, having one of her turns.'

'No, I think she's having a party.' Carolyn saw Sandy wince. 'You're limping.'

Sandy smiled ruefully and rubbed her ankle. 'I need a new pebble. Like to come for a walk on the beach this afternoon when these shenanigans are all over?'

'Yes, I'd like that. You're coming to the wedding, aren't you?'

'I don't know yet. I'm of two minds. I'd be the odd one out. Somehow I don't fit in.'

'Mother would be disappointed.'

'I know, that's what makes it so difficult. Can't stop now. I've got the downstairs loo to do. Your hair looks lovely.'

Carolyn dressed slowly and deliberately. It was like preparing for a ritual sacrifice. The only hope now was if the man turned up at the church and objected. She painted a mask on to her face, a dewy look that came straight out of a bottle. She was all ready except for her shoes. She couldn't find them. She tipped out all the shoes in her closet, pulling on some ancient scuffed disco sandals. They looked terrible.

'I can't go,' she said. 'I've no shoes to wear.'

'Where are the yellow satin slippers?' said Adele, bustling around. 'The ones that match the dress.'

Her mother finished dressing her as if she was a little girl again. Timmy was waiting in his white sailor suit, under strict instructions not to move or breathe.

'Let's go for a walk,' said Carolyn, taking his small clammy hand. 'Let's see what the garden is doing.'

'The garden is growing,' said Timmy.

'You're too bright by half. Watch it, my lad. You'll turn into a genius.'

'Bert's got a gorilla's head in the shed,' said Timmy, trying hard not to skip by her side. He liked Carolyn. She treated him like a grown-up.

'How odd. What's it for? Scaring off the birds?'

'That's right. He says it's for scaring the birds. It's horrible, with huge fangs and teeth and red gums.'

'I don't like the sound of it,' said Carolyn, changing direction away from the shed. 'Sounds like a silly joke.'

'Are we going in that big car?'

'Yes, when the bride is ready.'

'It's a vantage car.'

'Vintage.'

'Old, anyway.'

Carolyn could hardly believe that the ritual had begun, a relentless sequence of prearranged events over which no one had any control. The drive to the church, waiting in the porch for the bride to arrive, shivering in the sudden chilled atmosphere of the stone interior. Fiona arrived in a flurry of rustling skirts and veiling blowing in the breeze. She looked perfectly composed. It was Graham who looked worried, checking his side-slick in case the top hat had dishevelled it.

The organ broke into joyful music and the procession arranged itself. Timmy followed the bride, three paces behind. Carolyn drew up in the rear to keep an eye on Timmy. As she saw the back of the wedding dress, the penny dropped.

Carolyn nearly gasped aloud. It was an Emmanuel dress. Every trademark of the famous designer's was there. How had Fiona managed to afford an Emmanuel dress? It must have cost many thousands of pounds.

Carolyn caught a glimpse of her mother's face. Adele looked so sad, her eyes huge. Was she going to cry? Mothers did cry at weddings. Hal and his best man, Ralph, both looked suitably grave. Father Lawrence was robed to the hilt, the rich brocades of the Roman Catholic faith out of place in the simple country church.

No one said anything, no one challenged the marriage. There was a moment, definitely an electric moment, when Father Lawrence bade said objector to forever hold his tongue. An uneasiness filled the church, an atmosphere that could be cut with a knife. It was as if Father Lawrence expected someone to object. People held their breath, waiting, but nothing happened.

From then onwards, it was like a roller coaster. Carolyn remembered signing something in the priest's study. The best man made a joke and everyone laughed. It was quite a funny one, but she couldn't remember it.

Outside, an idiot with a video camera kept getting in everyone's way. Back at Tregony, the waitresses stood about with full trays of Buck's Fizz and champagne. The receiving line immediately grabbed as many glasses as they could drink before the guests arrived.

'It was all lovely, lovely.' Adele was laughing, dizzy with relief. 'Now, let's pray that the food lasts.'

Carolyn took off the hated slippers and wandered round in her stockinged feet. She was off duty now. She plied Timmy, who had developed a terrible thirst, with lemonade and straws. Nothing mattered any more. Fiona had fooled Hal. She had a father for her baby, and a golden ring on her finger to prove it.

She felt sorry for all the Vaughans: pity for Olive Vaughan, looking so hot and enormous; sympathy for Norman Vaughan, being lumbered with such a dreadful wife; desperately sad for Hal that she had not been able to save him. She could not find the courage in church to speak out, to bring the farce to an end.

There were speeches, cutting the cake. Carolyn threw her portion on to a flower bed. It would have choked her. She went over to talk to Hal as Fiona disappeared to change.

'Are you all right?' she asked. 'Feeling the strain?'

'A bit tired,' he said. 'I never knew getting married could be such an ordeal.'

'You don't look particularly happy.'

He half laughed. 'Well, what is happy? Do any of us really know? Nothing is clear-cut in life.' There was a sadness hidden deep in his eyes, as if he half knew.

'I'm glad you're my brother-in-law,' she said, dragging the words out from a ruptured heart. 'I really like you. I always have.'

'And I like you, little mermaid,' he said, touching her silver hair gently. 'Never swim too far away.'

Carolyn fled, shattered by the intimacy of his tender touch. She knew what she had to do. Somehow she had to free him, her beloved, her dearest, the only love of her life.

She went upstairs to her bedroom and chose the sharpest of her steel-pointed hat pins. She pricked her thumb with the sharp end. Blood oozed. This was for Hal, for his sake, for the man she loved . . .

# Six

S uccess did not come easily to Ralph. Quite the reverse. He had to inch his way up the ladder, every rung slippery with sweat and hard work and his own insecurity. He left school with good A levels, but with a widowed mother and younger sister to support there was no question of going on to university. He took a variety of positions, anything that was available.

He began working at Vaughan Precision Instruments as a despatch clerk under Mr Cartwright, an ancient employee who had not changed his methods for years. Ralph was submerged beneath a tidal wave of paper and forms, invoices and statements. It kept him busy, if not satisfied. Occasionally he saw Mr Vaughan, the owner, who was always pleasant. He even knew Ralph's name, which he found surprising.

Ralph met Hal Vaughan through an infatuation of his kid sister's. Susie had a part-time job at the sailing club after school, where she washed-up, made sandwiches and ogled all the bronzed young men. She was one of the boat groupies, a bunch of youngsters who hung about, wise beyond their years. Ralph hated the way she chatted up the young men at the club, wearing bright-pink lipstick and tight patched jeans.

'Hal Vaughan is just so dreamy, dreamy,' Susie sighed every time she came home from the club and flung herself in front of the television. 'And you should see his new car. A porch or something.'

'Porsche,' Ralph corrected. He had seen the sleek vehicle

too, parked in the yard outside the office. It must have cost a fortune, probably five times his annual salary.

'What I wouldn't give for a run in that car,' Susie went on, kicking off her shoes and shaking out her short, frizzed curls. 'I bet it can't half go. Sixty or seventy. I'd do anything for a ride.'

'Don't talk like that,' said Ralph. 'You're only a kid. Hal Vaughan is a grown man. He wouldn't be interested in you.'

'Oh no?' she replied archly. 'How do you know what he's interested in?'

Ralph was disgusted. He hated any signs of sexuality in his sister. It was a facet of their fatherless unit he found difficult to cope with, in himself and his sister. Sex was beyond him. He did not date girls and was afraid of the modern young women who inhabited the secretarial office of Vaughan Precision. They were always giggling and spent a lot of time repairing their make-up and wailing about laddered tights. He knew they laughed at him, called him Four Eyes behind his back, but he did not care.

It was Susie, in a bizarre way, who introduced him to the Vaughan family socially, and to Hal in particular. She had stayed late at the club, trying to pick up extra money. Ralph walked down to meet her as his mother did not like her coming home alone in the dark.

It was a pleasant walk down the narrow, cobbled High Street of Porthcudden to the harbour front. Parts of the fishing village were still quaint and old world. It had some fishing industry left, mainly herring, so there were boats preparing to go out night-trawling, and smaller private craft moored at the tiny marina towards the beach end where the club had its ramp and premises.

Ralph loved the sound of the breaking sea and the quietness now that most of the holidaymakers had gone. The lights were still on in the clubhouse, gleaming yellow on to the glittery shimmering sea. People were drifting out into the darkness.

He saw the clubhouse lights being switched off so he knew he had timed his arrival about right.

Suddenly he heard a man's voice quite clearly, sharp, raised in alarm.

'For heaven's sake, Susie! Cut it out. Hey, give me back my keys. Please.'

Ralph heard a car door slam, followed by an oath. Anger replaced the alarm in the man's voice.

'Get out of there, you young monkey. Come on. Move it. This is no time for games. I want to get home.'

Ralph quickened his step. He had a shrewd idea of the identity of the young monkey, though what she was up to he did not dare guess. He heard a gust of laughter, then some fragments of ribald remarks floated through the cool dark air, wafted to him on the westerly breeze. His heart fell.

As he neared the entrance to the club, he saw Hal leaning on his Porsche, arms folded, a look of black annoyance on his handsome face. A crowd was gathering round the car, some flicking cigarette lighters.

'What's the matter?' Ralph asked in a strained, gravelly tone.

'It's young Susie, from the bar,' said Hal. 'She's locked herself in my car and she's taking off her clothes.'

'I don't understand. She's only a kid,' said Ralph, dazed and bewildered.

'Kid or not, she's still taking off all her clothes,' said Hal. 'And in my car. It's no joke. I want her out. I want to go home now.' He glanced briefly inside, eyebrows drawn darkly. 'Hardly kid-shape any more,' he added.

Ralph went hot and cold with shame. He could see the vaguely pale skin of his sister's back as she divested herself of her few garments, tossing them on to the back seat. He saw her T-shirt fly over. People were peering in and laughing. Susie seemed to be enjoying all the attention, waving and posing as if for photographers. It was horrible. He had to stop it.

He made a dart for the hose that was used for sluicing down

the boats and dragged it round to the forecourt. Then he ran to the tap and turned on the water full blast, leaping out of the way as the hose snaked and reared up with the pressure. He aimed the jet of water at the Porsche, not stopping to think if there were any windows open. The water hit the roof, cascading in all directions down the windows.

The spectators leapt back with good-humoured laughter. It was all part of the strip show. Now there was nothing to see as water poured down the windscreen and side windows. Susie's shape was just a blur behind the miniature waterfall.

'Well done,' Hal shouted, who only just avoided a soaking. 'That was quick thinking. This girl's a real attention-grabber. Perhaps she'll get dressed now that no one is looking at her.'

Ralph redirected the stream to the ground, soaking his trousers in the process, and knocked on the car window. Susie's face peered at him, uncertainly.

'Get dressed,' he said, glaring.

She shook her head, so he directed the full force of the water at her window, the noise like a barrage of bullets ricocheting. It must have sounded terrible inside the car, quite frightening.

He tried it again. 'Get dressed at once,' he ordered loudly. He knew it was a case of wearing her down. She could be stubborn, but she must know she had lost and was now an object of ridicule. Eventually the passenger door opened a crack and a pair of legs in jeans appeared. Ralph tossed the hose aside and pulled his sister out. He was furious. He shook her till the curls bounced round her white face.

'You little trollop,' he raged. 'What do you think you're up to? How dare you behave like that in public? Whatever will Mum think when she hears? You're a proper disgrace.'

'Leave me alone,' she yelled, twisting herself out of his grip and beginning to run up the road. 'It's nothing to do with you, you prat,' she called back.

He ran after her. He was supposed to be seeing her home

or their mum would be furious. But suddenly he stopped, his chest heaving. If he went after her in this state he might do her an injury.

'Hold on, old chap,' said Hal, eyeing him. 'It was only a joke. Susie only meant it for a lark. No harm done. She's all right and my car's had a good wash.'

'I . . . I must apologize for my sister's behaviour,' said Ralph, his voice thick with anger.

'Oh, so she's your sister? Poor devil. What a handful. I've only a brother and fortunately I rarely see him. I say, you're absolutely soaked. You'd better hop in the car and I'll fit you out with some dry clothes.'

'There's no need. We don't live far. Besides I've got to see Susie home.'

'Don't I know you? Your face seems familiar.'

'I work at Vaughans.'

'I thought I knew you,' said Hal. He seemed genuinely pleased. 'All the more reason to come home and have a stiff whisky and a bite of supper. All this water sport has given me a ravenous appetite. We'll track Susie safely home first, make sure she gets in.'

Ralph was tempted. He knew Susie would be furious when she saw he was the one to get a ride in the Porsche. It would serve her right and might bring her to her senses. He rather fancied a drive in the car.

He gave a short, embarrassed laugh. 'I wouldn't say no to some supper. But I'm all wet . . .'

'Sit on this towel. We'll be at Rosemullion House in no time. This little baby just flies.'

That evening introduced Ralph to another world. Rosemullion House was beautiful. He was speechless at first, awed by the old house, its comfort and luxury. Hal was being polite to someone who had helped him out of a tricky situation, but they were of the same age and Ralph had a natural amiability that made it easy for him to adjust to new surroundings. He appreciated everything, and Hal found himself enjoying having a companion who was impressed and grateful. He offered to teach Ralph to sail.

Mrs Vaughan made him welcome. He was polite to her and listened to what she had to say, which was unusual for any of Hal's friends. Ralph was sorry for her. His mother was overweight too, and he understood her problems. And he knew what it was like to be laughed at.

It was difficult to talk to Norman Vaughan at first, as he was Ralph's employer. Hal soon decided that Ralph was far too bright for the job of despatch clerk to old Mr Cartwright, who held on to his job out of Norman's kindness to the family.

'You're wasted there, doing invoices and despatch notes,' he said. 'What would you really like to do?'

Ralph thought carefully before he replied. He had felt the same way for months and knew exactly what he wanted to do, but how would the Vaughans take it? They might consider it an impertinence.

'I'd rather like to take over advertising,' he said, going straight for the top job. Why not? 'The price lists and pamphlets are old-fashioned and hopelessly outdated. The catalogue needs reprinting. Its text is fuzzy and the drawings and photographs are not sharp enough. There are dozens of lost opportunities for pieces in the trade journals, new cruise ships being built, but I never see Vaughan Precision mentioned anywhere. And we need to advertise. Promote ourselves.'

'Hold on a minute, Ralph. You're going too fast. Do you know what you're talking about?' said Hal carefully. He knew his father was conservative about advertising.

'We produce first-class marine instruments, but the world doesn't know,' said Ralph enthusiastically. 'It's not enough to sell in a small perimeter. We're hardly known outside this country.'

'Could you produce a memo outlining your ideas, Ralph?' said Hal. 'I'll have a word with my father. He may not realize that this is an area in which we could be slipping.'

'Nosedived,' said Ralph.

A few days later, Hal came into the despatch department with a box file of pamphlets. He tossed it on to Ralph's desk.

'Redesign one of these and we'll have a look at it,' he said. 'But no promises.'

Ralph nodded. It scared him, but he knew he was right. There was too much black text in small print and the drawings were poor.

'They need more white, and clearer drawings,' said Ralph quickly before his courage failed. 'Better headings. Eye-catching. Bullet points.'

'Do it then.'

He stayed up all night. He redesigned all the pamphlets. The ideas poured out. He found he had a gift for tight words.

It was the beginning he had dreamt about. In a matter of months Ralph had taken over advertising for Vaughan Precision. He modernized their material and found a new firm of printers to carry out his ideas. He gave the catalogue a bold new look but still retained the image of a high-class, reliable product. He knew Norman Vaughan would not care for anything gimmicky.

His salary doubled overnight. He bought a car for himself and an automatic washing machine for his mother. Susie left school and went off to London. The last they heard of her, she was taking a secretarial course, learning computers.

Ralph was made welcome at Rosemullion House. He fitted in well and was helpful with any errand that needed doing. It was a warm summer's evening at Rosemullion when Ralph first saw Fiona Kimberley. She was coming off the tennis court, fair hair tousled, a rosy sheen of perspiration on her cheeks, long legs slim and tanned, the pleated white tennis skirt flirting around her smooth thighs.

She smiled at Ralph, who was carrying a tray of iced lemonade to the players at Mrs Vaughan's request. He stumbled, nearly dropping the tray. He felt that everyone could hear the glasses rattling.

He had never seen any girl so vitally alive. She was shining with good health and happiness. Nothing about her was false. Her hair, catching gleams of sunshine, was its true colour. Her face was devoid of artificiality, with only the merest touch of make-up. Her figure was naturally girlish and the cool white outfit was pure flattery. He fell irrevocably in love with her long before he knew she belonged to Hal.

He kept his passion a closely guarded secret. He knew he did not stand a chance. Hal and Fiona saw each other constantly. It was obvious that it was serious.

She called at the office one afternoon to wait for Hal. She found Ralph working under pressure, pacing his room, a paste-up of a new instrument on his drawing board. She came over to look at it, flowery in a pink summer dress and open-toed sandals.

'Don't look. It's not right yet,' he apologized. 'It's so flat. I can't get it to leap off the page, and it must. This new computer-controlled instrument is way ahead of anything anyone else has produced.'

Fiona peered at the clear black and white photograph of the instrument, wrinkling her nose.

'Navitte CP-2. What a mouthful. The illustration needs to be three-dimensional.'

'Yes, but how? I don't want to clutter the page. The message must be very clear and accurate.'

'Why not bring in a hint of the sea and the worldwide potential? After all, it is a marine instrument, and isn't seventy per cent of the world ocean?' She eyed his collection of paints and coloured felt pens. 'May I try something?'

'Feel free. I've dozens of proofs.'

She picked out a thick aquamarine pen and with a few light brush strokes washed in an uneven background of sea. Then she took a thin-tipped dark grey and added the faint outline of three ships: an ocean liner, a destroyer and a simple sampan.

They immediately gave life to the page, a feeling of the sea and the limitless use of the new instrument.

'That's brilliant,' said Ralph with resignation. 'You ought to be doing this job, not me.'

'Nonsense. I should know something about art. Anyway, I couldn't do all this technical stuff.'

'You run a gift boutique, don't you?'

'It's sort of half boutique, half art gallery. The shop's called Kimberley. I like to give local artists a chance to sell their work and to offer holidaymakers a slightly more up-market souvenir to take home. No Cornish pixies and wishing wells in my shop.'

'You're very talented.'

Fiona laughed, throwing back her head so that her hair swung in a shimmering curtain. 'No way, just lucky. My father raised the capital for me by selling off a piece of our garden, so there's no bank manager breathing down my neck. I can buy in what I like, invest in new work if I think the artist has talent. You can't get luckier than that.'

Hal appeared at the door, pulling on his jacket. 'You can't get luckier than me,' he said, catching the tail end of the conversation. 'This beautiful girl is coming to Minack with me tonight.'

'Drama under the stars,' said Fiona. 'What could be more romantic than an open-air theatre?'

'That's a long way to go,' said Ralph.

'Not in my new car.' Hal had recently acquired an Aston Martin.

'I hope you've got a cushion. Those rocks are hard.'

'Thanks for the reminder,' said Fiona, cheekily helping herself to the foam cushion from Ralph's office chair. 'You won't want this tonight.'

'Do you want to borrow my umbrella as well?'

They all laughed as if he had said something very witty.

It gave Ralph endless simple pleasure in the weeks afterwards to relive the way Fiona had borrowed his cushion, treating him as a friend that one could take liberties with, and that maybe she had sat on it. Although the thought of her slim rounded rear on the same cushion brought a blush to his face.

He grew a moustache to make his appearance more mature. It did seem to give him confidence.

When Fiona and Hal became engaged and moved into the estuary flat, Ralph was emotionally thrown, although he was never sure which event came first. He loved them both. Hal for being a genuine friend, good company and treating him as an equal, drawing him painlessly into his social circle. As for Fiona, for him she was the most wonderful woman in the world.

He was overwhelmed when Hal asked him to be best man at the wedding. The fact that the woman he loved was marrying another man scarcely touched him. The three of them were like a trinity in his mind. The reality did not sink in. It was something happening on another planet. He was pleased to have been asked and took more interest in the arrangements for the wedding than either the bride or the groom.

'We've no need to worry,' said Hal, slipping his arm round Fiona's slim waist. 'Ralph will be there to see to everything.'

Both families were grateful that Ralph was around to act as a go-between. If Adele wanted to know something, she phoned Ralph, not Hal. If Olive needed clarification on a point, she asked Ralph, not her son.

Three weeks before the wedding, Fiona turned up at the office. She wanted someone to help her put up some curtain poles. Hal had gone to the Far East on a long promotional tour. It was bad timing, but Fiona had accepted that perhaps he needed to get away from the now frenzied pace of pre-wedding preparations.

'I'll do it,' said Ralph, 'if you don't mind waiting ten minutes till I've finished this.'

'Can you put up poles?' she asked dubiously.

'For heaven's sake.' He grinned. 'I've been putting up things for my mum since I was ten. I'm the original DIY man.'

It was the first time he had actually seen the new ranch-style bungalow that the Vaughans were giving them for a wedding present. He enthused about it in a manner that really warmed Fiona's heart. He was impressed by everything, from the underfloor heating to the utility room.

'It's really smashing,' he said, wandering from one half-furnished room to another, sniffing in the smell of fresh paint and the newness. 'What a place to live! It's a palace. My mother would love it.'

'You actually like it?' said Fiona, almost wistfully.

'It's grand. Perfect for a young couple starting out.'

'I wish Hal thought so,' Fiona went on. 'I don't think he has even looked at it properly. He doesn't take any interest in the furniture or the fittings.'

Ralph came back from his wanderings, shaking off a silly dream. 'I'm sure he does, but it is a different way of life for him after Rosemullion House. That's a really big house and this is a bungalow. He'll adjust eventually.'

Just how different life would be, Ralph found out when he realized that two bedrooms were to be used: one pink and floral, the other an austere navy. It shocked him. He did not know what to say, but continued screwing in the supports for the rails, averting his face.

'It's all right,' said Fiona. 'You can say it. Why does Hal want a separate bedroom? Well, don't ask me, I don't know. It beats me.'

'I don't understand,' Ralph mumbled, his glasses misting. 'I thought married people normally slept t–together. You know . . . er . . .'

'Apparently not,' she snapped. 'My pink and white roses femininity offends his macho image.'

She flounced out of the bedroom leaving Ralph marooned on the top of the steps. He could not cope with the situation.

He did not have the experience to brush it off. Fiona returned with a bottle of white wine she had found in the refrigerator. She had two glasses.

'Look what I've found. A nice Hock. It definitely needs finishing up.'

'But I'm driving,' he protested.

'Rubbish, not for hours! You must be thirsty.' She poured out the wine and sipped. 'Join me. It's delicious.'

He drank the wine like water, hardly tasting it. Fiona was so close, so lovely in another of her flowery dresses, only this time it was silk that clung to her body, revealing all its delectable curves. He began to feel hot and uncomfortable.

'Come and help me put the duvet cover on,' she said. 'I bought it today for my room. Do you think it's pretty?'

'Very,' he said as they struggled to get the rose-sprigged cover over the padded quilt. But he meant her, not the duvet, which he hardly glanced at. They got into a ridiculous muddle with the billowing material. He was not used to changing covers. They still had blankets and eiderdowns at home.

Fiona came close, half laughing, trying to find a corner. Her perfume was all the flowers of the garden. Her straight, fair hair swung away from her face, giving him a glimpse of a soft, vulnerable neck curving into her shoulder. Such slim shoulders. Ralph could not help himself. It was all too much. Months of loving her shot to the surface and would not be denied a moment longer. As she brushed against him, his hands dropped the cover and his arms closed round her, pulling her clumsily against him. His mouth sought her face in a trembling kiss that told of years of loving and dreaming, of fantasies and hopes, tenderness and desire. His kisses were immature and tentative but Fiona made no move to stop him.

'Heavens,' she murmured in a small wistful voice, coming up for air. 'What's this all about then?'

But her arms crept round his neck, pulling his head down so that their lips met in a long, deep kiss. At some point, and

Ralph was not quite sure when, Fiona removed his spectacles and put them by the side of the bed. Nor did he understand how they came to be lying on the bed, their legs entwined, their hands exploring so gently and caringly, kisses deepening with each new pleasure, their warm breath mingling. Fiona began a slow, seductive exploitation of his innocent manhood.

Ralph was past thinking straight. All coherent thought disappeared. He gave himself up to the ecstasy into which Fiona was leading him. She was guiding him with a tenderness that was an utter delight. He was deliriously happy, swimming in a sea of rapture, each wave of feeling taking him higher and higher, ecstatic that she was giving him her lips, her breasts, her legs and then her most secret place. Fiona loved him in those moments, her own dear Ralph. She made sure it was wonderful for both of them.

Afterwards Ralph could not believe that it had been real, that it had happened. He lay in a stupor of euphoria, Fiona's hair splayed across his bare chest, her breathing soft and shallow. He felt a million dollars, like a king, like a lion. He had never known such happiness. Fiona had been so loving, responding to him with total abandon, meeting his demands with her own, her own passion a revelation. It had been an experience beyond any imagination.

She could not marry Hal now. Never. She could not possibly, not after this. Ralph knew it would take courage to cancel the wedding, but she must do it. Their own wedding would have to be something much smaller, much quieter, with only a few friends. Perhaps some little church, further along the coast. He would resign from his job but if he worked day and night he might be able to take on a mortgage for the bungalow. Fiona would want to live here. She obviously loved the bungalow, and anything she wanted, she must have.

He fell asleep into a fantasy dream, limbs heavy and sated, his arms around her lovely softness, the scent of her skin and hair in his nostrils. It was all so wonderful. He could only float in a vast inner peace.

When he awoke, Fiona had gone. He stretched out, lethargic and content, looking round the pretty room, at the poles he had put up, the frilly pink curtains waiting to be hung. Soon he would know this room so well; his clothes would share the white closet, his dressing gown would hang on the back of the door. No separate bedroom for him.

Fiona came in. She was fully dressed in her flowery frock and sandals. She had two mugs of tea.

'I found a tea bag,' she said triumphantly. 'I can't remember when we left that behind. Drink up, then I must go.'

Ralph pulled her down on the side of the bed and touched her face. 'You are very lovely,' he said. 'And you were so wonderful.'

'Good,' she laughed. 'So were you. You were great. I didn't know you had it in you. Our quiet little Ralph! Such hidden talent,' she teased.

'We've got to talk,' he said urgently. 'It's only three weeks till your wedding.'

'So?' Fiona slipped off the edge of the bed. 'There's nothing to talk about. Drink your tea and get dressed.'

'But we must talk, Fiona darling. We must decide what we are going to do. The future . . . There's our future.' He was totally confused by her casual reaction. The tea grew cold.

'What future? We don't have any future, Ralph darling. My future is with Hal. It always has been. I am going to marry him next month. Oh yes, this evening has been special, very special, I won't deny that and I'll never forget it. But sweetheart, it has nothing to do with marriage. It was just . . . a pleasant interlude.'

Ralph was shocked. His face paled, and his hand shook, spilling the tea on the rose-sprigged duvet covering him. 'An interlude? I can't believe it. You're joking, Fiona. I . . . I love you. You can't marry someone else.'

'Oh yes, I can. I don't love you, Ralph. You are my dearest friend but I'm not going to marry you. I'm marrying Hal Vaughan, and Vaughan Precision and Rosemullion House.

What have you got to offer me? Some semi in a backstreet, bringing up a couple of kids on your salary? No, thank you, Ralph. That's not going to be my life.'

'But just now . . .' he faltered. 'It was perfect. You can't turn your back on what we have just shared for the sake of money and status.'

'Why not? They're what matter. Sex doesn't last. It's gone in a year or two. Besides, there's nothing to prevent us meeting occasionally, if we want to. We could still meet somewhere, be alone,' she added with a wicked smile. 'Just you and me. Some quiet afternoon.'

Ralph sat up in bed, rigid with shock. He tried to struggle into his clothes. His beauty, his golden goddess, Fiona, his darling, had fallen from her pedestal. He gulped, trembling and cringing. He remembered with a flood of shame that Hal was his best friend and he had desecrated a relationship that had been so special to him. Ralph could have wept. At the same time he could not believe that Fiona felt so little after the ecstatic experience they had shared.

'I don't believe it,' he muttered. 'I don't believe one word of what you are saying. You must be in shock. Are you suggesting that we carry on, have an affair, after you and Hal are married?'

Fiona went over to the curtains waiting to be hung and shook them out. 'It was a silly joke. Of course I didn't mean it at all. I wasn't thinking. Being with you was so perfect, I wanted it to continue. What woman wouldn't? One doesn't often meet a man who knows instinctively how to make love.'

'But you'd still marry Hal,' said Ralph harshly, a pulse beating in his forehead. 'You would still rather marry someone else.'

'Yes,' said Fiona, sounding calm and decisive. 'I'm going to marry Hal. I want to be his wife.'

Ralph did not remember much of the drive home. He dropped Fiona off at the estuary flat. She gave him a light

124

kiss on the cheek but he would not look at her. He stared
ahead through the windscreen, unaware of the spots of rain
starting to cloud his vision. She took one look at his stony
profile and shivered, despite the warmth of the evening. He
looked like a stranger. There was thunder rumbling in the
distance and she hurried indoors. She hated storms.

On the morning of the wedding Ralph was kept busy. He
was to take the order of service sheets from the printers to
the church and check that all the ushers knew what to do. He
had to see that Hal was there on time. He had various bills
to pay that were the groom's duty.

Ralph had lost weight in the last few weeks and his hired
grey morning suit hung on him. His cheeks were gaunt. He
did not need a moustache to make him look older. Olive
began to wonder if he was ill. It was all a nightmare. He
had not been sleeping, agonizing over how he had cheated
his best friend. How he lusted after Fiona more than ever,
even though she had toppled from her pedestal and was only
a desirable mortal. He longed for her delectable body in a
perpetual agony of desire.

The church was cool and quiet. He wondered if its stony
chill might soothe his throbbing head. He spoke to the
grey-haired woman doing the flowers, but nothing he said
made any sense. What would he do at this wedding? Any
impediment, they always asked. Would he tell the gathering
at the vital moment that the bride had made love with him
less than three weeks ago? That she could not marry Hal.
That they loved each other.

'Is anything the matter?' Grace asked, pausing as she fixed
flowers on the pews. 'Are you all right, young man?'

'Sorry. Yes, I'm all right, I think. I don't know actually.
The flowers are lovely, really lovely.'

But when it came to that point in the service, Ralph could
not speak. He stood stiffly by Hal's side, his throat constricted
with a hard knot of grief. Fiona glanced across at him, her eyes

soft and pleading. He could not hurt her. He could not let her down. He knew that he only wanted her to be happy.

He went through his duties at the reception with a degree of efficiency. It was like acting, a part of him watching himself. He spoke to the elegant old aunt, drawn by something in her eyes. He had written a good speech and learnt it by heart. When the time came, before the cutting of the cake, he was able to deliver it with a smoothness that had everyone laughing and applauding. He saw Olive Vaughan's face approving and kind. Adele, too, looked relieved and happy.

Ralph could not take his eyes off Fiona. She was like a princess in a fairy-tale dress. She had never looked so beautiful. She did not look real. She was an ethereal creature, floating round a garden of flowers in an aura of purity and innocence. It was Hal who was going to defile that pureness.

'You forgot to say anything nice about me in your speech,' said Carolyn. 'You are supposed to mention the bridesmaid. It was all about Fiona and Hal.'

'I thought I mentioned the followers.'

'Was that supposed to mean me?'

'Sorry, it was indirect admiration. Forgive me. I was very nervous. And you do look very pretty.'

'It doesn't matter,' said Carolyn, offhand.

'That young man looks under the weather,' said Lady Elvina from the shade of the marquee. 'Do you think he's going to pass out? Perhaps it's the heat.'

'Who? Ralph? The best man?' said Adele. 'No, of course not. He's a very pillar of strength, a rock to lean on. I don't know what I would have done without him.'

'Look at him. He's ill. I know a sick man when I see one,' said Elvina, sipping her champagne thoughtfully. 'Someone has hurt him and hurt him badly.'

Ralph watched Fiona trip into Tregony after giving Olive a slice of wedding cake. His heart was pounding in his chest. How much time had he got left? How wisely could he use it? He had to talk to Fiona. His heart was pounding. He felt that quite soon it might explode in a nasty mess all over the marquee.

Fiona, Fiona . . . His silent cry followed her into the house. What was she doing to them, Hal and himself? Was she going to break both their hearts, ruin both lives? Tears came into his eyes and he blinked behind his spectacles. Fate was taking over. He felt nothing, only emptiness. He loved her so much. He smiled automatically at people in the garden, chatting, offering pieces of cake. He had no idea who they were. It was like an absurd dream, like the Mad Hatter's tea party. He hardly knew what was real and what was fantasy.

Something scratched his thigh. In his pocket he found his draughtman's dividers, a pair of measuring compasses, the twin points as sharp as needles. God knows how the instrument got there. He had been working late the evening before the wedding, his hired outfit waiting to be unpacked and tried on. It was part of the nightmare of the last few hours.

He stared into the empty hall of Tregony. Fiona was upstairs somewhere, changing. It was still not too late. The marriage could be annulled. His car was outside. She must say yes and then they could leave quickly and quietly together. They would soon be miles away.

He would persuade her, use his gift with words. She must see the sense in his argument. And surely Hal would understand that Ralph had only been trying to save him from unhappiness . . .

Ralph began to form his words. They had to be the right ones.

# Seven

Lady Elvina hated growing old. She thought it was totally unfair that someone who felt so young inside should look so ancient outside. She fought the encroaching years with all the armoury at her command. She dieted, exercised; she bought expensive anti-aging creams with collagen replacement; she had a few discreet lifts and tucks as well as a few discreet lovers. She was not sure which were the more beneficial, the young lovers or the operations.

Her passport said she was seventy-eight. Elvina could not bring herself to admit it was a lie. She felt exactly the same as she had at eighteen or twenty-eight or fifty-eight. A woman always ready for fun and excitement and new experiences. Her three husbands had added to the variety and spice of life, each in their different ways. She did not regret any of them. She only regretted that she had not had more. Elizabeth Taylor had had seven, or was it eight?

Elvina often felt that she should have started earlier. It was too late now for a number four. No one would look at her. Unless she found herself a toy boy, someone who would marry her for her money.

This made her laugh aloud as she sat by the big bay window of her elegant first-floor flat overlooking Regent's Park. She fancied a toy boy, someone handsome and bronzed with firm flesh and smooth skin, who would take her out to first nights and restaurants. He would not have to do much else . . . flatter her, bring her little presents, occasionally make her feel comfortable.

Elvina could not stop another throaty laugh. Her laugh had not aged, although she was aware that her girlish voice had deepened. She hated the brown liver spots on her hands, the wrinkled crêpey skin, fading blue eyes, dry and thinning hair. As for her sagging body, she looked at it as little as possible. She had the long mirrors in her bedroom removed, hoping that by some magic the scrawny brown envelope of skin would vanish from her bones, leaving the pale and luminous flesh that had once been hers.

Her first husband had been a soldier, a dashing sergeant who had died on the bloodied, scorching sand of the North African desert in the Second World War. Sometimes she had to look at the browning photograph of their wedding group in order to bring his face to mind. Poor, brave soldier in uniform . . . It had been so romantic, he going off to war and Elvina working in a munitions factory, despite those dreadful turbans they had to wear. His leaves had been wildly erotic, when they had scarcely ever left their hotel bedroom. They never had a home. There had not been time to make one.

She had taken a variety of jobs after the war to supplement a meagre widow's pension. It was whilst working in a draper's shop that she met Fred Goldblummer, an ambitious man of similar age, who realized that women were starved of clothes during the coupon rationing of the war, and that as soon as these restrictions were lifted, there would be a stampede for cheap, mass-produced clothes. Elvina was infected by his enthusiasm and hardly noticed that Fred was dark, Jewish and running to fat.

Fred Goldblummer opened his first dress shop in 1948. It was called Golds. The clothes were cheap and made by a factory up north, but they had a smart gold label inside that made the frocks seem more expensive. Elvina was one of the shop assistants. Fred was aware that Elvina looked better-dressed than their customers and she had a flare for clothes. She was a handsome woman, with sandy, reddish hair piled fashionably high and bright blue eyes that missed nothing.

He promoted her to manageress. By the end of the first trading year she was his mistress. By the end of the next, Fred had opened fourteen more city shops and married Elvina. She was an asset.

It was, first and foremost, a business partnership. Elvina worked hard improving the Golds chain. It was she who turned tat into elegance, and although Golds went upmarket, they never forgot their grass-roots customers and there were always special lines to be snapped up at bargain prices. Elvina introduced the distinctive gold carrier bags long before any other store used the idea as promotion.

'But what a waste of money,' Fred protested at first. 'Why give them an expensive bag? It's money down the drain. They'll just be thrown away.'

'No they won't,' said Elvina, knowing women. 'They'll carry them around so that their friends will know they shop at Golds. The bags will become a status symbol. Don't worry, they won't cost us a penny. One bag will be added to the costing of every garment.'

Elvina was right. Women bought to get a gold bag. They were used until the handles tore. She gave all the shops a facelift with luxury cubicles, good lighting, good mirrors, fitted carpets and assistants trained to be pleasant and helpful.

'I won't have assistants who intimidate the customers,' she said time and time again. 'Anyone who looks down their pert nose is out.'

She stopped wearing Golds clothes herself and bought from Chanel, Dior, Worth and Hartnell. They moved to a large double-fronted house facing Wimbledon Common, employed a cook and a maid. They had no children because Golds was their child.

Elvina became more elegant, her burnished hair more golden, bobbed, waved or bouffant as each new trend dictated, but Fred stayed the same: still swarthy, fat, sweaty and carefully wearing the same Savile Row suit till the buttons fell off. He was too tired at the end of a day to go out, but sat in front of their console television set with a large whisky and the accounts to work on.

Elvina looked elsewhere for entertainment. She was still young, full of energy and bounce. She wanted to see and be seen. She wanted to dance all night, and she did.

When Fred died from a stroke, collapsing in front of their newest and largest television set, Elvina played the grieving widow for about two months. Even that brief period was a strain, because she had already met Sir Peter Dawlish at Lingfield Races and was madly in love with his title, his distinguished profile, his estate in the country – and particularly his position at the Foreign Office. How he had managed to remain single in that social circle and elite marriage market was a small miracle. Elvina could not believe it. She found herself phoning him every day to make sure he was still a bachelor.

'An ambassador's wife,' she murmured to herself, marking the days off on a calendar. 'Lady Elvina Dawlish.'

Sir Peter was disconcerted when he discovered Elvina was in retail and thought her haste to discard her widow's weeds a little unseemly. Elvina immediately sold off the Golds chain of shops, which she had inherited, putting the considerable profit into gilt-edged stocks. She became the drab widow overnight, with downcast eyes and fluttering a mauve-edged handkerchief. This allayed Sir Peter's fears, and he promised they would be engaged by the new year and married the following spring. He kept his word. By then he was falling in love with her.

Elvina wore pink at her third wedding, Hartnell pink, a long frothy dress with a big shady hat covered in ostrich feathers. St Margaret's, Westminster, was packed with Sir Peter's friends and colleagues. There was not a shop assistant in sight, except outside on the pavement. Elvina's only guests were her younger sister, Madge, with husband, Tom, and their sweet daughter, Adele.

They cruised the Caribbean on honeymoon and it was on the balmy seas that Sir Peter fell truly in love with his ravishing copper-haired wife. He could hardly let her out of his sight. They spent the days mooning on deck together, the nights finding half-forgotten raptures in each other's arms. Elvina bloomed. The barren years dropped from her and she became a real beauty.

'I've never been so happy,' she said as he fastened a string of pearls round her pretty, tanned neck.

'And you'll always be happy, my darling,' he said, kissing her soft, bare shoulder with a new tenderness. 'I shall make sure of that.'

The diplomatic circle was all that Elvina had ever wanted. Wherever they went, they lived in the best of houses. When Sir Peter took up a post as chargé d'affaires in French Morocco, their residence was a palatial white villa on a hill with an army of servants, cool marble courtyards and elegantly furnished rooms. They entertained lavishly.

Sir Peter gave her a generous dress allowance; an embassy car was always at her disposal. Elvina could do as she pleased all day and every day. In return she was the perfect wife and hostess. If occasionally she fancied a younger man, she was discreet and always so charming that no one split on her. If Sir Peter knew of her little flirtations, he did not reprove her. Perhaps it suited him; perhaps her appetite was too much for him. After all, his job was strenuous and demanding.

'Reports, reports,' he groaned. 'The paperwork grows all the time. You go out and enjoy yourself, my dear.'

They lived all over the world. A difficult posting in Central Africa was followed by a Middle Eastern city where life was glamorous and their friends fabulously rich. Sweden was where Elvina acquired her furs, Japan where she bought jade. She liked European capitals best, for there she could really indulge her love of shopping.

But this idyllic lifestyle came to an abrupt end. Afterwards, Elvina was to wonder why all her husbands died suddenly;

none of them prepared her with a long illness or a stay in hospital. For each death, the morning began normally, with breakfast, newspapers, news on the radio, a bath, dressing to go out, and then by nightfall she was suddenly a widow.

It was a terrorist's bullet exploding in Sir Peter's chest that shattered Elvina's life for the third time. It was a mistake. It had been meant for the dark-skinned premier standing at his side at an official function. The terrorist's aim had been poor. A nervous tremor had invaded his fingers as he took aim on the shiny bald pate of the short politician. The bullet sped past the premier's ear and ripped apart Sir Peter's immaculate suit, spraying warm red blood over his surprised face and silvery hair.

Elvina packed in a numb daze and flew home with her husband in the freight compartment like a piece of excess luggage. There was an impressively solemn funeral as befitted the victim of such an outrage, and a memorial service at Westminster Abbey attended by everyone who was anyone, including the prime minister and the foreign secretary. Elvina hardly listened to the eulogies from the pulpit. Surely they were talking about someone else. It couldn't be her Peter.

'Sir Peter was a very special man,' people said to her, shaking her hand outside the abbey. Big Ben boomed midday, the echoing strokes the countdown to her demise. She was nobody now. She was not the ambassador's wife any more. In a month, even Sir Peter would be forgotten.

The state allowed her to live comfortably. Her pension was adequate and there was also Sir Peter's private fortune. She sold the country estate, which was damp and gloomy, and bought a villa in the south of France. Madge came out for holidays and so did her niece, Adele, who was growing into a beautiful young girl. Elvina enjoyed spoiling her and showing her off at parties. Despite the difference in their ages, Elvina and Adele had a lot in common. They both liked talking clothes and shopping, dances and parties.

Elvina grew very fond of Adele. She was like the daughter

Elvina had never had, and the white painted villa came alive every time Adele came for a visit.

'Darling child,' Elvina said, hugging the girl at Nice airport. 'So I've got you all to myself this time. That's wonderful.'

'Mother couldn't come,' said Adele. 'She sends her love, but you know what it's like. Dad expects her to spend Christmas at home.'

'Husbands!' said Elvina with a steady voice.

'I'd rather spend Christmas with you in the sun.'

'Of course, so would any sensible person. Escaping an English winter is the only civilized thing to do. Come along, my dear. You must meet my new friend. He's waiting to drive us back to the villa. His name is Andre. I'm teaching him English so that he can sell French antiques to the tourists at exorbitant prices.'

Andre was waiting by Elvina's open-top Daimler. He was tall and fair, skin tanned by hours on the beach. He had the profile of a Greek god but his manners were pure French. He took Adele's hand and brushed her skin with his lips.

'Enchanté,' he murmured.

'Andre is very shy,' said Elvina, laughing. 'I believe he's afraid of me. It will be up to you to coax him out of his shell, Adele.'

'What is this shell,' he asked, his blue eyes amused, 'that I am to be coming out of? Shall I like it when I come out?'

He was charming and Adele liked his shyness. He was so different to English boys. The only ones she knew were uncouth bores. Andre was a refreshing change.

'It's because you are so sophisticated, Aunt Elvina,' said Adele later as they were sipping chilled wine on the vine-covered terrace of the villa. 'No wonder Andre is terrified. He was brought up in a very strict provincial family, and antiques is a solid, respectable business. Suddenly he is catapulted into your frenzied world of parties and dances, swimming in the dark and ridiculous after-supper games.'

'His father sent him to me to be instructed,' said Elvina, wickedly. 'And I don't believe that young man is as innocent as he makes out. I'm sure beneath that charmingly shy exterior is a madly passionate Gallic nature.'

'Auntie,' Adele giggled. 'That's not true. Andre is a poppet. I wanted to teach him to jive this evening but he says it's not dignified.'

'Mind he does not have something to teach you,' said Elvina, remembering her reponsibility to her niece while she was staying under her roof.

'Don't worry. There's nothing I don't know about.'

But Elvina was not so sure. Adele had a genuinely open and trusting nature. Elvina felt sure that her experience of life was limited. She must keep an eye on her niece and her good-looking pupil. As the lazy days passed, it seemed she did not have any need to worry. Andre did not put a foot wrong. He was polite and attentive to Adele, never overstepping the mark. Gradually Elvina's fears subsided. The holiday flew by and Adele hugged her aunt goodbye with genuine tears.

It came as a surprise to Elvina when in the spring she received an invitation to Adele's wedding. She was marrying an estate agent called Graham Kimberley. It sounded rushed and Elvina worried that her niece was doing the right thing. Adele was too young to be settling down. It meant the end of the solo holidays which they had both enjoyed. Her visits would be quite different with a husband in tow.

Elvina did not go to Adele's wedding. She had an invitation to cruise round the Greek islands on a friend's luxury yacht. It was an opportunity she could not refuse. She sent her apologies and a generous cheque and went shopping instead for glamorous yachting clothes.

Adele never told Elvina what she spent the money on. She was disappointed that her aunt had not been at the wedding. She and Graham never visited the villa. Graham did not have much time for holidays with his growing business interests and he did not like going abroad, particularly to France.

When Fiona was born, Elvina sent another generous cheque and sadly reflected that she was not likely to see much of her niece now.

They kept in touch in a haphazard way. Elvina sent postcards from exotic places; Adele sent progress reports on her growing family. The generous cheques kept coming at Christmas, birthdays and christenings.

'Money, money, money,' Elvina murmured to herself as she uncapped her gold fountain pen. 'That's all I have to give anyone these days. I'm too old for anything else.'

A bout of influenza one cold January frightened Elvina into selling the villa and returning to London. She stumbled around the chilled rooms, coughing and shivering, hardly able to find the strength to dress or call anyone. Her dwindling staff kept out of the way, scared they might catch something.

It came to Elvina that she was paying out a lot of money for very little in return. She might as well have a centrally heated flat in London, cheer herself with visits to theatres and galleries, close up each autumn to spend the winter months in one of her favourite hotels around the world. At least she would get better service than from this lazy lot of servants.

On returning to London, Elvina rediscovered the Kimberley family, now grown-up. She had a guest bedroom that was suddenly very popular. Fiona had opened a boutique and art gallery in Cornwall and came to London frequently to buy stock or find manufacturers for a particular line she had designed.

'You can stay whenever you like,' said Elvina. 'Carolyn too. Your mother and I used to be great friends when we were both much younger. Oh, the beach parties, the dances . . .'

'That's great, Aunt El,' said Fiona. 'I'd appreciate a bed here. The personal contact is really important when trying to get a product made. It's no good relying on explaining by post, as I know to my cost.'

Fiona was like a young colt, fair and skittish. She had so much energy, bouncing around the flat, strewing it with samples and designs. Elvina was tolerant, knowing that Fiona would be off soon, like a whirlwind, leaving only a whiff of her expensive perfume in the air. A weekend of chamber music and concerts at the Grand Hotel in Eastbourne beckoned and Elvina was looking forward to reliving a little past glory in its Edwardian elegance.

'I will clear up before I go, Aunt El,' Fiona promised lightly. 'I can't help making a mess. I'm sorry.'

'Look at my desk,' said Elvina. 'It looks as if a bomb has hit it. This is worse than the Blitz. No one would think it was a valuable antique.' Her joking words were a premonition of the future, though she did not know it at the time.

A vaguely haunted feeling tugged at wisps of thoughts. Her memory was getting bad these days. The desk had been given to her by the young Frenchman that Adele had liked. What was his name? They had got on so well together, those two young people. She heard he had taken over the family business, becoming an international expert. Sometimes she saw him mentioned in the newspapers at important auctions. Was it Andre . . . ?

The bombshell came from the most unexpected quarter. And the true aim of the accusation, and its consequences, were the product of exceptionally clear thinking. It was a direct hit in every aspect.

Fiona arrived back one evening, bags bulging with china gulls and carved owls. She had had a hectic day trying to find a degree of quality along with an acceptable price. She would not stock rubbish in her shop, yet she knew there was a limit to the prices she could charge.

'My arms are falling out,' she groaned, throwing herself into an armchair and accepting a glass of dry white wine. 'Lugging all this stuff around on the buses and underground is no joke. Then I've to cart it all home again tomorrow. I ought to have a car.'

'But the traffic jams are terrible in London,' said Elvina. 'And there's never anywhere to park.'

'But you've got a resident's parking permit that you never use, haven't you? Most of the manufacturers I deal with are based in East London, or out in the suburbs. I waste hours walking around and trying to find the damned places.'

'You'll have to get yourself a little car then,' said Elvina, remembering the powerful purr of the old Daimler she reluctantly had to sell. 'When your shop is showing a good profit.'

'That'll be the day, when I make enough money,' said Fiona, sipping her drink. She pushed her feathery fringe out of her eyes and regarded her aunt thoughtfully. 'You did well for yourself, didn't you? Going from being Mrs Fred . . . What was his name? Goldblummer? Going from Mrs Goldblummer to Lady Dawlish in a matter of months. A fantastic leap up the social scale, wasn't it? How did you pull it off?'

Elvina's heart fluttered for a moment. What a strange remark for Fiona to make. 'I don't know what you mean, dear. It was the hand of fate, I suppose.'

'Poor old Uncle Fred,' Fiona went on, as if she had actually known him. 'The hand of fate, dying like that so suddenly, and you had already met Sir Peter, hadn't you?'

'Heavens girl, I don't remember . . . it was all so long ago. I met so many people. Let's find a more cheerful subject to talk about. This is too depressing.'

'I suppose being Mrs Fred Goldblummer is a depressing thought after being Lady Dawlish for such a long time,' said Fiona, gazing out of the window at the tops of trees in the park. There had been the slightest emphasis on the title. Elvina wondered if she had imagined it. A calculating look settled on the young woman's face that sent a chill through Elvina's brittle bones.

'I hardly think that's relevant,' said Elvina. 'My husband Fred has been dead for years. He had a stroke right in front of the television set.'

'What was on the telly?'

138

'What a question! How should I know after all these years?'

'You could find out,' said Fiona. 'The time of death would be on the police report, or the autopsy or in the coroner's records. Then you could ring up the BBC archives and find out what programme was on.'

'For heaven's sake, Fiona, I'm not particularly interested.' Elvina was beginning to get rattled. 'I don't think the police were brought into it. We called a doctor, of course. He had died a perfectly natural death.'

'Wasn't there a post-mortem?'

'No, there was not,' Elvina snapped. Her faded blue eyes sharpened. She sensed danger but she did not know what it was.

'Poor old Uncle Fred. What a way to go. Just bundled off like last week's washing.'

Elvina stood up abruptly. She could not sit still a moment longer. 'Fiona, I find this conversation rather offensive. I don't know why you are persisting in talking about my former husband. You never knew him. You can have no interest in him, so please stop.'

'But I feel as if I know him, as if I do have an interest in him, really I do.'

'Fiona!'

'Sorry . . .' Fiona sang out, trying to look contrite. 'I won't mention his name ever again.'

Elvina thought long and hard that evening but a horrid suspicion was growing. When it was time for Fiona to leave to catch an overnight train back to Cornwall, Elvina decided to test those suspicions.

'Fiona, I have been thinking about all your business trips to London. It must be tiring carrying all those heavy bags and boxes everywhere. You ought to have a car to get around in, so this is an early birthday present for you – with my love.'

Fiona took the cheque and gasped at the amount. She flung her arms round Elvina's withered neck and hugged her.

'Aunt El, thank you. That's marvellous. You are an absolute dear.'

An absolute fool, thought Elvina. But an old fool, and used to her comforts. It was too late to change now. She made a quick search of the flat but nothing seemed relevant.

Elvina also helped out when Fiona decided to extend the gallery side of her business by incorporating an old stone outhouse into her shop. It would cost a lot of money to whitewash the walls and put in some windows, Fiona hinted. Elvina paid up. Then Fiona fancied a bow-windowed shopfront with bottle-glass panes and an elegant cream canopy with the name KIMBERLEY emblazoned across it.

'It's just a loan, Aunt El,' Fiona wrote gaily. 'I'll pay you back when I get on my feet.'

By then I shall probably be on my knees, thought Elvina. Her bank manager thought so too. He was beginning to get worried. He sent a letter suggesting an interview, pointing out that she had not requested overdraft facilities and this was the third month she had been overdrawn.

'Sell some shares,' she told him over the phone. 'And don't bother me again with such trifles.'

But she was bothered. Her wealth was not a bottomless pit and she knew she had been spending heavily the last few months. Thousands of pounds had gone out, mostly down to Cornwall.

She began a systematic search of the flat to find some clue. What had prompted Fiona to make her remarks? The desk was an obvious start. Her cheque books revealed nothing, as she rarely filled in a stub. The bank statements told of a regular income and regular outgoings in the form of standing orders, but little else.

She ransacked the rooms in a sort of controlled panic. Somehow, somewhere she had been careless. Just some little thing she had overlooked, but which the alert Miss Fiona Kimberley had fastened on to with greedy talons.

Elvina's furs were kept in the guest-room wardrobe. They

were so beautiful. She ran her hands lovingly over their softness: a full-length mink, a sable, a fox-fur jacket. Crumpled
handkerchieves and theatre tickets were stuffed in pockets,
spoiling the shape. She went through the pockets, pulling out
all the rubbish.

A folded letter fell to the floor and her memory parted like
a curtain, revealing its typed contents as fresh and clear as on
the day she had received it.

'Dear Lady Dawlish,' it read.

> We feel we should bring to your notice the recent
> developments in electric wheelchairs. As your father
> seems to enjoy his outings in the grounds, we wonder
> if you would care to purchase one of these chairs
> for Mr Goldblummer? After all these years of being
> totally incapacitated, he has become exceptionally
> heavy, and any help for our nursing staff would be
> much appreciated.
>
> Yours sincerely . . .

Elvina closed her eyes and sat down on the edge of the
bed, the world spinning round her. She had not thought of
that evening in Wimbledon for so long; the hurried phone
calls, the drive through the night in an ambulance, the small
private nursing home. Then the very natural mistake made by
the matron in charge that Fred Goldblummer was her father,
a mistake which Elvina, in the confusion of the moment, had
not corrected. For years Fred had seemed more like a father
than a husband.

She had already met Sir Peter at the races at Lingfield.
When he began to show more than a passing interest in her,
the temptation became too much. Why not? Why shouldn't
she? Fred was paralysed, unable to speak. He would never
recover. She was still young and this was another chance
for life.

So Fred, her husband, conveniently 'died'. The funeral was

private. The only reminder was the standing order payment to the nursing home, which increased annually. She never went to see him. Apparently he did not recognize anyone, not even the nurses. He existed in a grey, mindless vacuum.

She married Sir Peter and they lived happily ever after. Until a stray bullet shattered the idyll.

Elvina put the letter down hurriedly. She was too old for scandal. The tabloid newspapers would love it, splash the bigamous marriage over the front page: AMBASSADOR'S WIFE HIDES VEGETABLE HUSBAND. LADY E IN FORTUNE FRAUD. The state pension she had been receiving for years . . . would they want it all back? Would she be proscecuted for fraud and sent to prison? Even an open prison would be unbearable. She could not share a bedroom or a bathroom with anyone, not at her age.

And Sir Peter's relatives would doubtlessly contest the will. They would want their rightful share . . .

The October stock market crash wiped out many of her investments, but she was too distressed to care. It simply brought her plans closer. Her money was running out. When it had gone, there was no point in living.

Fiona was worried though. She phoned her aunt to find out the exact state of her financial affairs.

'Oh, I'm not quite on the breadline yet,' said Elvina, knowing this was what Fiona wanted to hear. 'I've a few little nest eggs left. There's always my pension from the Foreign Office.'

'Ah yes, your pension. That's good.'

Elvina felt the balance of power shift. Of course, Fiona would not want the pension to suddenly stop. She would not want the source of plenty to dry up completely.

Elvina knew the true state of her finances, and devised a practical means of oblivion. She had a bottle of diazepam tranquillizers prescribed by a doctor who was totally taken in by her realistic symptoms of nervous fatigue. She carried them round in her crocodile handbag with a silver flask of the best five-star brandy. She would go out in a civilized way. She was not quite sure when or where, but she was ready for when the moment of highest drama presented itself.

When Fiona got engaged, Elvina's cheque book practically opened of its own accord.

'You'll want a really nice wedding present from me, won't you, dear?' said Elvina, not bothering to disguise the sarcasm in her voice. She was not frightened of Fiona any more. 'What would you like? Money, of course. You really prefer money, don't you? No silver toastrack or sherry tray from Mappin & Web would suit your expensive tastes.'

Fiona looked disconcerted for a moment but then she brightened up. 'Why don't you pay for my wedding dress?' she suggested. 'After all, it would be symbolic, you being the family expert on weddings.'

Elvina could have killed her then. But she sat on the surge of fury and bared her capped teeth in a silky smile. 'A perfect idea. I'll pay for your wedding dress. Just send me the bill. As you walk down the aisle, I shall be filled with pride and nostalgia, my dear.'

When the bill came from Emmanuels, even Elvina was shocked. She counted the noughts and laughed hysterically. All that money for one dress. It was more than the deposit on a flat or the cost of a small car. She made out the cheque with huge flourishes. This was going to be the very last payment. No more to the greedy Fiona.

Elvina enjoyed her overnight stay at Tregony before the wedding. Adele made her feel so welcome, she almost changed her plans. She was still very fond of Adele and they had a good evening together, laughing over old stories and sharing a bottle of French rosé. Adele looked tired around the eyes but it was not surprising. She had pulled out all the stops for her daughter's wedding. It was going to be the wedding of the year in Porthcudden, if not the whole of Cornwall.

Elvina did not try to sleep in the pretty guest room where Adele put her. It seemed a waste of time to sleep now. There was only sleep ahead. She propped herself up in bed wearing a coffee lace nightdress, sipping wine, eating the peaches which Adele had thoughtfully put in the room, and thinking about her long life. It had all been such fun! So many lovely male bodies. She could hardly remember their names, but she remembered their bodies . . . so beautiful and smooth, such firm backs and muscles. Surely St Peter wouldn't hold it against her? She laughed quietly at the unintended joke.

She skipped breakfast. No point in wasting good food. She took a long, leisurely bath, tipping in the last of her Dior perfume. The bathroom smelt like an Arab harem. Her silk outfit had come from a Paris fashion house many years ago, but it was timeless. It still looked fabulously expensive, and the matching shady hat was kind to her skin.

Adele was concerned when she saw her frail and elegant aunt coming down the stairs.

'I'm going to insist on you sitting in the garden with a coffee before Graham drives you to the church,' she said. 'And a little drop of brandy wouldn't hurt. We can't have you fainting in church. I couldn't cope with any dramas!'

'Sit by me, just for a moment,' said Elvina, catching at Adele's sleeve. 'I know you're madly busy but this won't take long.' She pulled the big diamond cluster ring from her bony finger. It was already loose and in danger of falling off. 'I want you to have this, Adele.'

Adele was aghast. 'No, Auntie, I can't take it. Sir Peter gave it to you. You always wear it. It's your engagement ring.'

Elvina pushed the sparkler on to Adele's third finger. It looked magnificent. 'I insist,' she said firmly. 'Humour me, please.'

Elvina felt happier than she had been for a long time, pleased that Adele was wearing her diamonds to the wedding. She caught flashes from the ring as Adele turned over the service sheet or adjusted her hat. Dear Adele . . . Adele . . . If only Adele had been her daughter.

She barely glanced at Fiona floating down the aisle in her magnificent dress. Instead she occupied her mind in costing it; the amount of fabric, lining, lace, pearl buttons, working hours, label. She almost laughed aloud when she was reminded of the labels and bags at Golds and how they had added on the cost. She put a gloved hand to her mouth, smearing her rose-pink lipstick.

The reception in the garden was lovely. The hydrangeas were banks of green but no blossom yet. An errant breeze stirred the salt-laden air. Gulls cried faintly from a distance.

Elvina sat like visiting royalty in the shade of the marquee where a waitress kept refilling her glass with champagne. So many people came to talk to her. They had heard of Adele's famous aunt. She did not touch the food – not even the wedding cake, which Fiona brought over with a show of affection. The bridegroom looked stern and handsome, and for a brief second Elvina was disturbed by his remoteness from the occasion, but it was not really any of her business. She was washing her hands of Fiona.

The champagne did its work well. Graham had not stinted on the quality. Elvina's brain was becoming more and more fuddled; flowers and people swam before her eyes and she wondered if she was going to be able to make it into the house. It would be very undignified to pass out on the way indoors.

The bespectacled best man was hovering by the marquee. He looked undecided about where he was going, too. Elvina beckoned him over.

'I wonder if you would mind helping me up the path,' she said. 'I need to powder my nose.'

'Your nose?' He sounded bewildered. 'Oh yes, take my arm.'

'Thank you. You're most kind. What a lovely wedding.'

'Yes, lovely.'

He deposited her politely in the hall of Tregony and disappeared as fast as the White Rabbit. Elvina sat on a tapestry chair in the cool shadows to catch her breath. It took a lot of courage when it came to the final moment. She fumbled with the clasp of her handbag, checking that she had the tranquillizers and the brandy. Her fingers closed over her manicure scissors. Sir Peter had bought them for her in Egypt. They were wrought silver, shaped like an ancient mythological bird, with sharp, pointed blades curved like a long beak.

Suddenly Fiona rushed through the hall, the dress rustling loudly and blowing in all directions. She did not see her aunt sitting in the shadows, but ran up the stairs, hitching up the billowing skirt with complete disregard for its cost, her long legs in pale stockings, coltish and provocative.

Elvina saw the flashing legs and an old, long-forgotten memory came to mind. She was back in her villa in the south of France. She saw the steep stone steps leading to the terraced vineyards above. She heard the sweet laughter of a young girl as Adele was chased in all innocence towards a flower-scented boudoir on the hillside.

The shock of the revelation cleared Elvina's senses with amazing clarity. It was all her fault. She had been so careless and thoughtless, encouraging the two young people to be together, ignoring how quickly young blood could be aroused. She and she alone was responsible for Fiona's conception and existence. She had created this female monster and allowed Adele to bear the burden. Well, if she could create, then she could also destroy.

Her fingers recoiled from the sharp points of the manicure scissors. Fiona had gone upstairs to change. Elvina stood up unsteadily, then fell back into the chair, clutching the carved armrests. The hall was spinning round her, her heart being squeezed, lungs wheezing for air.

She was breathing in shallow gasps as the stairs ahead rose like an escalator taking her into the unknown. It seemed she was climbing them in a daze, her legs moving without effort.

# Eight

Though neither of them were aware of it, Father Lawrence and Adele Kimberley were exactly the same age, born on the same day in the same year. This astrological coincidence may have had something to do with Father Lawrence's fascination with the family, an obsession which he kept carefully hidden.

It was Adele who first caught his eye, coming to church with her babies; such a pretty young woman with nice children. It made him shudder to think of her sleeping with that boorish husband of hers. Graham Kimberley looked like a turkeycock with his red neck and red hands. He did not know how she could endure it, or what had possessed such a fragile-looking woman to decide to marry such a pompous oaf. Father Lawrence never ceased to be amazed at some of the ill-matched couples he wedded.

His serpentine granite church in Porthcudden was one of the most ancient and beautiful in Cornwall. Its square tower had been a landmark for sailors for centuries. Holidaymakers came to photograph its tranquil setting and to walk over the gravestones of more than a hundred souls lost in one of the great wrecks off the coast. Two eighteenth-century smugglers lay buried close to the church wall. They had been caught by the Excise men hauling kegs of brandy up the steep cliffs from a narrow cove. The Excise men were short of time and short of temper after their all-night wait in teeming rain, so they exercised justice on the spot. The villagers found the two smugglers in a ditch

147

the following morning, their packs as empty as their white veins.

Father Lawrence kept the smugglers' graves well tended. Law breakers they might have been, but they had been unfairly executed. Only a rough-hewn red-streaked rock marked each grave, worn smooth now by the onslaught of rain and wind. No names, no dates, but still remembered.

Porthcudden had once been a prosperous tin-mining area, but all that remained were the ruins of old engine houses and chimney stacks. People like the Vaughans and the Kimberleys had generated money in different ways, business and property. Holiday homes were let at high rents, hotels sprang up like concrete mushrooms.

But fewer and fewer people came to the church on the headland. Father Lawrence called them the two-C Christians – they came for christenings and Christmas. Adele was not one of those; she came to regular services.

When his television screen erupted with close-ups of sores and pot-bellied children, starving babies covered in flies, dying in their mother's arms, Father Lawrence could stand the affluent complacency of Porthcudden no longer. He applied to the VSO, offering his services in Ethiopia. They wrote back, asking if he had permission to leave his present incumbency. He replied with an unpriestly and almost unprintable tirade against red tape, and in three weeks he was having injections and innoculations against malaria, hepatitus and smallpox. They made him very ill. Adele discovered him in his car, parked in a lay-by in a narrow high-banked lane of foxgloves, his face white and drenched with sweat.

'Are you all right, Father?' she asked, coming over to the car.

'It's some rather unpleasant injections,' he said, running a tongue over dry lips. 'They said there might be some side effects.'

'Are you going on holiday?'

'Hardly a holiday. Ethiopia. Three months, or perhaps six

months, it all depends. I've no medical training but apparently they think I might be useful burying the dead.'

Adele was shocked by his bluntness. She recovered quickly, cautious admiration coming into her eyes.

'How incredibly brave of you,' she said. 'We see those terrible pictures on the television. All we do is send a cheque; far too easy. But you're actually going to do something about it. You put us to shame, Father Lawrence.'

'That wasn't my intention, Mrs Kimberley,' he mumbled, equally disturbed by her frank praise as the sight of the wind blowing through her hair and the curving shape of her soft lips. He tried to pull himself together, to find a topic which would take his mind off her femininity.

'I want to give you some money,' said Adele, coming to the rescue. She searched in her purse and pulled out a twenty-pound note. 'It's all I've got on me. I know it's pathetic and won't save any starving child, but will you buy some medicine to take out with you?'

He did not tell her that he could only take one small rucksack of personal belongings; that the truck from Khartoum would be loaded with valuable supplies and volunteers were warned not to take a single item that was not essential.

'Thank you, Mrs Kimberley,' he said, folding the note away. 'I'll try to think of something useful.' He smiled his singularly sweet smile. Impulsively Adele held out her hand, and he took it. She did not know she was giving him more than money. She was giving him a vision.

The vision accompanied him on the plane from Heathrow to Khartoum. She sat beside him in the back of the rattling truck that took the newest batch of VSO workers the hundred miles to the refugee camp. It was the worst journey he had ever endured. The heat, the flies, the cramped conditions, a road surface that was endless miles of back-jolting potholes.

When they reached the straggling outbuildings of the camp, he could hardly walk. He staggered to the hut he was to share with three other men and crashed out on a camp bed, too weary and shattered to do anything but sleep. He did not even notice the bareness of the room, the lack of any amenities.

'Adele,' he groaned as his aching limbs collapsed with needle-shooting pains. 'Oh Adele, my dearest, pray for me.'

The rest of the culture shock came the next day. As he stumbled round the camp with the resident doctor, he realized that God's work was pretty useless in such surroundings. They were burying the bodies faster than he would be able to hold burial services. There was no time to waste in that stifling heat. They had to be buried fast. What did some foreign service mean to these emaciated people? The men and women stared at him with their huge yellowed eyes and he felt a fraud. They would not understand a word he said.

Three days later he went to the medical officer in charge of the camp. Father Lawrence had already lost his priestly look. His shirt and trousers were sweaty and dusty, his boots covered in sand, his skin beginning to redden under the fierce, desert sun.

'For God's sake, give me some proper work to do,' he said. 'I'm useless here. They can't eat prayers. I'm not worth the stale bread you feed me or the ghastly brown brew you call coffee. There must be something else I can do.'

The doctor recognized the stress and anguish in the priest's face. It was a normal reaction to arriving at the camp.

'You help us all with your presence, Father. We need spiritual food too, to enable us to carry on with our work. It's important to the medical team. A group of nuns will be arriving soon. They will be glad to find a priest here.'

'It's not enough,' said Father Lawrence, staring out at the burnt landscape and the flapping fawn sea of makeshift huts and tattered tents. 'What good will prayers do for these people? I could be on my knees twenty-four hours, day and night, and it won't save a single child.'

Adele would not be proud of him now, hot, weary and

muddle-headed. He even smelt. He could feel sand in his clothes, taste sand in his mouth.

'Go to the food distribution centre tomorrow morning and find Sister Grey. She'll show you how to make up the liquid protein feed for the children and how to feed those too weak to do it themselves. And don't forget to wash your hands, again and again. Every child is a potential source of infection.'

The brown babies were pot-bellied with huge eyes. They urinated in his arms but he learnt how to make up their feed, how to hold them, croon a prayer or two as they sucked weakly on a bottle.

Eight weeks later Father Lawrence was in the camp hospital with dysentery. He lost two stone in weight. His skin hung on him like crinkled leather. There was no question of him doing a second term of three months. When he was well enough to be moved, they sent him home. He returned to Porthcudden a hero, though he knew he had been a failure. He knelt on the cold stone steps of his old church listening to the sound of the pounding sea, praying for some ease to the pain and humiliation.

Adele Kimberley was one of the first to welcome him back, though he had deliberately kept out of her way. He could not face his vision. She, who had been at his side throughout those nightmare weeks. Surely she would know the truth.

'You've lost a lot of weight, Father Lawrence.' Adele was shocked by his appearance. His face was haggard and a bad colour. 'Anyone can see you've been really ill. Thank goodness you've come back to Porthcudden. Not a moment too soon.'

'It's nice to be home.'

'I'm not going to ask you what it was like. It won't help. None of us could continue our lives for a minute if we thought about the starving millions in the world.'

'We are all helpless,' he said wearily.

'Come and have supper one evening next week. You need building up.'

'Thank you, that would be very nice. I am grateful to be able to drink clean water from a tap.'

'Would Thursday do?'

'Perfect.' He could sense that she wanted to ask what he had spent her twenty pounds on, a natural feminine curiosity. 'By the way, I bought a stock of glucose tablets with your donation. They were much appreciated.'

She flushed, embarrassed. 'Oh well . . . something at least. Hardly anything though. Not worth mentioning.'

His smile deepened and he turned away to hide the lie. Her note lay neatly folded in his wallet. He would never give it away. He had put twenty of his own money into a charity box at Heathrow. The whole world was a charity. It did not really matter where the money went.

He kept his secret admiration for Adele well hidden. No one suspected, least of all Adele. When she came to him with plans for Fiona's wedding, it was all he could do to write the details in legible handwriting.

'I want it to be a really wonderful day for Fiona,' said Adele, a touch of wistfulness in her voice. 'A day to remember. One she will never forget. Something to carry with her into the future for when times are hard.'

'Surely hard times are not in store for Fiona,' said Father Lawrence, averting his eyes from Adele's slender neck. 'Hal Vaughan will inherit the family business. It seems to me she is making a very secure marriage.'

'Oh yes, and they are very much in love.'

He nodded. What was love? What did he know of married love? Nothing. Was it this gnawing in his loins, this cruel waste of passion, the torment of every dark night?

'There's so much to do,' said Adele with enthusiasm. 'I've so many plans, just for one wedding! I shall be worn out.'

'Perhaps they'll elope and save you the trouble,' he suggested.

'Not a bad idea.' Adele laughed, showing her pearly teeth. 'But I think Fiona has her heart set on a big wedding with all the trimmings, all her friends there. We're going to hire a marquee for the garden. That'll save a lot of tramping through the house.'

'It will indeed, Mrs Kimberley.'

'I think after all these years you could call me Adele,' she said as she left, pale lilac skirt swirling round her slim legs like the petals of a sweet pea.

'Adele,' he said, swallowing hard. He repeated her name aloud after she had gone. 'Adele . . . Adele.'

The arrangements for the marriage went ahead with detailed planning. The two-way path between Tregony and the church became a joke. Graham was amused at the amount of time Father Lawrence found necessary to spend at Tregony.

'Anyone would think it was his daughter getting married.' He grinned.

'He's being kind,' said Adele. 'He's merely taking an interest in the two young people, in Fiona and Hal.'

'But are Fiona and Hal taking any interest in the religious significance of their vows? Have they been to see the priest yet?'

'That's none of our business,' said Adele. 'I'm only responsible for the practical arrangements of this wedding, not the moral aspects.'

Father Lawrence could have told her that neither bride nor groom had requested instruction, or even an interview. He did not expect them to. It was an old-fashioned idea these days. He would only tell them things they did not want to hear, concepts they would ditch immediately outside his front door.

The days leading up to the wedding had a bittersweet flavour for Father Lawrence. Adele flitted in and out of his life like a gorgeous butterfly. She wore such pretty clothes in pastel colours: lilac, pink and blue. He let himself think she was wearing them for him. Her soft hair was shiny like a chestnut and she smelt of flowers, light and fragrant. He could almost make himself believe that she was coming to see him.

He agreed with everything she suggested, though sometimes he invented some little hurdle, to make her stay longer, or come back another day, or to see the little droop in her spirits that made her look young and vulnerable. It was a kind of play-acting in which Adele did not know she took the leading role.

'There'll be flowers everywhere,' she said. 'All yellow and white. That's my colour scheme. Grace is going to make your church absolutely beautiful.'

'Absolutely beautiful,' he repeated, nodding, noting how today she had tucked her hair behind her small ears for coolness. 'But the carpet mustn't get wet. Any spilt water would make it go mouldy. And it would cost a fortune to replace.'

'I'll mention that to Grace,' said Adele, jotting it down in her notebook. 'I'm sure she'll be careful.'

The day before the wedding he was summoned to the confessional box by the little bell. He was somewhat irritated as it was late and he was not expecting anyone.

He let himself into the box, crossed himself and slid aside the door from the grille so that he could hear the voice. The face, as always, was in shadow, but he knew instinctively that it was a woman.

'Yes, my daughter?' he began.

'Well, this is a bit awkward,' said the woman. 'I've forgotten how to begin, it's been so long. Oh yes, I have sinned, Father. Hear me, for I have sinned.'

'How have you sinned, my child?' he said, waiting to hear the usual list of lies and petty dishonesties. He hoped it would not take too long. He still had his Sunday sermon to write.

'It sounds a bit silly saying it out loud,' the voice hesitated. 'I'm getting married soon, very soon, and . . . well, I'm pregnant.'

Father Lawrence was not shocked any more. He had heard it many times. He had lost count of the number of pregnant brides who had stood before him at the altar, wearing varying degrees of straining seams.

'Then we must bless this union and the soul of the unborn child,' he said. 'It is by God's grace that you are giving a united parenthood to this baby.'

He heard a suppressed sigh. It did not sound penitent. 'I don't really understand what God's grace has got to do with it,' the woman said. 'It doesn't seem terribly appropriate. I'm going to have a baby and I'm getting married. The two events are not connected.'

'By getting married you are absolved from sin, my daughter.'

'No, no! You don't understand. The baby is someone else's baby. The man I'm going to marry is not the father.'

Father Lawrence felt a wave of anguish. How could people be so callous, so careless with each other's feelings?

'Does he know? Your fiancé?' Father Lawrence asked, at a loss.

'No, of course he doesn't. He'd be furious. He'd kill me.'

'Aren't you going to tell him?'

'No, I'm not. And you can't, can you? Anything told to you in the confessional is sacred, isn't it?'

'Can't you marry the real father of your child?' It was clutching at straws. Father Lawrence knew the answer before he had even asked the question.

'Marry him? Heavens no, I don't love him. It just happened. It was a stupid mistake.'

Father Lawrence could not imagine how such careless intimacy could happen, but then he was not an expert. It was not like catching measles. The young woman expected forgiveness. A dozen Hail Marys – was that enough for foisting a bastard child on an unsuspecting young husband?

'Can't I have forgiveness, Father?' A first sign of anxiety had crept into her voice. 'I'm getting married soon, and I'm sorry, truly I am. Very sorry.'

'I suggest you pray for God's forgiveness on the altar steps for one full hour with all your heart. Think seriously on what you are about to do,' he said coldly. 'On your knees, no cushion and no day-dreaming.'

'A whole hour? Father, I haven't got time! I'm getting married tomorrow and I'm madly busy.'

'You could pray for nine months and it still would not atone for the deception you are planning on the man to be your husband and on the true father of your child. That is a grave sin and you must find an honest path.'

'Oh well, it was worth a try. I might have known you wouldn't understand. Thanks anyway.'

'Bless you, my child,' he said, making the sign of the cross. 'May you find wisdom and redemption in your hours of prayer.'

He heard a brief chuckle from behind the grille.

'Thanks again, Father. See you in church.'

There was a scrape of a chair and the tap of high heels leaving the church. He sank back, his hands sweating. He knew who the woman was. It was Fiona, the bride of the morrow. Adele's daughter.

He slept little that night. Fiona's confession had brought the wedding into sharp, vivid focus. It was no longer a glorious pageant created by the magic wand of his lovely Fairy Queen. The reality was that it could not go on. He could not allow it to go on, yet his vows of silence gagged him. Adele's eyes, so trusting, seemed to plead with him . . . It was her day too. All her plans, all her hard work, her pride and joy in her daughter. He could destroy it all. He could destroy his love for her with the same weapon so that he would be free of her enchantment once and for all. It became a confused dream and he awoke drenched with sweat, his fists clenched into hard knots.

He ate no breakfast. He prayed in his room but there was no answer. He wandered into the coolness of the church where that Grace person was doing the flowers. They were like funeral flowers, their heavy scent masking the smell of death. Had Fiona knelt for an hour on the altar steps? Probably five minutes and then she'd be off.

'Good morning, Grace,' he said. 'A busy morning.'

'Good morning, Father,' said Grace. 'Absolutely frantic. I've the marquee to do as well, back at Tregony, and it's a big one. I'll be glad when today's over, I can tell you.'

'So shall I. I find these fashionable receptions a little overwhelming. But I'm sure Mrs Kimberley has organized everything down to the last printed napkin.'

'It's going to be a very hot day.'

The ridge of high pressure had registered and Lawrence retrieved the thin, lightweight black suit he had taken to Ethiopia. He had hardly worn it. There was still sand in the trouser turn-ups. It needed a good brush and hanging in the air.

The wedding itself was almost dream-like. It seemed to begin of its own accord, wafted along on waves of music. Adele's music. He heard himself conducting the service, the familiar words, somehow injecting sincerity and enthusiasm into his voice. Nothing sounded true to his ears. Once, he caught Adele looking at him curiously and he wondered if she, his vision, had detected something strange and unnatural in his conduct.

He could hardly look at the bride. She was in an enormous dress like an overblown lily that filled the width of the aisle. Her perfume was cloying, expensive, her face made up like a doll. She spoke in a voice he recognized, with a kind of controlled speed as if she wanted to get the wedding over quickly.

'Are you all right, Father?' Adele whispered as the couple were signing the register.

'It's very hot. These robes are unsuitable.' He emphasized the last word, but of course Adele could not know why.

'They must be awful,' she sympathized. 'Soon be over.'

Next came the photographs outside the church. Guests

157

trampled over the graves of the lost souls and the smugglers, their cameras clicking. Father Lawrence stretched his skin over his teeth as he stood in line with the family and some idiot with a video pranced around ordering everyone to 'smile please'. He couldn't smile. It just would not happen. There came a point when he could not stand the crowd of grinning faces any longer and he escaped into the coolness of his church. He staggered to a pew and sat down. It had been the most dreadful wedding of his entire priesthood. He could not remember ever being more disorientated or disturbed.

His robe caught in a pew-end floral arrangement and sent it toppling to the floor. Some loose daisies spilled on to the carpet. The upturned green plastic Florapak and chicken wire were like some obscene green pudding. Their ugliness revolted him. He found himself stamping on the mesh until it was a flattened mess of plastic foam and crushed flowers, a dark stain spreading on the carpet.

Suddenly he could not stand the cloying smell. It sickened him. He had to rid his church of it, to cleanse the holy place. With a sad, high-pitched wail, he tore down the floral arrangements, grinding the flowers into the carpet with his heels. He sent the hanging baskets on wild, giddy swings as he pulled them off their hooks, tearing out the stems and flower heads. He flung the massive altar flowers down the steps, grunting and gritting his teeth, a hard glitter in his eyes as he destroyed their defenceless beauty.

He stood panting amid the wreckage, his pulse racing, heart pounding. The church was strewn with devastation. He wished it had been Fiona in her great lily dress under his heel.

He tore off his wet, spattered robes and shakily put on the jacket of his black suit. He combed back his disordered hair, and, breathing heavily, went outside for some air.

'Do you want a lift to the reception, Father?' someone asked. He nodded his thanks.

The garden of Tregony seemed an alien place with the huge

marquee dominating the lawn. Father Lawrence drank two glasses of Buck's Fizz in as many minutes before he realized that the orange juice was laced with alcohol. He began to float. He nodded benignly at other guests, hardly recognizing anyone, his eyes constantly searching for glimpses of Adele. She was all he cared about.

He stood gazing at a bed of large pansies. They seemed to be watching him. He nibbled at some food but was unaware of what it was. He was beginning to feel ill. He did not listen to the speeches or watch the cake being cut. His suit smelt of dust and it was no surprise to find a disposable syringe in his top pocket, hygienically sealed. For some minutes he was back in the refugee camp, tasting the sand, smelling disease, seeing babies dying around him with their saucer eyes and bloated bellies.

There was an ampoule of morphine with the syringe. He could not remember being given them or putting them in his pocket. One of the medics must have left them in the wrong jacket when they were eating in the mess hut. It was the only explanation.

Father Lawrence took out the syringe and ampoule and examined them. He still remembered how to use one. Perhaps the morphine would remove this agonizing pain. It had to be injected into a vein. He would find a vein in his arm.

He sleepwalked towards the house, seeking shade and privacy and somewhere to sit down. He loosened his collar and started to pull off his jacket.

'Doing an ecclesiastical strip, Father?' teased Fiona gaily as she passed him. 'I don't blame you. I might even join in the fun!'

He paused with the ampoule hidden in the palm of his hand. He knew now where it had to go. Right into the heart.

# Nine

**B**uying Tregony was the biggest piece of luck in the whole of Graham Kimberley's life, though he would never admit it. He put it down to his business acumen and skill as a negotiator. If cheating an old couple out of the real value of their house could be called business acumen, then Graham was loaded with it.

He had sold his own three-bedroomed semi-detached in Streatham on the spur of the moment. One day a skinny Asian shopkeeper walked into the branch office of the estate agent's that Graham managed. He dumped a small suitcase on a desk and opened it, smiling with pride.

'I wish to buy for my family a house now, namely today,' he said.

The case was full of used notes. Graham had never seen so much money. In half an hour he had sold his own house to Mr Jaboorhi. He took the man round in his car knowing Adele would be out at work and Fiona at playschool. Mr Jaboorhi was charmed. Adele had good taste and everything in the house was of the best quality and colour co-ordinated.

'I take it,' said Mr Jaboorhi, admiring the frills and quilted ties on Adele's lined curtains. 'Just as it is, please. Curtains, carpets, complete.'

'That can be arranged,' said Graham heartily. 'Thought you'd like it.'

When Adele came home from work, having first collected their daughter, and laden with shopping from the supermarket, she found they had been made homeless. She was speechless. She reheated a shepherd's pie for supper, peeled carrots and opened a tin of peas, hardly able to believe the announcement.

'How could you? Graham, how could you?' she said over and over again. 'Our home. And we've only just got it how we want it. No, no, no . . . we can't sell now.'

'Too late. It's sold. It's far too good an opportunity to miss, Adele. A cash sale, and Mr Jaboorhi was prepared to pay well over the odds. We'll be able to move somewhere really nice like Caterham or Purley.'

'Purley! I don't want to live in Purley.'

Fiona started to cry. She didn't like her parents shouting at each other.

Graham knew he had made Adele really angry for the first time in their marriage. But he simply could not resist the sight and feel of all that money. Money now safely paid into a holding building society account, awaiting the exchange of contracts.

He stared at the ceiling of their bedroom that night, unable to sleep. Adele had not come to bed. She was downstairs ironing Fiona's clothes for the morrow, banging the iron on the board.

'Leave it, can't you? Come to bed.'

'I will not leave it,' said Adele through clenched teeth. 'Fiona always goes to playschool looking nice.'

'She can go in a creased dress for once.'

'She cannot.'

'You spoil her. You work your fingers to the bone.'

'People are critical of working mothers. The slightest sign of neglect and I'd get it from her teachers.'

'You won't have to work now, Adele, not with this windfall,' said Graham, grabbing his chance.

She had a tight look about her face that really alarmed Graham. Perhaps he had gone too far. But it was done now. He would have trouble extricating himself from the sale and might lose his job if Mr Jaboorhi complained to Head Office.

It was an unwritten rule that employees didn't sell their own houses in preference to properties on the books. Perhaps they could stay with Adele's mother till they sorted out a new home.

The next morning at breakfast Adele was unusually quiet. She gave Fiona her Weetabix and milk, then honey sandwiches. Graham trod carefully. He did not want to upset her any more. She'd come round. Let her get used to the idea.

Adele made herself a mug of black coffee and stirred in a sweetener. She looked Graham straight in the eye.

'If, as it seems, you have sold the roof over your family's heads and we are to move, then we are not moving to Purley or Caterham or any other soulless suburb. We are moving to Cornwall.'

'C–Cornwall!' Graham nearly choked on a mouthful of toast. 'Adele, are you out of your mind? It's hundreds of miles away. What am I supposed to do? Commute every day?'

'No, though the train service is getting better. You complain enough about the Streatham branch stifling your ambition. Well, be ambitious and ask Head Office for a transfer. They've got a south-west area office. Or get another job. There's more than one firm of estate agents.'

'This is sheer nonsense,' said Graham, spluttering. 'I'm not moving out of London.'

'Yes, we are. You've sold the house, remember? And I'm serious. It's either we move to Cornwall or we stay here.'

Graham opened his mouth to object. They had four to five weeks in which to pack up the house. This was not the moment to tell her that he had included extras like the curtains in the sale. She had spent hours at her sewing machine making them.

'All right, I'll ask. But it's a ridiculous idea.'

'No more ridiculous than selling this house. Drink your milk, Fiona, or you'll be late for playschool.' She led Fiona to the sink and washed her sticky hands and face. 'You'd like to be able to play at the seaside, wouldn't you, Fiona?'

'Yes, Mummy.'

Graham did not want to move to Cornwall. He thought of himself as being in the upwardly mobile bracket before the phrase was ever coined. He dressed in style, drove a good car, ate out. Everyone living in Cornwall was a yokel with straw in his hat and clotted cream coming out of his ears. It was a backwater.

He was surprised when Head Office welcomed his tentative enquiry. Their Truro office would soon be needing a new manager and it was sound policy to send someone with London experience. Salaries were not quite so high as London, but then house prices were lower.

'Big properties frequently come on the market, estates and land. You wouldn't only be dealing with suburbia and fishermen's cottages. It could be an interesting job for the right man. Let us know, Kimberley, by Monday morning, as we shall be advertising the post next week. You'd get expenses for moving.'

They parked Fiona with Adele's mother on the Friday night and drove down to Cornwall. Graham grumbled all the way. He was not used to long-distance driving. Eventually they stopped somewhere on Bodmin Moor so that Graham could catch a nap.

'Be all right if you'd learned to drive. You could have shared the driving.'

'You've never let me touch your precious car.'

'Quite right, too.'

He huddled into a corner and tried to sleep. He was aware of Adele getting out of the car and strolling off the road. She looked very relaxed, hands dug deeply into her pockets, her hair ruffled. She was going to watch the dawn coming up over the moor, she said. Daft. One dawn was the same as any other dawn.

She was drinking coffee from a thermos cup when he awoke, stiff and cramped. He eyed the steaming cup.

'Thanks very much for mine,' he said.

163

'You were asleep.' She poured out a second cup and stirred in some sugar. 'Mind, it's hot.'

'Surprise, surprise,' he said sarcastically. 'Tell me something new.'

By the time they reached the Truro office, Graham's spirits were recovering. They had an excellent breakfast at a roadside cafe. He was impressed by the solid air of respectability of the Truro office; the mahogany fittings, the big desks with leather tops, the deference of the staff to someone from London. It made the Streatham office look quite tatty.

He was also impressed by the variety of property that they were handling. They had just sold a Rosemullion House to a local man which had cost nearly a million. Though they were not in the market for a Cornish manor house, Graham could see they might pick up a very nice place for themselves. Far bigger than anything he could afford in the Greater London area. Perhaps a year or two down here wouldn't hurt his career or his pocket. Buy a place, do it up, sell at a profit.

Later, as they strolled through the thriving town with its elegant Georgian and Queen Anne houses and the graceful three-spired cathedral, Adele asked if there was time to take a look at the sea.

'Well look, there's the sea.'

'No, I mean the real sea, with waves. That's a river estuary. We could find somewhere to stay, bed and breakfast perhaps. We could relax for the evening then drive back on Sunday. There'll be far less traffic.'

Graham was feeling generous towards Adele now, conveniently forgetting that it was his own reckless action that had left them homeless. They were enjoying a ploughman's lunch at a pub with a good Stilton and beer.

'We ought to take advantage of being on our own for once,' said Adele, tucking her arm through his. 'It's not often that we don't have Fiona with us.'

Graham turned the car south and they found a small fishing village where everything was neat and tidy and the harbour curved like arms embracing the sea. Beyond the quay the high tide was throwing up spumes of spray, drenching them as they walked along the top, feeling very brave.

Adele turned her face to the powerful cliffs where small thatched cottages clung to the hillside. 'It's so beautiful here,' she said.

Graham happened to think that Adele looked very beautiful then, fresh and dewy. That night, in the brass-knobbed bed, under the eaves of the best front room of the cottage, Carolyn was conceived.

When they moved out of their house, Graham came down to Truro in advance of Adele. She stayed at her mother's with Fiona and their furniture was put in storage. Tregony came on the market and he knew instinctively that Adele would love it. He soon realized that the old couple had no idea of the value of their property and he could not believe his luck.

'It's a big detached house,' he said on the phone that evening. 'Four double bedrooms, two excellent reception rooms, a poky, old-fashioned kitchen, but several adjoining sculleries that could easily be knocked into, making a big kitchen and breakfast area. The bathroom is out of the ark but a good size again. High class, secluded road on the outskirts of Porthcudden. I could drive to work every day.'

'Sounds all right,' said Adele cautiously. 'But how can I tell without seeing it?'

'It's got a really big garden, nearly a couple of acres. More than we could cope with, but we might be able to get planning permission one day to sell off a building plot.'

'I like gardening,' said Adele.

'That's the first I've heard of it. You wouldn't want to soil your lily-white hands.'

'How do you know?' said Adele. She was not feeling too well. 'We didn't have much of a garden in Streatham.'

She took the train down to Truro with Fiona in a pushchair. Graham drove her out to Tregony and she fell instantly in love with the house. She saw all the drawbacks but they did not matter. She wanted to get her hands on the house and transform it into something elegant and lovely. She was not dismayed by the narrow, dark kitchen, or by the antiquated plumbing. She saw the dreadful wallpaper stripped off and the walls restored to white plaster and oak beams. She would polish and stain the oak floors and stair treads, improve the uninteresting front face with an arched porch and overhead balcony. She had always wanted a balcony. The porch would be filled with plants and flowers whatever the season.

She stood speechless at the views from the upstairs windows. A pale sky, lucid sea and a glorious setting sun set fire to the garden wilderness.

'Can we afford it? The other houses in the road look expensive.'

'Prices are much lower in Cornwall,' said Graham.

Adele took Fiona into the garden. The fussy flower beds and rose trellis were overrun with weeds. It looked neglected. Fiona ran down the lawn on her sturdy legs, chasing a butterfly, uttering little cries of delight.

'It's really lovely,' said Adele. 'I can see so many ways of improving it.'

'As good as done,' said Graham. 'It's ours.'

Graham did not feel he had cheated the old couple. He paid them their asking price, feeling he had saved them the hassle of showing strange people round the house. They did not need the money. They were going to live with their son. It was all arranged.

Those first few months were the happiest ever for Adele and Graham, despite sharing Tregony with builders, plumbers and decorators. Bert appeared from nowhere, determined to put the garden to rights. He and Adele seemed to strike a friendly distance and Adele was glad of his help now that her pregnancy was slowing her down. Graham let her organize all the alterations; he was far too busy at the office. He joined the Rotary club, played golf, sat on committees. When

Carolyn was born, they both felt they had lived in Cornwall for years.

'I did the right thing, didn't I?' he insisted. 'Selling the semi and moving down here.'

'I suppose you did,' said Adele, not inclined to argue. She had a lovely house, a sweet new baby daughter, and a beloved garden.

Tregony took on a distinctive look with Adele's flair. The arched porch added a softness to the front; the sombre grey stone walls were painted white. A new garage was built on for two cars and the old attached garage space turned into a utility room. The drive was widened to a pleasant curve and the garden simplified, much to Bert's satisfaction.

'You should have seen how it was once,' he often said. 'Best hydrangeas in Cornwall. Big as dinner plates. Lawns like velvet.'

The balcony leading from her bedroom was Adele's special joy. She often sat there in the sunshine, by herself, thinking.

Years later Timmy came along. Graham always reckoned Timmy was an accident after a particularly good golf-club dinner. It seemed a bit late for another child. Fiona was sixteen, almost grown up. Carolyn was twelve. It was a big gap but Adele was thrilled. She loved her wide-eyed, funny-faced son.

'There's a box of old baby clothes in the loft,' said Adele when she came home from the maternity hospital. 'I'd like to sort through them and give the best away. There were several young unmarried mothers in the ward who have practically nothing for their babies.'

'Serves them right,' said Graham. He was heavier now, with florid skin, hair thinning. He did not enjoy going up into the loft although they had an aluminium loft ladder that pulled down. He hated stepping off at the top, where there was nothing to hold on to. He had a touch of high blood pressure that worried him.

He pulled down the ladder and climbed up carefully,

putting on the loft light as soon as he could reach it. Adele was more nimble at going up into the loft; why couldn't she have done it, or Fiona? That girl didn't do anything to help around the house, always off down the sailing club to see her new friends.

The dormer window let in some light but he still stumbled among the unwanted furniture and stored boxes, some of which had not been opened since their move down to Cornwall. It was ridiculous the way Adele hung on to all this old stuff. She was too sentimental. They ought to clear it out and have a garage sale.

He opened a few of the dusty boxes: clothes, books, letters, ornaments, oddments belonging to her parents who had died years ago. It was all rubbish. He tore open another cardboard box, the lid of which had been glued down and the whole thing tied up with string. Must be the Crown jewels, he thought contemptuously.

It was full of faded postcards of France, photos of Aunt Elvina's villa, programmes, newspaper cuttings, tickets, guidebooks to chateaux, shells, souvenirs of Adele's youthful holidays with her aunt. There was a diary too, full of enthusiastic accounts of beach parties and dances, trips to the local market to buy cheese and pastries, sunbathing, swimming with someone called Andre.

Graham laughed aloud. It was so juvenile. He was unrepentant about reading Adele's diary. No one should be allowed a private diary. He read on. It was obvious she had had a crush on this Frenchman. Some foreign wimp. But then his laughter stopped abruptly. Sweat broke out on his forehead. He slammed the diary shut, then with fumbling fingers opened it again to check the dates of the holiday entries.

His escaping breath was like the hiss of a snake. He staggered to the top of the ladder and hurriedly began his descent. At the third rung from the bottom, his foot slipped, missing the rest of the rungs. He fell heavily on to his back and lay, sprawled out helplessly, pain swamping everything from his mind.

Adele came running up the stairs. She had heard a loud thump.

'Graham, what's happened? Are you hurt?'

'Bloody hell,' said Graham through gritted teeth. A red sea of pain choked him.

The hospital consultant diagnosed a fractured vertebra. Graham was on his back in a spinal cast for weeks. Then he had to wear a steel corset. It was the end of his golfing days.

He said nothing to Adele, but he blamed her. He stoked up his revenge. It was a morbid green disease that festered inside him like an ulcer. He would make her suffer. She would be sorry. He put part of the garden up for sale to spite her, then at the last moment took it off the market. Meanwhile he channelled the same spite into making more and more money. The more wealth he had, the more powerful he would be.

When Fiona left school she wanted to start a gift boutique in Falmouth. Graham encouraged her. She had a bright business mind and Adele's gift for anything artistic.

'I'll find you a nice little shop going cheap,' he said.

'I don't want any old dump you can't offload,' said Fiona. 'It's got to have class.'

'Would I do that to my own daughter?'

'Yes, you would. And can you lend me the cash? I don't want to be burdened with an expensive mortgage.'

'I could sell off a bit of the garden. It would make a decent building plot. Your mother made such a fuss last time, I had to take it off the market.'

'Don't tell her then.'

'That's the ticket,' he winked. 'She's got far too much garden to look after.'

Adele said nothing when Fiona accidentally blurted out about the sale. She knew it was useless arguing with Graham.

His temper was unpredictable. She watched the fence going up, wondering what else he had not told her. She watched the slow building of the chalet, felt sad about its long emptiness.

When Adele became friends with Sandy, their new neighbour, Graham could not resist pointing out that he had been right.

'I told you so,' he said. 'Better to have a friend to chat with and ask round for coffee; better than all that gardening.'

'Perhaps you're right. Sandy's a really nice person.'

'Of course I'm right. Aren't I always?'

Their life at Porthcudden was comfortable and stylish. Both girls joined the sailing club. Adele did a lot of work at the church and as much of the garden as Bert would allow. Timmy grew into a happy boy, going to the best private school in the locality. Tregony was an open house for everyone. Adele stocked the big freezer with lasagne, moussaka, pizzas, home-made Cornish ice cream and fruit from the garden. She could rustle up supper for any number at a moment's notice and serve it with elan.

Graham had mixed feelings when Fiona started going out with Hal Vaughan. He was envious of the young man's position in Cornish society, of Rosemullion House, of the money he spent so casually. And he was good-looking in a dark, serious way. Graham enjoyed being on equal terms with the Vaughans, meeting the parents socially, name-dropping whenever the occasion presented itself, which it did frequently.

But he was outraged at first when the young couple started to live together, a combination of suppressed envy and hypocrisy. Adele would never have consented to such an arrangement with him. She had insisted on marriage first, though she had once allowed him to stay overnight when her mother was away. It had been the height of daring for those rigid days. Their one night together had not been all that successful. He had put it down to Adele's inexperience, not his own clumsiness or lack of imagination.

When Fiona and Hal got formally engaged, Graham's first thought was the appalling cost of weddings. As the bride's father, he would have to foot the bill. He suggested something restrained and quiet, about twenty guests, with the reception at a good hotel. He soon discovered that Adele and Fiona had quite different ideas.

'I'm marrying a Vaughan,' Fiona stormed when he objected to the size of their plans. 'Not some little clerk called Smith or Jones from your office.'

Graham was very hurt. The Truro office was the pride of the company. They advertised selected properties with colour photographs in *Country Life* magazine.

'But a marquee is going to cost a fortune. And all those people . . . Do we have to have so many?'

'Yes, we do. I want everybody who's anybody to come. Sell off a bit more land,' Fiona suggested.

Graham tried to find ways to cut costs, but the more he trimmed, the more Adele and Fiona added. At least the drinks were left to him. He ordered a good champagne, mainly because he was determined to drink a great deal of it himself and cheap ones gave him indigestion.

'Buck's Fizz,' he said to the wine retailer. 'Plenty of orange juice. That's what goes down well.'

'That's right, Mr Kimberley. People will be thirsty. They always are at weddings. It's all those endless photos and hanging about.'

'I ought to check the flowers with Grace,' said Adele a couple of days beforehand. 'I can't get her on the phone, and they must be yellow and white, even if they are difficult to get. It doesn't matter what they cost. Will you drop by her place on your way home? And remind her about the archway. Do you know someone who could knock up an archway for outside the church?'

'I'll do it myself,' Graham grumbled. 'No point in paying.'

'Well . . .' said Adele doubtfully. 'If you've got time.'

'Doesn't matter what it costs . . .' Graham groaned as he drove along the high-banked lanes, trying to find Grace's smallholding. 'I'll be overcharged. Bound to be. And they'll all be dead by the next day.'

His temper was not improved by meeting another car headlong and having to reverse quite a long way to a passing place. Even then their wing mirrors scraped.

'Not meant for cars,' he shouted out of the window.

He turned into Grace's yard, nearly running over a cat that was basking in the late sunshine.

'Damned cat!'

Grace was nowhere around. He stamped about, not appreciating the array of flowers, their scent glorious in the warm sunshine. The sea was close by, the pounding on the rocks like an aerial symphony. He saw nothing, heard nothing. He itemized only the sheds in need of repair, a broken wheelbarrow, the ramshackle yard. The greenhouse was a shambles, with plants and seedlings in every stage of growth. He nearly fell over a tray of yellow pansies on the ground.

He picked them up. They had big heads, nodding cheerfully like faces. This Grace woman was bound to overcharge him. It was only fair if he made his own justice. He put the tray of pansies in the boot of the car. Adele would be impressed. She had been going on about the lack of yellow flowers to plant in the garden.

The cat watched him with narrowed eyes from the safety of a bush. He would tell Grace when she got home. He mistrusted the man. His shoes smelt bad.

Bert and the gorilla mask was the peak of a fraught week. Graham sacked Bert on the spot with relish. He had wanted to be rid of the man for years. Bert's intractable dourness had always been an affront to his own success.

The morning of the wedding was pandemonium. Tregony was full of people and Graham had had to listen to Aunt

Elvina droning on all evening about her embassy days and her French villa. He was in a foul mood when he went to bed, tossed and turned, kicked the bedclothes off. Adele lay curled and mouse-like at his side, never moving, wide awake.

He struggled into the hired morning suit, swearing they had sent the wrong size.

'You might have put on weight since you were measured,' said Adele, trying to fasten the waistcoat.

'Never. I've lost weight. All the worry.'

The vintage Rolls was perfection on wheels. Even though it had been Adele's idea, Graham enjoyed riding in the gleaming vehicle to the church, everyone admiring the unusual sight, smiling and waving. He was full of pride, as if he owned the car, a ducal beam on his face. Fiona was done up to the nines as usual. So much dress, there was hardly room for Graham on the seat. She looked different, hair in curls, frank blue eyes that saw right through him. Disconcerting eyes.

The wedding service was a lot of mumbo-jumbo. Graham only pretended to listen, wearing a special solemn expression for the occasion. That priest fellow was looking at Adele. No wonder he'd been round to Tregony so much; he couldn't take his eyes off her. Perhaps he ought to drop a hint to the bishop.

Back at Tregony, Graham went straight to the kitchen for a quick slug of champagne. He drank it out of a mug. In no time at all there seemed to be crates of empty bottles by the back door.

'Hold on,' he told the caterers, panicking. 'Go easy with the champagne. Take round trays of Buck's Fizz.' He eyed Aunt Elvina. 'And don't give any more to that old girl in the marquee. She's had enough already.'

The waitresses exchanged glances. The old dear could have as many glasses as she could carry, as far as they were concerned. They weren't going to spoil her day.

'Yes, Mr Kimberley,' they said. Outwitting the mean old jerk would add some spice to the function. They kept a running tag in the kitchen. 'Five down to the old girl, sixth coming up!'

Graham had written and rewritten his speech a dozen times. It was the moment he had been waiting for all these years. What better revenge, with all those important people here – the Vaughans and their posh friends, Father Lawrence, Carolyn and Timmy. Adele would never be able to show her face again in Porthcudden. She would be shunned. A warm current of pleasure coursed through his veins. It would serve her right. She was going to get her deserts now. She looked sweet and innocent in her silky blue dress, smiling and being a pleasant hostess. Soon everyone would know what a fraud she was.

The time for the speeches arrived. Graham had eaten well, partaken amply of the champagne, declined coffee. He was riding on a high. Everyone kept saying what a wonderful wedding. He had not felt so good for a long time.

The best man struck the side of a bottle several times with a silver spoon. 'Ladies and gentlemen,' said Ralph, 'pray silence for the father of the bride.'

The chatter died away to a murmur, glasses clinked. The guests looked expectantly at Graham. The waitresses refilled glasses in readiness for the toasts.

'Ladies and gentlemen, friends and relatives,' said Graham, heaving himself to his feet. He was perspiring and the stiff collar was cutting into his neck. The expectant faces swam around in a bright haze.

'We are here today to say farewell to my little girl as she begins the voyage of life with Hal. My little girl,' he repeated fondly, swinging round to look at her. 'Such a radiant bride, so pretty as a teenager and delightful as a baby. I often wondered then if she was real. She was like the child of a mermaid, fathered by some gallant French fisherman on a balmy Mediterranean seashore. Perhaps a love child, an ethereal creature more part of a dream, a youthful fantasy.'

Feet began to shuffle. There were raised eyebrows. Graham

had obviously drunk too much champagne. He was getting maudlin and fanciful.

'How do we know where we come from?' he asked his audience. 'We believe our parents are our parents. We take it on trust that we are who they say we are. Look at Fiona here. Tall, fair, blue-eyed. And look at me. Short, fat and freckled!' People laughed to hide their embarrassment. 'And I once had ginger hair. How did I come to father such a lovely girl? It must have been a miracle of the genes. She was indeed a seven-month miracle because, as you probably don't know, Fiona was a premature baby. She was a complete surprise to me and Adele. Especially to Adele.'

Adele had paled. He could see her grasping the stem of her glass so tightly that at any moment it would snap.

'Hal is a fine young man and we are glad to be united with the most esteemed family in this part of Cornwall. But their marriage must be based on truth. This truth, ladies and gentlemen, is essential to their happiness. I am about to give you that essential truth.'

He caught the movement of a hat. Aunt Elvina was looking at him sharply. She knew all right, the old witch; she'd probably known all the time.

'So before toasting the happy couple, I have one important announcement to make.' Graham cleared his throat and paused. He had rehearsed this bit a thousand times. He was word-perfect. Adele would cringe under his condemnation; Fiona would be shocked, her love for her mother turn instantly to loathing and hatred. The Vaughans would be mortified. He looked round triumphantly at his captive audience, a long, lingering look of controlled malice. It was a long pause.

'Raise your glasses, please,' cried Ralph loudly, leaping into the breach of what he thought was a memory lapse. 'To the bride and groom, Fiona and Hal.'

The guests rose to their feet with enthusiasm, relieved that the dreadful speech was over. They drank to Fiona and Hal, clapping and cheering, looking round for refills.

Graham started to splutter. 'But I haven't finished.' He glared at Ralph.

'Sorry, Mr Kimberley. I thought you had.'

'Well done, darling,' said Adele, carefully concealing her emotions. 'It was very revealing.'

He wrenched his sleeve from her hand. 'Damned fool! That damned fool! He spoilt my speech.'

'It was quite long enough, Daddy,' said Fiona with her usual bluntness. 'Everyone was getting restless.'

'I have not said enough. Not nearly enough!'

Graham sat down and tossed off a gulp of champagne. He was fuming. His moment had gone. Forever. Down the drain. The climax of years of planning was ruined. He glared at Adele.

'I was going to tell them,' he hissed. 'I was going to tell them about you and Andre.'

Adele rose without a word. Her glance was withering. 'You don't have the remotest idea,' she said at last, walking away.

After the other speeches and the cake cutting, Graham roamed the garden like a caged beast. He was losing control fast. He saw Bert sliding away behind some bushes. What was that imbecile doing here? He'd been sacked. He saw Carolyn talking earnestly to Hal, but hurried past with barely an acknowledgement. Lady Elvina was nodding off. She looked like a puppet, her face caked in make-up. Everyone was still drinking; they were opening the reserve crates. Damn it, he'd sue the caterers if they overcharged.

Fiona ran up and kissed him on the cheek. A wave of perfume hit him. 'Have you drunk too much? Going in to change, Daddy. See you soon.'

'You will indeed,' he growled.

He followed her slowly, taking a roundabout route towards the house. Adele was going to be punished now. He had fed and clothed her bastard child for long enough. She thought she had got away with it, coming back from her French holiday, all sweetness and light, encouraging him, wanting to get married, anxious to settle down. He had been taken in by the soft soap, the gentle, pleading voice, the warm young arms round his neck. She must have been laughing at him all the time. Fiona was Andre's child, some damned Frenchman. It was in Adele's diary. She had written it all down; her joy, her fear, her panic.

He removed the streamers of white nylon ribbon from the bonnet of the vintage Rolls and rolled them up. 'You don't mind, do you, old chap? Just want a souvenir.'

He knew nylon was very strong. It would not snap. Fiona's neck was slender. He could probably break it with one hard jerk.

He went upstairs to the master bedroom and closed the shutters and curtains, loosened his collar, waistcoat and waistband. He'd wanted to do this too, for years. She wasn't his natural daughter, so what did it matter? She was anybody's . . . he fancied a bit of rough.

'Fiona,' he called out. 'Come in here a moment, darling. I want to speak to you. It won't take long.'

# Ten

Cornwall was the gritty lifeblood flowing through Norman Vaughan's veins. There was no place so vibrant or so mysterious. All its wealth of legends, turbulent past, spectacular scenery and sweeping seas were invisibly fingerprinted on his spirit.

From boyhood he had loved walking through the swathes of sea mist that suddenly enveloped the coastal paths and turned the most familiar landscape into a mystical place. He never minded the rain. It seemed to invigorate him. It was a fickle, exhilarating climate that challenged him to walk miles, bare-headed, often without a coat, not caring how wet he got.

His mother scolded him, but his father, another true Cornishman, told her to leave the boy alone.

'It won't hurt the lad,' he said. 'Not Cornish rain.'

The longest period Norman was ever away from Cornwall was the years he spent in the Navy. He never regretted those years, sailing the great oceans, for they reflected his love of the sea. But he was thankful when his time was up and he returned to his father's business, Vaughan Precision Instruments. It was small, very specialized and old-fashioned. Norman was an injection of new life and the business expanded rapidly. By the time he was married to Olive and the two boys arrived, the orders were rolling in and the name was respected in marine circles around the world.

'Put your money in property,' his father had said, so

Norman bought Rosemullion House and let Olive have a free hand in its decoration and furnishing.

But the transaction was not quite so prosaic. Norman had known of Rosemullion House for years, admired it from afar, visited the gardens on the annual open day. He had often stood, enraptured, by its mellow pinky-grey stones, never imagining that one day he would own it. Now it was his, every inch of verdant grass, every wind-bent tree, every pitted stone.

It was a recurring moment of pride as he drove home each night. That first view of Rosemullion House always caught his throat. Sometimes he wondered if he was dreaming and he would wake up, back in the plain red-bricked villa he had shared with Olive when they were first married.

He was so lucky, he thought, as he drove his Mercedes more slowly along the winding drive to savour the moment of arrival. He had two fine sons, a thriving business, a good wife and the house of his dreams. That love had gradually evaporated from his marriage did not seem too important. He had everything else.

As the sun hid behind a scattering of evening clouds, the pink of the stone changed to a pale dove grey, and the twinkling octagonal glass panes in the four mullioned bay windows turned to black mirrors. The carved stone gables were silhouetted against the sky like lace. Great banks of hydrangea bushes, blue, pink and mauve, stirred in welcome. The flowers were at the stage Norman enjoyed the most, when a few florets were open wide and the rest of each head was a tight cluster of buds.

In his study in the south-facing turret, Norman had a 35mm telescope mounted on a deep window sill. He watched the tankers and cargo boats at anchor in Falmouth Bay. He observed them for hours, absorbed by their slow manoeuvres, wondering if they were fitted with navigational aids made by his firm. It made him feel proud of his work and his contribution to marine safety.

He was fascinated by fierce and wild weather; winter brought eighty-mile-an-hour gales that tore at the countryside and turned the sea into a seething cauldron. He often went out and stood in the teeth of a black gale, thinking of all the wrecks that littered the coast, of the lives lost.

Olive did not understand his fascination with storms. There was a lot about Norman that she did not understand, though their marriage was solid enough on the surface. He and Olive entertained frequently in the panelled dining room that overlooked the formal lawns. Olive liked cooking and supervised the menus. They also gave Sunday noon drinks parties, out on the lawn if it was fine. They were a quick and civilized way of repaying hospitality and meeting new people. Sometimes they had parties on-board their cruiser, or took friends fishing.

Entertaining was practically all that was left of their marriage; a shell of sociability. They never slept together, had separate bedrooms, rarely ate any meal together. In the evenings Olive watched television while Norman gardened or went for long coastal walks with one of his dogs.

Norman knew to the day when his life changed, when feelings he had thought dead suddenly flared back into life. He met Alexandra in a torrential rainstorm, literally bumping into her outside the station, their umbrellas locked into lethal combat as each struggled to get free.

'Sorry,' said Norman.

'Sorry,' said the woman.

He tugged at the bent ribs of his umbrella, flicking a shower of rain all over her face. She sprang back and her umbrella snapped inside out, drenching his sleeve.

She wore a maroon sou'wester that protected her face from some of the rain, but her lashes were spiky with moisture, cheeks dewy, eyes dark with amusement.

'If we go back into the station we can sort out these umbrellas,' he said. 'They seem to be out of control.'

'A case of instant attraction,' she said as he carried the

pair of entwined umbrellas under cover like a limp bouquet. 'Shove at first sight.'

Now, closer, Norman was struck immediately by her fragility. He was so used to Olive's robust size that he had almost forgotten how slender a woman could be. This young woman hardly looked strong enough to hold up an umbrella, let alone cope with a downpour.

She was like thistledown, pale-skinned, dark hair scraped back from a smooth brow. She had a serenity that calmed all sense of irritation.

'I think they're both broken,' he said quickly to stop himself from staring at her.

'Never mind. It doesn't owe me anything. Just put them in a bin.'

'What will you do? It's still chucking it down.'

'Don't worry. I'll treat myself to a taxi.'

She started to walk away. Norman watched her disappearing among the passengers with a failing heart. It was a long time since he had felt stirred by a woman's looks. The slim, rain-drenched beauty had confused him thoroughly. The way she had smiled, her delightful low laugh, the dark luminous eyes full of warmth and interest. Yes, that was it, thought Norman. She had looked at him as a person, as if she thought him interesting. But that was ridiculous, of course. He was fifty, grey-haired, his face lined, and she was young.

A cruising taxi slowed as he stood thoughtfully on the pavement, his coat becoming patchy with damp as the rain seeped through. The passenger door opened and she said, 'Do you want to share? Taxis are like gold dust at the moment. I was lucky.'

*No, I'm the lucky one*, he wanted to say as he climbed into the dark, damp cavern and sat beside her. She was smiling a sweet, generous smile that could shatter hearts at six paces. The effect on Norman, sitting only inches away, was cataclysmic.

'This is very kind of you,' he said, as tongue-tied as a teenager.

'Not at all. I'm merely repaying a kindness,' she said, taking off the sou'wester and shaking back long dark hair. 'We have met once before.'

Now that Norman could see her clearly, he remembered. He remembered that moment on the cliff with a jolt of alarm and a fear that quickly subsided. She was obviously all right and at ease with herself and the world. She had a tranquil confidence that evoked an aura of calm water and he was gladdened by the knowledge.

He nodded slightly, not wanting to remind her of the previous circumstances. He wondered how far he dare go before she laughed at him or gave him the brush-off. It was a step of such delicacy, and it was so long since he had made any overture to a woman. He had almost forgotten how.

'Perhaps this deserves some kind of celebration,' he said clumsily, feeling awkward and an old fool. He would not blame her if he got a straight refusal.

'It doesn't exactly merit a celebration,' she said slowly as if aware of his predicament. 'But I wouldn't say no to a really hot cup of coffee.'

'Scalding! I know the hottest coffee in town.'

She laughed. 'Let's hope they don't object to two drenched customers.'

'I'm sorry my umbrella behaved so badly.'

'I'm not,' she said softly.

It was the beginning of the happiest period of Norman's life. Rosemullion House, Olive, his sons, all faded obliquely into another dimension. Only this was real, seeing Alexandra, listening to her, talking for hours, falling more and more irrevocably in love with her as each day passed. He returned to Rosemullion House in a kind of daze after seeing her. He moved, worked, spoke like an automaton. He lived only for his next visit to London and meeting Alexandra.

That she came to care for him was a constant source of

wonder. He could not see his own mature good looks, the thickness of his silvery hair, the kindness in his seafaring eyes. His caring attitude was important to her. She soaked up the unexpected small attentions, the notes, the calls, the kind lifts, the realization that her welfare and opinions really mattered.

She in return became the perfect mistress: discreet, undemanding, independent. She hated him paying for anything.

'I have more money than I know what to do with,' he told her, easing a restaurant bill from her fingers.

'Good. Then you can give it away.'

'I'll do that if it'll please you, but first let me pay for this meal.'

The giving away began in a totally unexpected manner. A series of phone calls started to plague Norman at home and at his office. They were unpleasant and disturbing but he did not tell Alexandra. He could not bear having her worried or upset. Nor did he inform the police. They would want to know the nature of the calls and a step like that would be difficult to keep from Olive. Norman wanted to keep his marriage intact for his sons' sake, and for Olive. He did not intend to hurt her. He knew he was being selfish to want Alexandra as well.

It was not surprising when the abuse turned to demands. Norman had expected it to come eventually.

'I'm closer than you think,' the ingratiating male voice said. 'I see you but you don't see me. Right amusing, ain't it? You don't know when I'm there.'

'Nor do I care,' said Norman icily. 'Get off the phone and leave me alone.'

'Now, now, don't be nasty when I'm being right friendly. Of course, I might be persuaded to stop phoning if I went away for a little holiday, say America. Now that would be nice. I might be gone a long time. I suppose a couple of thousand would see me through.'

Norman knew he was being foolish to pay up, but the money meant nothing to him. He was buying time with Alexandra.

He took the packet of fifty-pound notes to Waterloo station and left them in a left-luggage locker and posted the key to a PO Box number in Reading. He tried to keep watch on both the Reading shop and the locker, but it was hopeless without causing suspicion at home or worrying Alexandra. Besides, Norman was not sure he wanted to see the man. The voice was unpleasant enough.

'Is something worrying you?' Alexandra asked as they strolled along the embankment from the Festival Hall. 'I don't believe you heard a note of that music.'

'It's nothing,' he said. 'Just busy at work. Our CP-2 model is going so well. Hal and I can hardly handle all the orders. And the machine shop are working overtime. I ought to buy new equipment, take on more staff.'

'Don't work too hard, darling,' she said, taking his arm. 'Leave a little time for yourself.'

The promised holiday in America did not last long. The man went through the money in no time. Norman had paid his fourth payment to the unknown blackmailer when there was a series of accidents at sea. A fishing boat foundered off The Lizard; two small tankers collided in the English Channel; a schooner was found going round in circles near the Greek islands.

The insurance investigators were mystified. There was nothing amiss with the boats and the weather conditions had been reasonable. Then a ferry went aground off the Isle of Wight and passengers had to be rescued. This time the marine investigators found a common denominator. The vessels were all fitted with the latest Vaughan navigational instruments, including the computerized Navitte CP-2. They took away sample sets from the workshops and found that fifty per cent were rogue. Norman immediately called in the entire production. They had been sold all over the world and the cost in sales and reputation was astronomical.

Hal was aware of the situation but kept the worst of the news from his mother and Fiona. He believed Norman had ample resources to weather the crisis. The testing system at Vaughans was completely revised.

Norman took out a second mortgage on Rosemullion House in order to meet the claims. He told no one.

Only Alexandra sensed that something was seriously wrong. Norman's face grew haggard with worry as he saw his business and home slipping through his fingers.

'I've some money saved,' she said. 'Let me lend it to you. Please, Norman, you must let me help.'

'My dear child,' he said with a gruff laugh. 'I couldn't take your savings. Besides, it wouldn't be enough, a mere drop in the ocean. The only way out is to sell up. The house, the business, everything.'

'Do it then. Sell up. Start again.'

'How can I? Olive needs Rosemullion House. It's her anchor. Hal's job is important, especially now he's getting married, and apparently Fiona can't live anywhere but in a brand-new bungalow overlooking the estuary that's going to cost me a cool three hundred thousand pounds.'

'Tell them you can't afford it,' said Alexandra. 'Surely she'll understand if you explain.'

'I've a feeling she wouldn't,' he said, taking Alexandra's hand and putting his lips gently to her fingers. 'Not everyone is like you, my dearest.' Sometimes he loved her so much he could barely breathe.

'Oh, Norman,' she said, tears rushing to her eyes. 'You shouldn't be worried with all this hassle. It will blow over. I know it will.'

'Perhaps.' He did not mention the batch of photos he had received in the post that morning. Pictures of Alexandra and himself walking arm in arm, stepping into a taxi, going through the swing doors of a Park Lane hotel. He was caught by her loveliness in them and then sickened by the thought of their being followed, photographed, spied on. There was a brief note. The negatives were for sale at £1,000 each. There were twenty-three photographs, almost one complete film.

Norman was preoccupied all that evening, wondering how he could save Rosemullion House, the business, and being with Alexandra. The one unnecessary expense and drain on his dwindling resources was this damned bungalow that Fiona had set her heart on. Why hadn't he promised them a silver canteen of cutlery and a cheque like any other father? Because he wanted to keep Hal, he supposed. He had already lost one son and he did not want to lose another. Jonathan had shrugged off all parental ties. Norman had been going to offer Hal a partnership in the business . . . but a partnership in what now? It was a drowning wreck. He did not want Hal to go down with it.

They were lunching in their favourite riverside pub when Alexandra told him that she would not be seeing him again. The food grew cold on their plates. Norman felt the blood draining from his heart as she stumbled over words.

'I know something is seriously wrong,' she said. 'I'm an added complication and I don't know why. If you can't tell me what's wrong then it would be better if I stayed away from you until everything is sorted out.'

'No, Alexandra, don't say that. I can't live without you. You're the only thing that keeps me going.'

She shook her head. 'I know I'm right. You've too much to cope with at the moment. Our love affair can be no pleasure now. I'll always love you, Norman. Please believe me. I'll never forget you, never stop loving you.'

'Don't go, please don't leave me . . .'

'It will help if I'm out of the way. It's going to hurt me too. I shall miss you so much, but I'll manage. I did before we met. And it'll be the best for you, and that's all that really matters. I won't be far away.'

Olive was in a complete flutter on the morning of the wedding. She had had her hair done but it still looked like a bird's nest. Norman could hardly bring himself to look at her outfit. It was a disaster. He had not realized how fat she had become. He listened to her wheezing as she climbed the stairs and was concerned. She ought to see a doctor.

Hal had gone out early to go sailing, snatching a last chance to get away from all the preparations. It seemed a rash thing to do with the wedding only hours off, but Norman did not blame him. Norman was shattered by Alexandra's decision. Nothing else really registered.

The post that morning brought a letter from his bank. They were not happy about the huge mortgage he had taken out on Rosemullion House, especially as Vaughan Precision Instruments might be on the verge of bankruptcy.

'You were perfectly happy banking my money when Vaughan Precision was riding high,' said Norman irritably, phoning the manager at his home.

'Yes, but things are a little different now, Norman,' said the manager. 'Money is tight and we aren't a charity. You've been drawing out huge amounts of cash. Your overdraft is quite unacceptable. You'll have to do something about it, or we'll call in the mortgage.'

Norman ran a hand over his forehead. He could feel a headache beginning to throb in his right temple. Where were his tablets? This was no day to have a migraine. 'I've had some personal problems.'

'That may well be,' said the manager, sounding like a pompous headmaster. 'But we don't let problems get us down. We do something about them. A fairly substantial cheque by Monday morning would be appreciated.'

From the window Norman saw Hal returning in his car. He was wet, jeans and shirt soaked, hair glistening with water.

'I'll call you back. I promise I'll do something by Monday.' He put the phone down and hurried out into the courtyard.

'Are you all right?'

'Just a slight accident.'

'Did you capsize? Are you hurt?'

'It was nothing, I tell you. I only got wet.'

'Don't let your mother see you or she'll have hysterics.'

'I'll go in the back way. Thanks, Dad.'

Norman found his tablets and swallowed them with cold water. Olive was sitting primly in the drawing room in all her finery, sipping pale cream sherry and nibbling clotted cream chocolate fudge.

'Is it time to go?' she asked for the third time.

'Soon,' said Norman. 'Soon.'

Norman showered and changed into his hired grey morning suit. A tall, grim-faced stranger stared back from the mirror. He put on the grey topper and took it off immediately. It made him look like an undertaker. He did not know how he was going to get through the formal performance of the day. All those people he would have to be polite to . . .

But this evening he would be alone. He would take the coastal path with old Jock and strike out along the cliffs, feast his eyes on the towering granite rocks, let the thunder of the tumbling seas block out the tumult in his mind. Perhaps the magic of Cornwall would do something for his failing spirits. Perhaps he would meet Alexandra.

'It's time to go,' he said, coming down the stairs.

Olive tipped up the last of her drink and grabbed her handbag, knocking the dish of fudge as she stood up.

'Slow down,' said Norman, patiently. 'We haven't got a train to catch.'

'Is Hal ready? Ought I to go and see if he's all right?'

'Hal's a grown man. I think he can get himself dressed. Ralph is here to drive him to the church.'

Norman drove the Mercedes to the church on the headland with Olive prattling away in the back seat. He parked and then escorted Olive into the crowded church. He hardly noticed who was there. He did smile at Adele, who he thought was a sweet, pretty woman and far too good for Graham Kimberley. He hardly recognized the straight, stiff and relentless back of his son waiting near the altar. He was aware of the heady scent of flowers everywhere.

Fiona's arrival came as a surprise, as he had been miles

away and did not hear the heralding music. What was it all about? This pomp and ceremony so that Hal and Fiona could live together, when they had already been living together for several months. He thought of Alexandra and the lines on his face softened. She was all he lived for.

Fiona did not look the same girl. She was like one of those extravagant crinoline dolls some people put over telephones or on spare loo rolls. Norman was more used to seeing her in tennis shorts, swinging a racket, laughing as she missed an easy shot.

This overdressed fairy princess was not that carefree girl at all. Perhaps Fiona had got cold feet and run away, leaving a doll as a stand-in.

Norman guided Olive out of the church after the service for the photographs. She was unsteady and had smudged her mascara with maternal tears. The whole thing was being videoed as well as photographed. Norman saw some boring evenings ahead when they would be invited round to view the wedding all over again.

A small boy in a sailor suit stood lost among all the grown-ups. Norman vaguely remembered there was a small Kimberley child. Perhaps this was him.

'It'll soon be all over,' he said to Timmy.

Timmy was looking bewildered. His mother seemed to have deserted him. He couldn't see her. He didn't know what he was supposed to do next. He looked up at the man.

'Come and stand over here with me,' said Norman. 'We'll be getting in the way. They just want the bride and groom and the bridesmaids now.'

'I'm a bridesmaid,' said Timmy, confused.

'Then perhaps they'll want you in this one.' He pushed the boy forward to join the group.

'It's all so beautiful,' said Olive, sniffing. 'Such a lovely wedding. It's very moving.'

Norman stood dutifully in the receiving line back in the garden of Tregony, waiting to shake hands with hordes of people he did not know. He had managed to down two aspirins with some water before the invasion of guests arrived from the church. It was going to be hard work.

People were deferential to him. He was known for being the richest man in that part of Cornwall. He owned Rosemullion House and Vaughan Precision Instruments. He was a man worth cultivating.

Norman nearly laughed aloud. What would they think if they knew he was almost bankrupt? There was no money left. The bank would call in the mortgage any day now. He would have to sell the boat and the Mercedes. Whatever he scraped up would hardly dent his overdraft.

He knew he would see her soon. Even with the size of the garden and the crowd of guests, even with her favourite habit of hiding under a huge hat, she could not dodge him forever. Norman caught sight of Alexandra across the lawn. She was standing alone like a slender-stemmed flower, beautiful.

For a moment the world stopped; all his firmly dammed emotions rose bubbling to the surface like a newly opened bottle of champagne. He did not care who saw him. What did it matter now? His reputation would soon be in shreds. He strode across the lawn, shouldering people out of the way, oblivious to everyone.

'Alexandra,' he choked, taking both her hands. 'It's you. My darling. My dearest girl.'

They looked at each other for a long minute, shattered by their meeting, hearts racing wildly, almost lost for words.

'How are you?' said Sandy at last.

'Missing you like hell,' he said simply.

She nodded, understanding. She did not withdraw her hands. They hung on to that fragile touch.

'You didn't shake hands with the bride and groom.'

'I came round the back way because I saw you in the line-up. I couldn't face you, shake your hand.'

'Why did you have to leave me?' he asked.

'I had to, Norman. I could see the worry was killing you.

190

What had been so good was somehow working against you. You were torn between your family commitments, the business worries, and me. I couldn't be that kind of responsibility to you. The price you're paying is too high. I couldn't stand by and let it happen.'

'The price I'm paying,' he repeated with an edge to his voice. 'I suppose you could say that.'

'I love you too much to let you destroy yourself.'

'This is all nonsense. I can't live without you, Alexandra. I know that now.'

'You'll have to, my love.' Sandy squeezed his hand gently.

'I've nothing left. My business is almost bankrupt. Rosemullion House is mortgaged to the hilt and I'm being blackmailed. Everything I've worked for all my life is in ruins. All I have is you. Don't take that from me, too.'

'Ah, Mr Vaughan!' A voice intruded into their presence. 'Now here's a nice group for the video. Stand closer, please. The groom's father and, shall we say, a good friend? Now let's have a right pretty smile, lady. Anyone would think it's a funeral.'

Izzy bobbed about on his sneakers, video camera perched on his shoulder. He zoomed in on Sandy's stricken face.

'Don't call that much of a smile. Right gloomy! Let's have another shot. Can always edit it out.'

Suddenly Norman recognized the voice and the irritatingly repeated catchword. He swung round on the stocky young man, flattening the palm of his hand against the video lens.

'So it's you, Izzy Cartwright,' he raged, almost incoherent. 'I knew I'd find you one day. Izzy Cartwright, the son of my old friend. Your father's my oldest employee. I can't believe it. You've been to my house, been fishing with us. We've treated you like one of the family since you were a boy. And you're nothing but a dirty blackmailer! Right? Right?'

Norman snatched the apparatus off Izzy's shoulder and

sent it hurtling through the air. It crashed spectacularly on Adele's rockery among the Giant Suncrested pansies.

Izzy paled but stood his ground. 'You'll be sorry you did that, Mr Vaughan. Right sorry. You see, I've still got the last photograph and that's a right beauty. And it's going to cost you a packet along with my broken equipment. I don't owe you anything, Mr Vaughan. All those years of patting me on the head, being kind to a motherless boy, keeping my dad on in some rotten job in your office. You did it to make yourself feel good. Well, how you do feel now, Vaughany old chap? Who's on top now?'

'What does he mean? What's happening?' cried Sandy, distressed by Norman's violence. 'Will someone tell me?'

An ungovernable fury eroded Norman's usual good sense and composure. He thought of his beautiful old house, its rose-grey stones so peaceful and welcoming; his father's business left to him on trust; the lovely woman beside him that he could not have. And this miserable worm of a youth was milking him of his last few pounds.

Izzy backed away. He turned and ran. Sandy was saying something to Norman, her hand on his arm, restraining him, but Norman could not hear her properly.

Fiona drifted across his blurred vision, a glimpse of shimmering silk and light, laughing. The chalky whiteness reminded him of the ridiculously extravagant bungalow he had been forced to buy for the newly-weds. If only he could lay his hands on that capital . . . £300,000 by Monday morning. If he could hand the deeds over to his bank manager, it might save him.

He wanted to be saved.

Through a bright haze he saw the gleam of a silver ice pick lying on a barrel of ice. It blinded him momentarily, distorting his vision with dazzling zigzags. Half of him acknowledged that a migraine was starting and he knew that in a few minutes his vision would be restricted to a blaze of flashing lights.

The other half was sickened by what he must do. He

must do it for Sandy, for sanity, for some sort of peace and happiness. And he had to be quick. He could hardly see what he held in his hand; the encroaching migraine was relentless and unstoppable, splitting his mind.

# Eleven

It was three weekends of non-stop house-hunting that wonderfully cleared Hal's mind. The pleasure of Fiona's vivacious company was stifled under the weight of estate agent's lists clutched in her eager hand.

'Daddy's been wonderful,' she said, climbing into the Porsche with enthusiasm. 'He's picked out the cream of the bargains, although I suppose as your father is buying it for us, we need not bother ourselves too much about the price.'

They did not look like bargains to Hal. They were a dreary bunch of suburban villas, crumbling vicarages, jerry-built conversions, flaking cottages, damp farmhouses. All manner of blots and sores on the brooding landscape competing with the ancient ruins of prehistoric tinworks and nineteenth-century engine houses. They no more compared with Rosemullion House than did a nettle to an oak.

'They're awful, awful,' Fiona wailed. 'We can't live in any of these dumps.'

Hal agreed. The flat overlooking the estuary had been different. Its smallness had been part of its charm. It was like playing a game, living in a doll's house, making do in a primitive cave, with the fun of camping, caravanning. Every time they bumped into each other in the minute kitchen it was a joke, cue for a hug and a kiss.

But now Fiona wanted a real house. As they looked at dearer and dearer houses, Hal's heart fell. He was going to be a property owner. He would have to maintain said property, mow the lawn, fix fuses, paint walls, clear the drains. The prospect appalled him.

When they returned to visit Tregony, tired and dispirited, it was all wedding talk. Did Hal like the printed invitations? Should the names be handwritten in scroll or copperplate? Silver or gold ink? Had his mother finalized her guest list? Did they want a Teasmade or a toaster from the Forresters?

'You ought to make up your mind,' said Adele. 'They want to know what to give you.'

'Teasmade,' said Fiona.

'Toaster,' said Hal.

Hal tried hard to show an interest in the arrangements. Adele was putting her all into the wedding. It was as detailed as a coronation or state opening. The Earl Marshal could not have done a better job. Hal felt unnecessary, in the way, a male encumbrance. It did not matter who stood at Fiona's side in church, as long as some man was in the right place, wearing the correct style of morning suit.

When Fiona found the new hillside bungalow development, she set her heart on living there immediately.

'It's wonderful! There's only one left so we've got to make up our minds fast. Everything's brand new. No one else will have slept in the rooms, bathed in the bath. And it's got a utility room. Oh Hal, say you like it.'

She went on and on about the utility room as if no housewife could possibly survive a wash day without one. Hal roamed the bare and empty cubicle, sniffing the smell of paint and fresh plaster, while Fiona planned where to put the washing machine, the tumble-dryer, the dishwasher.

'And this'll be our bedroom,' she said, sweeping open the door to a front room that looked out on to an unmade gravel road. 'It'll be lovely. We'll have it decorated in pink, with a pink duvet. Roses, I think. I love roses.'

'Where's my bedroom?' he asked.

He had always had his own room, ever since childhood. His room at Rosemullion House was a living museum of sports achievements, holidays, sailing trophies, university pranks. It lived and breathed Hal Vaughan. He did not care to be transplanted into a room painted pink.

'This'll be our bedroom, where we'll sleep,' said Fiona, surprised. She twined her arms round his waist and pulled him close. 'Remember, darling, we're getting married. We're making it legal. First Saturday in July.'

'I understand that this is to be your bedroom. Paint it pink, purple, whatever makes you happy,' he said. He strolled back through the bungalow, throwing open doors and peering inside. 'I'll have this room,' he said. It was the only one with a view of distant fields and hedges.

'But that's the guest room.'

'I'll move out every time there are guests,' said Hal with irony.

'This is ridiculous,' said Fiona. 'And very hurtful. Don't you want to sleep with me? You like it well enough at the flat. There was a time when you couldn't wait to move in. Any bed, any time.'

'I don't always sleep with you,' he reminded her. 'If I come in late or have a lot on my mind, I sleep on the sofa, you know that.'

'I suppose you'll want your own bathroom next,' she flung at him. 'Somewhere private and to yourself.'

'Good idea,' he said. 'We'll have an extra one built on. You'll have more room for your make-up and it won't matter how long you soak in the bath. There are advantages, Fiona.'

Hal said it with a finality that closed Fiona's protests for the time being. She had not expected him to have pre-wedding nerves. He was always so calm and decisive. It was one of the qualities that attracted her.

'At least we can tell your father we've decided on this modern bungalow,' she said. 'It's a very generous gift, though I suppose he can afford it.'

With the bungalow settled, Fiona began to drag Hal round

furniture stores and carpet shops. On fine sailing days, he was forced to make domestic choices. Oatmeal carpet or pale grey? Oval table or square? Walnut or pine? His mother had bought most of the furniture for Rosemullion House, and the price paid rather than good taste had led her in the right direction. His father sometimes came home with an elegant bureau or cabinet picked up at house sales when an old property was auctioned off.

Rosemullion House had grown and developed round Hal like a beautiful, mellow shell; shrugging it off for this bare, featureless bungalow was a painful business. If all this furnishing had to happen, then he did not want to be involved. Any day now Fiona would be asking him what colour tea cloths he preferred, or whether the Brillo pads be kept in a jolly china frog. It was slowly driving him mad.

'Father, are you really sure about giving us the bungalow for a wedding present? We've all this trouble blowing up about Navitte CP-2. Why don't we forget it and take out a mortgage like any other young couple?'

'Because you're my son, that's why. I promised to buy you a house and I always keep my word.'

'You don't have to. We could look for something cheaper and smaller.'

'Cheaper? I can't imagine you living anywhere smaller, either. Fiona would have a fit! She's enjoying herself, playing at housewife. Let the girl be.'

Hal snatched at a trip to the Far East like a drowning man. They had a lot of valuable customers in Bangkok and Singapore that Norman did not want to lose.

'But a mere month before your wedding? Are you sure?' Norman asked. 'There must be so many last-minute things to check.'

'Adele has it well in hand. She's the supremo in charge. I've just got to turn up on the right day, at the right time, wearing the right pair of pants.'

'What about the bungalow? Surely there's a lot to do there, getting it straight.'

'Probably,' said Hal indifferently. 'But it can wait. Fiona knows exactly what she wants. I'm better off out of the way. Fiona gets mad because shopping bores me. I think I ought to go to the Far East for Vaughan Precision, to convince our customers that we mean what we say; that it'll never happen again; that a rogue computer is every firm's nightmare. Besides, I need to get away from all these preparations.'

Norman understood. He remembered his apprehension before marrying Olive, the feeling of being trapped by all the arrangements, and that had been a simple, country wedding, with no fuss. There had not been any money about then.

'Well, I would certainly appreciate your going, Hal. There's the goodwill involved. I can't go. There's too much to do here. And we must negotiate ourselves into a position where we can do business with these people again.'

'We will, Father. There's nothing wrong with the rest of our instruments. Navitte CP-2 could have happened to any firm. It was just bad luck.'

'No, not luck, lad,' said Norman. 'It was my fault. I should have run more checks before promoting it so widely, more stringent tests before they left the premises. I took a chance. My mind was elsewhere. Preoccupied. Fatal for a middle-aged man.'

Hal thought his father had aged a lot in the last few months. His silvery-grey hair had lost its vigour, and the furrows and gaunt shadows had deepened. He seemed to be withdrawing from the family, becoming more and more of a private man.

Hal could see a lot of himself in his father. He liked being alone, the solitude of sailing. He enjoyed the days when he crewed for his brother, Jonathan, before all the local girls descended on the sailing club. That's how he met Fiona. And Carolyn! How could he have forgotten Carolyn? There had been a time when she followed him around like a puppy, always eager to help with any chore, from painting a hull to bailing out a dinghy.

Those had been carefree days. Sometimes he wondered how he had got into this marriage situation. He loved Fiona but he did not love this glorification of marriage. The pomp, the fuss, the meaningless vows that two-thirds of couples did not keep. How could he know how he would feel in ten, twenty years' time? It was like a long-range weather forecast. Unpredictable.

'You don't look too happy, Hal,' said Adele, bustling into the kitchen at Tregony with a tray of empty coffee cups. 'Is all this wedding hassle getting you down?'

'Not really. I think you're doing a wonderful job. I'm so lucky to have you as a mother-in-law.' He smiled slowly. Adele was a surprising bonus. He really liked her, particularly when she was sitting and doing nothing. Her hyperactivity must be compensating for something, or be a kind of defence. She was always busy.

'We're having some trouble with one of our products,' he went on. 'I shall have to go out to the Far East to settle the complaints.'

'What, now? Just before your wedding?' She looked a little perturbed.

'I'll be back in time, I promise you.'

'You'd better be,' she said. 'Fiona having hysterics in church would be no laughing matter.'

He nodded, pretending to be amused. But he already knew what it would be like. Fiona had hysterics when he told her he was going away. He had never seen such a performance. No one in his family was temperamental. Olive was placid, his father serious and Jonathan casual. They rarely argued.

Fiona had flown into a rage that had shocked Hal. She stormed at him, calling him names, questioning his motives for going, accusing him of not helping with the preparations, of leaving everything to her. Finally, worn out, she began to cry till her face was red and distorted with tears.

'You're trying to get away from me but I won't let you go.' She hiccuped. 'You don't want this wedding. You'd rather live in a poky flat near the river.'

He could hardly agree. He consoled her as best he could and promised to bring back a piece of ivory for their new home.

'That would be nice,' she sniffed. 'Something elegant to put on the mantelpiece. A centrepiece.'

'I'll find something really special,' he promised, though he had his doubts if anything could improve the appearance of the modern fireplaces uniformly built into all the bungalows on the estate.

They travelled to London together and said goodbye at Victoria station. Fiona could not go to Heathrow as she had an appointment with a supplier, and then she was going to stay overnight with Lady Elvina. The noise of the station bustle isolated them from the crowds.

She was weeping as she clung to him. 'I'm going to miss you so much,' she sobbed. 'Come back soon, earlier if possible. I can't bear you being away from me. I'm always afraid something will happen to you.'

'Nothing will happen,' he reassured her, trying to unwind her arms, which were throttling him. 'I'll be all right. Just take care and don't overdo things. We don't want the bride looking exhausted.'

'I've got the most gorgeous dress,' she said, brightening, a gleam in her eyes. 'Wait till you see it. I'm going for a fitting tomorrow.'

'Busy girl,' he grinned.

'Give me a phone number so I can phone to check if you've arrived all right.'

'You're not going to phone Bangkok, Fiona. I'll give you a ring.'

'Will you phone every day? Please.'

'No,' he said firmly. 'Not every day, but when I can. I'm not promising anything.'

'What a selfish attitude. One little phone call . . .'

He prised himself away from her and with a final kiss escaped to take the underground train to Heathrow. The big jumbo waiting on the tarmac seemed like a haven, though he half expected Fiona to pop up at his side demanding just one more kiss. The clang of the cabin doors closing was a welcome sound.

Though his visit had a serious purpose, Hal could not help enjoying his freedom. Cornwall was a million miles away. It could have been on another planet. Fiona and the Kimberleys rolled off his shoulders like a millstone. He had little time for sightseeing; he would have to come back some day. He wanted to see Thailand's most sacred place, the Temples of the Emerald Buddha, go for a trip down the Chao Phraya River. Not once did he imagine bringing Fiona with him. She seemed to have vanished into the mist that hung over the polluted brown river every morning, and evaporated with the day's blistering heat.

He only remembered at the last moment that he had not bought the promised piece of ivory. He found the ivory district of the crowded shopping streets, where the goods on display ranged from the cheap and nasty to exquisite pieces worth a fortune.

In a gloomy corner store, Hal found the figurine of a Thai dancer. It was only four inches high but perfect in every graceful detail. It had obviously been carved by a craftsman.

'Velly beautiful, sir,' said the shopkeeper, emerging from the shadows. 'Worth ten times price I am asking.'

Hal raised his dark eyebrows. 'Really?'

'But she is flawed. Such beauty flawed, sir, is a thousand pities.'

'Isn't all beauty flawed? Is it new?'

'Oh no, not new. Velly old. Belong old merchant family. Old Bangkok house pulled down for hotel. Not estimable antique, you understand, sir, or price would be hundred times.'

Hal liked the little dancer; she was delicate and graceful with a childlike face, her hands in a traditional Thai pose. He looked carefully to see if he could detect the flaw.

'You like? I show you flaw. Velly honest.'

She wore little anklet bells; a miracle of carving. One of the bells had broken off. Hal reached for his wallet.

'I'll have it anyway,' he said. 'Can you wrap it, please? It's a gift.'

'Lucky lady will like,' said the shopkeeper, grinning.

Hal wished he could be sure. The figure was so small and dainty. It would be lost on that modern mantelpiece. It should really be displayed behind glass. There was an old wall cabinet at Rosemullion House that would show it off perfectly.

Hal thought about Fiona constantly during the return flight, every airborne minute reducing the miles between them. He remembered to buy her favourite duty-free perfume, some brandy for her father. He did not know what to buy Adele.

Fiona was not at Heathrow to meet him. He phoned Tregony and then her boutique, but she was out. He caught the train home, dismayed to find that her voice dominated his thoughts and that suddenly he was dreading seeing her again.

The realization made him feel ill. Two days before his wedding and he did not want to see the bride. It was cold feet, he told himself sternly as he stared out of the train window. Perhaps Fiona was feeling apprehensive too. If they talked and laughed about it, perhaps these fears would disappear.

He took a taxi from the station, driving straight to Tregony. Fiona ran from the house and flung herself into his arms, face flushed, eyes bright.

'I rushed home as soon as I heard you'd phoned! Darling, darling! I've missed you so much. You were horrid to go away for such a long time, leaving me all alone.'

They did not sound the words of someone with cold feet or wedding nerves. Hal looked at her face closely for any signs, but her eyes were especially bright and she was her usual bubbly self.

He did not answer her question, but dug into his pocket for the small parcels. Fiona shrieked like a little girl on Christmas morning.

'My favourite perfume. Darling, how gorgeous. And my ivory! Fancy remembering when you had so much on your mind.' Her fingers closed over the silver box embossed with red dragons. Inside, the figurine poised her slim legs on a bed of crushed black velvet. A sweet waft of Eastern incense reached Hal's nostrils and he was transported back into the shadowy shop, reliving his first joy at finding the dancer.

'How perfectly sweet,' Fiona enthused. 'What a pretty little thing. Thank you, sweetheart. And did you get something special for our lounge fireplace?'

'This is it. This is special,' said Hal.

Suddenly the air was charged. Fiona's displeasure was tangible but she kept it in check.

'But it's rather small,' said Fiona after a pause. 'You can hardly see it. And isn't it second-hand?'

'It was handmade by a craftsman. It's unique and came from the home of a wealthy merchant. Surely your artistic sense can appreciate its beauty?'

'That may well be,' she said, unable to keep the disappointment out of her voice. 'But I wanted something special. Something big and expensive that people would notice and remark on.'

'Shall I nip back and change it?' Hal offered.

'Don't be silly. Well, I suppose this'll look nice somewhere but it's not at all what I wanted. Let's go to the bungalow. I've done masses since you've been away.'

A great weariness settled on Hal. The last thing he wanted was to traipse round the bungalow he was beginning to detest, having to admire curtains and lampshades. 'I've been travelling for the last day and night, Fiona. I'm jet-lagged. I couldn't face another mile. If your mother doesn't mind, I'm going to flake out in the garden.'

'Can we go sailing soon?'

'I have got a lot of paperwork to clear up.'

'I haven't been sailing for ages. I need some sea air and some excitement. What about Friday evening?'

'There's my stag party.'

'Oh, that'll be awfully boring. It'll be the same people you see all the year. Cancel it.'

'My friends,' he corrected gently. 'You'll get plenty of sea air on our honeymoon. I'd better check that the *Sea Sprite* has been provisioned, or have you done it?'

'Heavens no, I've been far too busy with the bungalow.'

'Of course,' said Hal, drowsily, stretching out.

'We won't need much food,' he heard her saying. 'We're going to eat out. Most of the marinas have club houses or big hotels nearby. I'm not a galley slave.'

When he awoke late in the afternoon, the shadows were lengthening into a swansdown dusk and he could tell that Fiona had gone. The garden had a tranquillity that was not there when she was around.

'The men are coming to put up the marquee tomorrow,' said Adele, arriving with a tray of tea, home-made scones, strawberry jam and a dish of clotted cream. 'It'll be all hell let loose.'

'Fiona?'

'Gone to get the dishwasher plumbed in.'

He groaned. 'A dishwasher – for two mugs?'

'You heard her. She's no galley slave. Besides, Fiona has to have everything. I thought you would have discovered that by now.'

'Including me,' he said without expression.

'You'll be very happy,' said Adele. 'I'm sure you will. Fiona is very young. She'll grow up.'

'Whilst I am aging rapidly.' He smiled at his future mother-in-law. She looked somewhat harassed, her hair windblown, a smudge of earth on her cheeks. She had been gardening as he slept. 'It's very kind of you and Graham, the way you are allowing your garden to become Wembley Stadium. I hope the hordes don't trample on your flowers.'

'I shall make on-the-spot fines if people so much as use the flower beds as ash trays.'

Something made Hal reach out and touch her arm quite briefly. It was odd because he was not a touching person.

'Adele,' he said in some confusion. 'You're wonderful. If anyone disturbs a single petal, I shall personally take them aside and sort them out.'

'Thank you, I hereby appoint you on garden patrol. I hope you won't be overworked. We don't want Fiona to feel neglected on her wedding day.'

They laughed together, a last laugh.

The day dawned very early for Hal. He had not been able to sleep properly. The previous evening had been his stag party at the sailing club, nothing wild, just a few friends drinking beer, Ralph practising his speech, making dreadful jokes. Fiona turned up unexpectedly in the middle of it, much to everyone's embarrassment. She wanted to check if Izzy would be at the church as well as the reception.

'There has got to be a complete video of everything,' she said, unaware of the sudden hush in the hilarity.

Hal steered her out of the door. He almost asked if she wanted Izzy to come on the honeymoon. 'He'll record every shot you want,' he said evenly.

'Darling, I've just had a wonderful idea! Let's go for a sail now. We haven't had any time together since you came back. It's a lovely evening and very romantic. Please, Hal.'

'I can't leave my guests, you know that. Perhaps someone else will take you.'

'I'll take myself then. I'm capable of handling a small dinghy. I don't need your help.'

'You shouldn't go by yourself,' said Hal. 'Not at this

time of night. Go home, Fiona. There's no point in being foolhardy.'

She flounced away from him, making for the car park. Hal watched her with pain in his heart. He would have liked to go sailing, too, to get back to how he used to feel about her.

He knew exactly what he was going to do when he awoke early. He put on jeans and a sweatshirt, let himself out of Rosemullion House and drove down to the sailing club. Porthcudden was deserted but for a few aimlessly wheeling gulls and some solitary cats. He took out his favourite sailing dinghy and hoisted the sails. The rhythmic slap of water on the bows and the fresh wind helped to clear the cobwebs. He steered the dinghy into the wind and the craft took a fast course across the bay. It was exhilarating, his hair blowing in all directions, the old shirt flapping against his chest, spray flying in his face. At moments like these, he could envy his brother Jonathan.

He sailed back, his mind almost numb with chill from the wind; goose pimples on his bare arms. He prepared to bring the dinghy into the shallows before jumping into the water to pull her up the slope.

A flash of white caught his eye. It was purely by chance. It could have been anything, a pebble, a bone, a crumpled plastic bag. He swung the dinghy round and peered into the quivering green depths. The dinghy was in about four feet of water, but a sudden ray of light pinpointed the object clearly through the distortion.

The cramp was physical. It gripped his guts. Without hesitation, Hal let go the tiller and tipped himself overboard. He groped blindly among the pebbles and sand on the seabed. Scrambling to the surface, he gulped in air and went down again, his heart thudding.

On the second surfacing he had two handfuls of sand and debris. He held a soggy mess of silvery cardboard with smudged red dragons. In his other hand lay the fragile Thai dancer, never to dance again, a leg broken off at the knee.

206

Hal had never wept in his life, but tears stung his eyes as he trod water with the precious load. He washed the grains of sand off her face, removed a slimy strand of seaweed from round her neck. It could have been an accident. Fiona could have gone sailing after all and unknowingly dropped the figure; perhaps she had been showing it to someone and it fell out of her hand.

The drive back to Rosemullion House was accomplished in record time. He drove recklessly, clipping hedges, slicing the heads off wild flowers, giving a cyclist a near heart attack. He slowed down then, ashamed of giving way to his feelings.

An air of constrained bustle hung over the house. Breakfast was buffet-style as most of the staff would be going to the church. They were hurrying about their duties, self-conscious in their best clothes.

Hal had no appetite for food. He drank two cups of strong coffee and took another up to his room. He stood the figurine on the window sill but she could no longer stand unless propped up. Hal felt exactly the same. Helpless. As he got dressed he wondered if he was someone else, not Hal Vaughan at all.

'Still got time to run,' Ralph joked as they drove to church. 'Motorway to Penzance; twenty minutes on the helicopter to the Scillies. In an hour we could be fishing.'

'Brilliant idea,' said Hal. 'You've obviously forgotten the ring and this is your cover-up plan.'

'How did you guess? And I've checked twenty times at least.'

The church was very cool despite the number of people already seated in the pews. The hats turned as Hal entered, nodding like flowers. Light streamed through the stained-glass windows in a river of rainbows.

Adele greeted him with an encouraging smile. If Adele had been twenty years younger, he would have been marrying her, he thought wryly. No mother-in-law jokes about Adele.

He had a feeling that it would be the father-in-law who was the joke.

A loud series of chords on the organ announced Fiona's arrival. She began the walk down the aisle on her father's arm. Hal could hear her coming . . . the swish-swish of her dress . . . like the wheels of a tumbrel approaching.

She stopped by his side in a wave of heady perfume and smiled up at him. She looked radiantly beautiful, all sparkling and luminous, as unreal as a Gainsborough painting.

'Dearly beloved,' began Father Lawrence.

They repeated the ritual of the vows without fault; Fiona's voice clear and bell-like. Hal did not recognize his voice. It had changed, become deeper, gravelly. For better, for worse, for richer, for poorer . . . What was he saying? Till death us do part?

'Those whom God hath joined together, let no man put asunder,' said Father Lawrence solemnly.

They proceeded to the vestry to sign the register. There was quite a crowd in the small, cold room. Fiona paused, pen in hand, before signing for a photograph to be taken.

'Mrs Hal Vaughan,' she declared to the world with a theatrical flourish.

The three words seemed to bounce off the walls of the enclosed space. Someone laughed nervously. Hal could not tell if it was Carolyn or Ralph. They both looked strained.

Hal bent to add his signature. As he uncapped his pen, he heard two further words: 'At last!'

Fiona was smiling at him again but it was not a smile laced with love. It was a smile of pure, calculated triumph.

He recoiled physically, almost stepping back on Carolyn's toes.

'Sorry. Did I hurt you?'

'Don't you know?' said Carolyn softly. 'She's got what she wanted.'

Snippets of long-forgotten remarks began to float back into his mind. 'What a gorgeous house! Hal, you're so

lucky to live here . . . living like a lord! Are you going
to stand for Parliament? Oh, you must, darling . . . with
your connections . . . no trouble getting elected. One day
I suppose Rosemullion House will be yours. Imagine me,
lady of the manor. Sir Hal Vaughan, for services to industry!
What fun! An American takeover? Is that likely? You could
be bought out. Millions.'

'Hal, are you all right?' It was Carolyn again.

'It's a bit hot in here,' he said, though he was clammy
with cold.

Fiona clamped on to his arm and they were soon walking
down the aisle to more strident music. His feet were like lead
weights that needed manually lifting with each step.

'Smile, darling,' Fiona was saying between her teeth.

'Mrs Hal Vaughan,' said Hal, unbelieving.

'I know, darling. You're stuck with me now.'

The congratulations, the group photographs, the confetti . . .
More remarks tumbled into his thoughts. 'The drawing room
at Rosemullion ought to be in old gold. All this land and no
swimming pool? I've always wanted a pool. And a jacuzzi.'

Fiona laughed and waved as they drove back in the vintage
car. 'This is like being royalty. We're going to be Cornwall's
First Couple.'

And I'm the first step, thought Hal. It was his name she
wanted, that was all, the status of being a Vaughan and
Rosemullion House. She married him for a house.

She ran across the lawn at Tregony, skirts billowing and
veil floating like some huge moth. She took two glasses of
champagne from a waitress.

'It's going to be champagne all the way from now on,'
she laughed. 'Your father keeps a good cellar, doesn't he?
And your mother is wearing some really lovely jewels today.
I haven't seen them before, have I?'

'I believe they are kept in the bank,' said Hal. He could
see the working of her mind quite clearly. She was already
trying on the diamonds, roaming the cellars.

The receiving line was forming and Hal forced himself to be pleasant as their guests began to arrive, but there was nothing he could do to unstiffen his face or relax his muscles. He had frozen into an overdressed robot.

Thank goodness he had learnt his speech. It tripped along easily, raised a few laughs, was mercifully short. They cut the cake together, the knife finding it hard work to slice through the icing.

Fiona grimaced. 'Adele ought to complain. This cake's dreadful, and so mean. Hardly any fruit in it. Mostly glacé cherries, awful. Whoever made it? Was it your old house-keeper?'

'She's been with us a long time and we wouldn't dream of replacing her,' he said sharply.

Fiona looked at him, startled by his tone of voice. 'What are you talking about? I didn't say she had to go.'

'Sorry, thoughts wandering. Forget it.' The knife was stuck with dark crumbs and a currant. It reminded him of the debris from the seabed. 'Did you go sailing last night?' he asked.

'Heavens no. It got too dark, remember? What a funny thing to ask. I drove home and had an early night. I'm going in to change now. It's time we left. I can't wait for us to be alone . . . Really alone.'

Jonathan would have seen through her. His brother would not have been so blind. Hal watched her trail across the lawn, stopping to talk to Lady Elvina, then exchanging a word with his mother. Breaking the figurine had not been an accident; she must have thrown it into the sea.

Carolyn came over to him. She looked unusually pale. 'I'm worried about you,' she said. 'Perhaps it's jet lag, or maybe you're sickening for something. What's the matter?'

'Don't worry about me, Carolyn,' he said. 'I'll be all right. I'll survive.'

He thought of the sea muttering on the rocks and the suddenness of a freak wave that could take a life. He was being swept along by such a freak wave, any moment now to be hurled against the rocks. The great cliffs of granite had stood for aeons. What was his life in comparison? Nothing much. It was a mere flicker of an eyelid.

He hesitated before following Fiona into the house. The hall was cool and shadowy. He began to climb the stairs, stooping automatically to pick up an ice pick which had been dropped on the landing. He knocked on the door of Fiona's room.

'Who is it?'

'Hal.'

'Come in, darling. You don't have to knock. After all, you are my husband now.'

She flung open the door. She had not begun to change and was still in her wedding dress. Someone had brought her a cup of tea on a tray. Voices floated up from the garden. The room was full of slanting sunshine.

'Husband?' said Hal. 'I think sacrificial lamb would be a more accurate description of my role.'

'What an odd thing to say. Sacrificial lamb? Whatever do you mean?'

'I think you know,' said Hal bluntly. 'I must have been blind and certainly very stupid. I have only just realized why you married me. It's not because you love Hal, the man inside this suit. You love what I represent in your eyes. Rosemullion House, Vaughan Precision, status, a name. I don't matter at all. I could have had three ears and a hump and you would still have married me.'

'But you haven't got three ears and a hump, and you're very handsome. This is absolutely ridiculous,' said Fiona, the laughter fading from her voice. 'What nonsense. You've obviously had far too much to drink.'

'No, I haven't. I'm quite sober. You gave yourself away today. I saw the triumph in your eyes when you were signing the register. I should have known it when I found the Thai dancer. She wasn't big enough or showy enough for you, was she? So you threw her away.'

'It was an accident,' said Fiona hurriedly. 'Getting in the boat.'

'An accident? You said you didn't go sailing. What's the truth? I think you stood at the water's edge and hurled it with all your strength.'

Fiona sat on the bed and stretched luxuriously, her eyes half-closed with some secret, a new smile of cunning touching her lips.

'Well, it's too late now,' she said. 'Whatever you think.'

'No, it isn't,' said Hal. 'I'm going to get this marriage annulled. It's finished before it's even started. I'm leaving now, walking out without you. The *Sea Sprite* is fuelled and provisioned and it'll be weeks, maybe months, before I return. You can tell people what you like, but I'll be in touch with my solicitors first thing on Monday morning from wherever I happen to be.'

Fiona's face went white, her eyes darkened. Her breasts heaved with distress.

'You can't do that.'

'Yes, I can,' said Hal. 'So goodbye, Mrs Vaughan. You're only going to be Mrs Vaughan for a single day, so make the most of it.'

He turned to leave but as he did, Fiona leapt off the bed and lunged at him, her nails clawing his face, her mouth distorted into a scream of rage.

'You're never going to leave me,' she gasped. 'Never, never! I won't let you. You're mine. Everything that's rightfully yours is mine too. I won't let it all go. I won't. I want it. I'll kill you first.'

'Stop it, Fiona. Don't be foolish.'

'I'm never going to let you go. You'll see, you can't walk out on me.'

She clung on to his clothes, all pretence gone. She was consumed with animal fury. He struggled to get out of her limpet grasp as she fought to pull him towards her. A clatter of loose change fell out of his pocket, scattering over the floor.

Fiona made a whiplash-spring for the ice pick and swung it up into the air like a dazzling sword.

Hal caught at her wrist in a lightning movement. As they fell together in a heap on to the bed, Fiona let out a small cry of utter astonishment.

Two uniformed policemen stood in the garden at Tregony, their patrol car parked further down the road, behind the guests' cars.

'I'm sorry to trouble you at a time like this, Mrs Kimberley. I'm Sergeant Routing and this is Constable Peters. I understand there's been some trouble at the church.'

'I beg your pardon?' said Adele blankly, eyes glazed with shock. 'What church?'

'The church, ma'am. The church where your daughter's wedding has just taken place. It's been vandalized.'

'Has it?' she said, not understanding a word.

Then she remembered what she had found upstairs and why she had been screaming. Part of her mind worked automatically, forming the right words. 'I think you had better come in . . .'

# Epilogue

Nothing was ever quite the same for anyone after Fiona's death. For some, things improved; for some it heralded change, and for a few life was shattered.

Grace got her new wheelbarrow, then a new van, and began specializing in exotic plants. It was the mandrake plant that started her interest in rare species, and now at the Chelsea Flower Show she wins prizes. She went, by accident, to a talk about auras and healing and energy centres, and discovered that she has a special gift that can help the sick.

People now come from all over the country to be with Grace, and the track to her smallholding is becoming like a pilgrimage. One day she dug up the mandrake plant and burnt the roots. Although she felt nothing beyond relief as the acrid smoke filled her nostrils, she noticed that Titus fled and hid under her bed.

Olive lost a lot of weight during the divorce proceedings and the preliminary hearings before Hal's trial, and afterwards she had little spare money to spend on alcohol. Her notebook of detailed dates and times gave Norman's lawyer quite a shock. But the new, slimmer Olive is happy enough in the narrow, converted white-stone fisherman's cottage in which she now lives. Word of her talent for cooking is spreading, and she is in demand to cook other people's dinner parties, and being paid well for it. But Hal is the pivot of her life and she is sure that he will return to her one day.

As Olive's confidence grows, she is beginning to experiment with dishes and sometimes she tries them out on the retired accountant who lives in the cottage next door. He is encouraging her to put them into book form and has lent her his ancient typewriter.

Norman and Sandy married immediately after the quickie divorce was finalized. Despite knowing that their affair was illicit and that they should be consumed by guilt, that feeling has quite escaped them. They live on air in the south wing of Rosemullion House. The rest was sold off and turned into a conference centre, full of young people coming and going, studying everything from alternative medicine to creative writing. Vaughan Precision is small again and Norman spends a lot of time walking the dogs and gardening, content to be showing his beloved Cornwall to Sandy.

Sandy's foot is growing stronger, and some days it does not hurt at all. Her reputation as a choreographer still takes her to London, but her happiness is so complete that she is less and less inclined to leave Norman. She knows their time together may be limited and that every new morning is precious.

The day of the wedding will never leave Sandy's memory. She had found Norman on the stairs, head in his hands, half blinded by a migraine, and taken him next door to her home. She left him in her darkened bedroom to rest and sleep, then returned to Tregony. It was she who took care of Adele and Timmy in those first few traumatic hours and days, and shouldered the burden of running the household for her friend.

Carolyn lived in a vacuum for a year, not really doing anything with her life, moving aimlessly from job to job, her flair for designing hats quite gone. It was ironic. Even in death, Fiona had succeeded in taking Hal from her. Then one day, in walked an older, craggier version of Hal, bronzed and bold, who swept her off her feet in three weeks of unorthodox courtship. He was totally unconventional, completely his own master, and in no time at all turned Carolyn's life upside down. The moment he saw her pale face and her pale mermaid's hair, he knew he was never going to let her go.

215

It was Jonathan Vaughan, back from the jungles of Borneo, on a refuelling stop before another trip abroad. Carolyn went with him and they were last heard of in Fiji, making a wildlife film and ecstatically happy.

Fred Goldblummer died in his sleep soon after the wedding and with his death the remaining guilt vanished from Elvina's mind. She celebrated by going on a luxurious world cruise. Halfway across the Indian Ocean she had a heart attack at the captain's table and died as she would have wished, beautifully dressed in grey pleated chiffon, a glass of champagne in her hand and in good company. She even died elegantly, merely slipping down in the gilt chair with a faint sigh, hardly spilling a drop of her Bollinger Special.

Only the solicitors knew about the generous insurance policy Sir Peter had taken out on Elvina's life. All of the money went to Adele, together with a few pieces of furniture, including the antique bureau, which she learnt to treasure. In one of the drawers, Adele found a crumpled letter in splintered English from Andre, thanking Elvina for her liberal reception during an unforgettable summer. It was then that Adele discovered that the lovingly polished bureau was a gift from Andre.

For a while she daydreamed about what Andre might be like now but the image was too faint. Their love had been a youthful holiday romance and that's how she wanted to remember him, tall and boyishly handsome, his skin like satin, breath like blossom.

The money was enough to give Adele independence, to be able to leave Graham and start a new life. She found a small house, white and covered with climbing roses, with a garden that stretches down to the sea.

For a while she took on the running of Fiona's boutique because no one else had time. But now her interest is being kindled and she is beginning to develop the gallery side, letting the touristy trade fade away. She likes encouraging young artists and finds a certain peace in their uncomplicated company.

Graham eventually brought home a new wife to Tregony. She is a fitness freak and had the lawn dug up for a hard tennis court and then the rest excavated for a lagoon-shaped swimming pool and patio. Bert throws rubbish in the pool whenever no one is looking, and makes potholes in the surface of the tennis court with a shovel.

Bert never really understood what happened that day. He simply turned up for work the following morning as if he had never been sacked. Some days he feels more and more like a tree and simply stands motionless with his head thrown back, drinking in the sun with a thirst that is never quenched.

The Mark 2 wife rules Graham with a skinny, bony hand, calcified by hormone replacement therapy, and even his side-lick is starting to look harassed. The chauffeur of the vintage Rolls remembered that Graham had asked for the white ribbon as a souvenir and it did not take the man long to spread this item of salacious gossip round the county. Graham bluffed it out, but his social status suffered.

Hal is still awaiting trial on a manslaughter charge in Exeter maximum security prison. He was refused bail for complex reasons. His counsel intends to plead not guilty and is fairly optimistic. Forensic evidence showed that the path of the ice pick's entry was consistent with Fiona falling on it while it was clasped in her own hand.

There was a witness to Fiona's death, who, despite being under age, was able to give a clear and lucid account of what he heard in the bedroom, but not of what he saw, because he saw only two pairs of feet moving about.

Timmy had been hiding beneath Fiona's bed. Bored with the reception, he had been planning to surprise her with the gorilla's mask. It was one of the many odd things the police discovered in Fiona's bedroom, along with a cooling cup of tea loaded with poison, a single wilting rose on her pillow, coins scattered all over the floor and a carefully folded length of white nylon ribbon, twisted and tied into a hard, strangler's knot.

To fill in the time, Hal is taking an Open University course in maritime history. He does not know what he is going to do with his life. Despite being in prison, he has a sense of escape, of release. He has vague plans of sailing somewhere distant, seeing the world, of savouring freedom, finding another ivory dancer.

Ralph is emigrating to Australia. He vows that he will never marry. He does not know that one day he will meet an older woman who will make him laugh and show him how the hurt can be healed.

Father Lawrence has taken the entire burden of guilt on to his own shoulders and spends many hours praying on the hard stone steps of the church. If only he had done something, anything, Fiona would still be alive. He should have broken his confessional vows, stopped the wedding, saved that unborn child. Even his fragrant and lovely Adele has gone from his life. He prays for her constantly, tortured and lonely.

Adele is taking the longest to recover, if she ever can. Fiona was her child, her first baby. She grieves inwardly for her wayward eldest daughter. Her hair has gone silvery-grey and she has lost the bloom of youth from her cheeks. She lives only to care for Timmy, to nurture him as he grows up, and takes pride in the young man he is becoming.

She often remembers her thoughts on the morning of the wedding. *I am imprisoned*, she had thought then, *and tomorrow I will be free.* But that had not come true. With Fiona's death, the iron bars had thundered to the ground all around her.

Sometimes, when she is on her knees, planting seedlings in her new garden near the sea, she looks to the open crystal-clear sky that stretches above her. And, like a flower unfolding, she knows with certainty that one day the cage will open and she will fly away.